O BRAVE NEW WORLD . . .

The touch of my thumb on the security plate activates it. Must be mine. The screen clears. Words swim up:

YOUR NAME IS JOSHUA ALI QUARE. HIT RETURN.

I do.

WELCOME TO 2109, JOSHUA, YOU MADE IT AGAIN. READ THE NEXT PART CAREFULLY.

YOU ARE ON MARS. THE YEARS IS 2109 AND YOU NO LONGER WORK FOR THE KGB, MURPHY'S COMSAT AVENGERS, NIHON-AMERICA, OR THE ORGANIZATION. THERE IS NO MORE SOVIET UNION, NO MORE EUROPEAN COMMONWEALTH, AND NO MORE UNITED STATES OF AMERICA. EARTH IS COMPLETELY CONTROLLED BY RESUNA. YOU ARE PHYSICALLY JUST OVER SIXTY YEARS OLD. A NEW IDENTITY HAS BEEN ESTABLISHED FOR YOU AS "REAGAN FOSTER HINCKLEY," A JOKE WHICH YOU AND MAYBE A DOZEN HISTORIANS WILL GET.

Tor books by John Barnes

Kaleidoscope Century
A Million Open Doors
Mother of Storms
Orbital Resonance

Kaleidoscope Century

John Barnes

A TOM DOHERTY ASSOCIATES BOOK
NEW YORK

This is a work of fiction. All the characters and events portrayed in this book are either products of the author's imagination or are used fictitiously.

KALEIDOSCOPE CENTURY

Cover art by Bob Eggleton

A Tor Book
Published by Tom Doherty Associates, Inc.
175 Fifth Avenue
New York, NY 10010

Tor Books on the World Wide Web:
http://www.tor.com

ISBN: 0-812-53346-1
Library of Congress Card Catalog Number: 95-6319

Second mass market printing

Printed in the United States of America

0 9 8 7 6 5 4 3 2

Kaleidoscope Century

I

What Rough Beast

i

I wake up for the fourth time I can remember. The first two times were longer ago. Each time I got up, drank water, and took a piss. I think the third time I was looking for a dark-haired girl, maybe ten years old. I might have known her name, and called it. I don't think she was there. I'm not sure.

I know the third time, the time before this, I wandered around the room. There was a battered old werp in the corner, its case dented and scraped, all sorts of stickers and slogan plates pasted and glued to it. I didn't get farther than noticing it was there and wondering if it might be mine. I felt sick and tired so I went back to bed.

I'm awake and much better now. The dreams from before are fading. I sit up in bed and think, *My name is Joshua Ali Quare, and I have a whole life behind me, but I don't remember much of it.* This is normal. I think.

In the mirror by the toilet, my image is hideously thin, muscles wasted as though by a long fever, immense dark circles under my eyes.

My hair's gray, face lined, beard grizzled. I had thought

I was about twenty or twenty-five, possibly younger. Clearly not.

I wish the girl would come back and explain. If I could remember her name, I would call for her.

What baffles me most is that I seem to be in Martian gravity. Not as low as the moon's but lower than Earth's, anyway.

How do I know how much gravity the moon, or Mars, has? The Augmented Shuttle Mission never even left for Mars, and that was just an orbital mission, a near approach to Phobos that would have arrived on my thirtieth birthday. I was planning to get drunk with my friends and watch it.

Inventory of the room:

One steel door, with handle, unlocked, leading into a kitchen.

In kitchen: airlock door with stamped logo that reads SEARS MARSHACK. SEARS OF WELLS CITY, LTD.

One window looking out on a darkening pink sky and reddish dunes streaked with gray and brown, beyond which a lake—or an arm of the sea?—rolls with lead-dull waves impossibly big and slow.

Bed. Smells like I had a bad fever in it for a long time.

Toilet. Foul. Probably missed it a few times while I had the fever.

Sink and drinking glass—christ, I'm thirsty. I take another glass of water before I continue.

Rack: ten shirts, four pairs of pants, socks and underwear on top shelf. Most of it still in the package.

Bathrobe hanging on corner of rack. I put that on.

Fresher in the corner. I must remember to stuff the sheets into it soon.

Recycling shower, must use that too.

Mirror over toilet.

Werp in the corner, in a case that looks more like an old-fashioned portable typewriter than anything else.

Small box, beside the werp, with a key in its lock. A space allocation box, what they give you before you get on a ship, it fits into the slot at the end of your bunk, you have to fit all the belongings you're taking into it.

They *used* to do that. Nowadays spaceships have a bigger space and weight allowance than airliners had when I was young. I just use it because it's a convenient container. It's mostly empty. I know because it's mine.

I feel a rush of memory, much of it confusing, little of it useful. I thought at first that I recognized low gravity because I read so much sci-fi when I was a kid. I don't seem to remember anything reliably after I was about twenty or so, though all sorts of things lurk at the edge of memory. Most of my past seems to be in the corner of my mind's eye, vanishing if I look directly at it.

No, I know about low grav, had experience with regular, no-, micro-, and low. Definitely.

When?

I think, *that box contains seven things.* A brass key, a Boy Scout knife, a bar napkin with a name and phone number on it, a book of matches from Gwenny's Diner, a picture of a young girl, an Army dog tag for John Childs, and a plastic white knight from a cheap chess set. At once I have to know. My fingers scrabble over the surface, find and turn the key. Tears in my eyes—I don't know what that's about.

They are all there, inside, and the first thing I do is lift up the Boy Scout knife and press my face to its cool handle. I recall that it is rusted shut and I can't unfold the blades anymore. Touching it makes me feel better, but I am still crying. I heft the brass key in my hand. My mother gave it to me the last time I ever saw her—a key to the kitchen door. I squeeze it so hard that it bites my flesh, and that feels good, and comforting.

The name on the bar napkin is Anastasia, and I know that wasn't her real name, but I don't remember anything else. The phone number's an old-fashioned ten-digit one, from back when there was local and long-distance. The area code's for Supra New York. I don't remember when phone numbers changed to twelve digits, either, or when SNY was built.

I have an odd feeling that I might be John Childs. The dog tag feels strange; it's on a chain and I slip it around my neck for a moment, before taking it off again with a shudder that I can't quite explain.

I don't know what Gwenny's Diner was, but handling the book of matches (they are very deteriorated and I don't think they would light) makes me feel sort of warm and safe.

When I hold the white knight in my hand, my fingers begin to do a strange little maneuver, like a magician passing something, so that the knight flows around the fingers. I don't understand why I do that. I feel nothing much emotionally but I keep the knight moving.

The little girl is the one I was looking for. I'm pretty sure of that. The picture is a color holo, not the ribbed kind I remember used to be in cereal boxes, but just a flat piece of paper, about two inches square, no slick surface, into which I can look and see a three-dimensional image of the girl. I turn it over and sure enough, there's the back of her head. By angling it around I can see the picture was shot in a basketball gym, using three cameras, and that the photographer was trying to squat in one of the blind spots and not quite managing it—I see one of his sneakers, his checked pants, his red jacket, and just a little of his curly brown hair and mustache. I'm sure I never met him.

Over the girl's right shoulder, with the paper almost perpendicular to my eye, I can see the other kids waiting to be photographed.

I turn it back over and look at the girl. Long dark hair

hangs limply, most of the way down her back. Her chin is just a little prominent, though whether that's a feature she will keep when she grows up, or a freak of being about eleven and very thin, isn't clear. Just a bare suggestion of breasts shows through her thin pullover. She looks uncomfortable, like the gym was cold or perhaps she just didn't want to be photographed. Maybe it's not a school photo but a shot for a refugee i.d. or something.

I can't remember her at any other age. I don't know whether, when I woke up the time before, I was looking for her because I could reasonably expect to find her, or because I was out of my head and raving about things that had happened long ago.

More things are pressing into my memory, and for one moment I'm breathing hard, afraid of being overwhelmed . . . but the surging memories never quite break through to the surface and explain themselves.

I turn to the battered old werp case and open it up. Inside, the werp looks like it's seen better days; there's a prominent dent in the keyboard and the screen has two stains that won't wipe off with my bathrobe sleeve.

The touch of my thumb on the security plate activates it. Must be mine. The screen clears. Words swim up:

YOUR NAME IS JOSHUA ALI QUARE. HIT RETURN.

I do.

THIS IS YOUR WERP. MANY OF YOUR MEMORIES ARE IN HERE. PASSWORD CHECK: WHAT DID YOUR FATHER CALL YOUR MOTHER THE VERY LAST TIME YOU SAW HIM?

The question startles me. I speak the answer aloud, "A Commie cunt." I reach to type it in but apparently the werp has voice processing because it's already responding.

When did werps get voice processing? And when did werps come along, anyway? When I was younger there were only laptops, and I sure couldn't afford one.

The screen scrolls up:

WELCOME TO 2109, JOSHUA, YOU MADE IT AGAIN. READ THIS NEXT PART CAREFULLY.

2109? But that would make me one hundred forty-one years old. . . .

Memories flood back, now, more than before, and I bend forward to read the document:

YOU ARE ON MARS. THE YEAR IS 2109 AND YOU NO LONGER WORK FOR THE KGB, MURPHY'S COMSAT AVENGERS, NIHON-AMERICA, OR THE ORGANIZATION. THERE IS NO MORE SOVIET UNION, NO MORE FREE SOVIET ASSOCIATION, NO MORE EUROPEAN COMMONWEALTH, AND NO MORE UNITED STATES OF AMERICA. EARTH IS COMPLETELY CONTROLLED BY RESUNA. YOU ARE PHYSICALLY JUST OVER SIXTY YEARS OLD. YOU HAVE ONLY FRAGMENTARY MEMORIES OF YOUR FORMER LIFE AS JAMES NORREN, NOR DO YOU RECALL MUCH OF YOUR FORMER LIVES AS JASON TESTOR, BRANDON SMITH, ULYSSES GRANT, FRED ENGELS, EURIPIDES FREDERICKSON, ELISHA TESTOR, OR KINDNESS O'HART. A NEW IDENTITY HAS BEEN ESTABLISHED FOR YOU AS "REAGAN FOSTER HINCKLEY," A JOKE WHICH YOU AND MAYBE A DOZEN HISTORIANS WILL GET.

Below that: directions. On the morning of Thursday, June sixth, if I haven't reported in yet, someone will come to see me and take me to Red Sands City, where I can get a hotel room, activate a bank account, and get my new life underway.

June 6 is ten days away. Today's Memorial Day, I think, then laugh. Who would remember?

The werp says there should be food in the kitchen. I open the door. Fridge, stove, cabinets, sink. Pressure suit on a rack. The airlock door has an elaborate warning sign about conserving air and proper airlock procedure, so I guess whatever's outside isn't fit for breathing. I still don't remember Mars having water, let alone a lake.

In the fridge I find a lot of packages with labels that

don't match their small square shapes: things like "rabbit," "peas," "onion soup," all of them in packages the size and shape of the small package of Velveeta Individual Slices. I look around and see that the gadget that I had thought was a microwave is a "Westinghouse *Foodzup! Reconstitutor.*" Taking a wild guess, I toss a square labelled "tomato soup" and another labelled "Four grilled cheese sandwiches" into it—it looks like a microwave inside, but who can tell?—carefully putting "tomato soup" into a large bowl first.

The readout on the reconstitutor says "select finished or prep for manual." I have no idea so I select "finished" and push the button.

It hums for about two minutes, then chimes. I open the door. In the large bowl I had put the square package of "tomato soup" in, there's a small, covered bowl, and it's full of hot tomato soup. A stack of four grilled cheese sandwiches sits on a plate, though I had not put any plate in there with that package. And there's no sign of the wrappers from the food packages.

I move the food to the table, sit down, eat. It's wonderful.

After the meal, I'm tired. I go back to bed. When I wake up again, it's dark, but I remember everything from before. I check the clock on the werp and find that I am up at 5:00 A.M. local time, or whatever time the werp was set to.

I've slept a long time. No hope of getting back to sleep. I turn on the lights—strange to see pools of yellow light on the Martian soil outside the windows—and go into the kitchen.

Plenty of square packets labelled "coffee, one liter pot." A dozen labelled "eggs," "hash browns," "bacon," "toast." I put one of each into the reconstitutor, not putting a plate or bowl underneath this time. I set it for "finished" and start it running. A coffee cup? A few in the back of one cabinet, all white, small circle on each side of them, and fine print in the circle. I hold the cup at almost arms' length to see the print clearly—I wonder if I have any reading glasses anywhere? And why I'm not surgically corrected?

The text reads: "The use of coffee is associated with bowel cancer, genetic damage, and several disorders of the nervous system. If you are a proven frequent and/or irresponsible coffee user you can be denied health benefits under the Uniform Care Act of 2094."

So some things have changed a lot, others have gotten more the same. I rinse out the cup. The reconstitutor pings.

I move the hot plate of breakfast and steaming pot of coffee to the small kitchen table, sit, and eat. I have to work on gaining back some weight. Whatever's going on, you can't fault the chow.

After I've finished the solid food and poured the second cup of coffee, I get the werp from the other room. Supposedly my history's in here; so far I have a list of seven names, besides my own, apparently aliases I've used at one time or another. And I have my seven objects.

I get up and get the space allocation box, so it's sitting next to me as I begin to read at the werp. I don't want to let the box get far from me, or the werp either.

When the sun comes up I am still reading and scanning. Tens of thousands of separate documents in the werp. Doesn't look like I've been much of a diary keeper, more of a collector, just grabbing up anything that seemed interesting. The werp camera seems to have been used mainly to take short videos of friends. Mostly they just wave and say "Hi" without identifying themselves. Also homemade porn—several shots of women, mostly undressed, right after sex, looking bored. A couple of them are saying things like, "That will cost extra." Several holograms of enormous, sagging breasts, shot up close so that all I can see is the breast.

I find four more pictures of the little girl whose picture is in the box, one each at ages nine, ten, thirteen, and eighteen. Her name was Alice.

The text documents don't reveal much. I wasn't much of a writer. When I do write it's mostly things like shopping lists. From these I learn I like Iron City beer.

Every so often, I find my own voice, usually just audio, sometimes with the video focused on my face, always talking urgently and urging me to remember, not to forget . . . something or other.

I try identifying the dates on all the documents. Perhaps if I read them from earliest to latest, I will learn something.

The one hundred and fourteen earliest ones all have the same date and time, Friday, October 8, 2021, 1745 GMT. One says "Guide note." I cue it up. It says all the other documents were copied from a stack of loose paper, video tape, photos, and cassette tapes that "Brandon Smith" had been carrying with him for a long time. I look about thirty in the note. I say I hope the "Reconstruction-issue" werp will hold up. The werp I have is not nearly that old, I'm sure—werps in those days did not have built-in cameras or holography. Or at least "Reconstruction-issue" werps didn't.

I keep working at it, as the sun comes up over the Martian beach outside. I take a minute to get up and stretch, look out the window at a bright point in the sky—Deimos, probably. I can't see it moving visibly. The small white sun climbs up out of the water toward the moon. It's a windy day and the waves out on the—lake? bay? sea? whatever—are bouncing about crazily. I feel ill looking at them.

Pull the curtains. Reconstitute another pot of coffee. Keep going. I have more than one version of my early life. They can't all be true. But the different versions all seem to be supported by fragments of my memory.

Taking a break from the early documents, wandering at random through all the others, I see a note, dated 2093, called "Inconsistencies." I call it up and discover it's a short clip of myself—looking not much younger than I look now, though it's twenty-six years in the past—talking earnestly into the camera, stopping every now and then for a pull on a beer. "Start with a list of questions. Is the girl in the picture named Anastasia, Bambi, or Alice? Is she my daughter, a girl I befriended, or perhaps my wife or girlfriend at a younger age? Could she have had more than one identity and more than one role?

"Did I get the Boy Scout knife from the body of John Childs, as I seem to remember, or was it a gift from someone? If a gift, who from? And how did it get rusted shut? I remember both finding it after several years of not having it, and burying it in the ground once. Did I do any of that?

"I think I make up stories based on the few documents I have and the few memories that leak through. Some of them are dreams I think. Then the stories end up in the document files looking just like everything else. Wish I was better at keeping records. Even with stuff from within this lifetime, I'm not even sure which files in here now are by me and which ones I edited when I moved them to the new werp. I just don't know. Sorry."

My image clicks off. I sit, stare at the screen for a long time, get up, look out the window. Late afternoon. Don't know any more than I did by mid-morning, just know it more ways.

At least I have some idea what's behind my being here. One of the earliest documents, if it's a real one, says I come back into the world differently every time a "transit" happens. Maybe this time the transit made me a better writer. I'm not sure, but I'm sitting here typing.

I wonder when and where I learned to type. I don't recall being able to when I left home. I couldn't do shit when I left home, if you want to know the truth.

I want to know the truth.

I sit and type as the sun sets on the other side of the

building. Now that the waves aren't so big I leave the curtains open.

The water never gets blue here on Mars—except right at sunrise and sunset when the sky is sometimes briefly deep blue and the water reflects it. I keep looking up at the window, away from the werp screen, because I don't want to miss the moment when that happens.

ii

I was born in 1968. Till past 2000, you could say practically everything about me by saying that my mother was a black lawyer's daughter and my father was a white ex-con with a political history. Grandpa got Daddy out of jail for the ACLU, and lived to regret it (I heard him say that himself). Mama was an activist, passionate in her battle to overcome everything about the past, in her early twenties in 1966 when they married. She was ten years younger than Daddy, and Daddy was the big, strong, handsome, innocent man that had written two books in prison.

Except he wasn't innocent. He liked to rub Mama's nose in that. He had brains, looks, and a lot of charm when he wanted to, but he was guilty as all hell of the rapes he'd been convicted of. He hadn't been convicted by a proper procedure, was all. It was only that *if* he'd been innocent, he'd've gone to jail anyway. Hence the "matter of principle"—which is a "technicality" you agree with, as Grandpa used to say—that was known to lawyers as *Quare v. Tennessee.*

He was huge—a tall man, with a deep chest and arms like iron. Gray-blond hair in tight curls. Fine-boned face always red from the sun, from drinking, and probably from whatever he was doing to his lungs with all the Camels he smoked, lighting each one off the previous, so there was always one clenched between his bared, yellow teeth. From the time I was able to remember him, he had a permanent squint, as if he always looked into the sun.

I remember his voice was soft, even, and polite around Mama's parents, and that whenever he got onto a tear working on a book, he'd barricade himself into his little office and just type away for hours. He never finished one after getting out of the pen, though. He claimed that without being locked up he didn't have the incentive to revise.

My mother was light-skinned, anyway, and as a result I was one of those people of no definite race that you see everywhere now. Call me ahead of my time. When Daddy would get drunk and mean, he'd sometimes call me "that little half-nigger" in front of Mama, just to hurt her, which was why he did most things as far as I could tell. I don't think I invented my memories of him hitting me, or her; I don't think there's much exaggeration in my believing he raped her twice a week during all the years they were married. Maybe it was different back before I could remember.

Mama stayed. If there were a god, he might know why. Maybe the shame of the mistake she'd made, a bright, talented, beautiful woman giving herself to a big, vicious ape with a smooth line of talk? It couldn't have been fear it would come out. It *was* out. I saw Grandma Couandeau bandaging Mama up when I was seven, and I already knew that was nothing you wanted to ask about.

I was never close to Daddy's size. I had Grandpa Couandeau's build, slight and small. I hated Daddy as much as I would ever hate anyone, and I fell asleep dreaming of beating him up and throwing him out of the house. It never happened.

I was a third-generation Red Diaper baby. Andre Couandeau, my grandfather's father, had joined the Party in the 1920s, and, at least according to family legend, died under a cop's nightstick during the sit-down strike at Firestone ten years later. Mama, in her stroller, had attended Paul Robeson's last concert in America, claimed she remembered the backs of the longshoremen and truckers as they stood down the Legionaires "for free speech." She always told me, "You get free speech when you get the power to stand up for yourselves. Till then all you have is *tolerated* speech, Josh, no matter what they tell you in school."

We argued a lot about what I got taught in school, because I saw no sense in arguing with teachers. I was perfectly willing to agree with Mama that it was all bourgeois lies, but I didn't see any reason why I should have to correct it. Not when I could quietly drift along in the back of the room, ignored by everyone, and keep my concentration on basic issues like saving up for a car out of my job at McDonald's. It was okay with me that we went to CP stuff all the time, and the demonstrations were kind of fun, but it was like being born a Witness or a Mormon—you weren't exactly like the people around you, but you weren't *not* like them, either. You just had a slightly different set of adult friends and links to different families than other kids did.

When I was little, Mama's cell used to meet at the house, but that stopped pretty soon because Daddy was not what you could call "reliable." I get the impression he was never invited to join the Party. Anything that excluded him rankled him, but he mostly confined himself to claiming he was going to turn Mama in (even though the Party had been legal for years) "for the reward." Then he'd laugh and say he was just kidding.

Now and then they'd ask him to talk to a meeting about his time in prison. He'd tell the same stories, all from his first book, over and over.

He was also jealous, I think, of Mister Harris. I think of him that way, even now, *Mister* Harris. In Mama's and Grandpa's eyes, this was the most important person they knew. Mister Harris "traveled," which meant he drew a stipend from the Party and went from cell to cell on regular visits. Kind of a circuit preacher, kind of a beat cop.

Mama and Grandpa were both on the state Central Committee. Grandpa was known on sight to Gus Hall. Mama had shared a hotel room once, at a conference, with Angela Davis, but somehow Mister Harris was more important. It took me a long time to figure out why.

I left home forever on my sixteenth birthday. Two of the earliest documents I've got—both audio recordings of me reciting as much as I could about my own past—agree that it was my sixteenth birthday.

I passed the driver's license exam at 3:50 P.M. that day—the earliest moment after school it could be managed. My score was perfect, which was no surprise since driver's ed and auto shop had been my only "A" subjects. That meant I had to run to make McDonald's in time for my job, with so little time that I couldn't even pass by the house, just a few blocks out of my way, where a beautiful little silver RX-7—merely 120,000 miles and only six years old—was parked, for which the owner wanted just $1600.

The guy was holding it for me—$2200 in my account, $1600 for the car, $45 to register it, $12 plate fee, first insurance payment $130—two days and that car was mine.

Like most kids I knew, I was working five hours a night, piling up cash so I could have things. Might as well. They didn't teach shit in school. If you took General Math and General Science you didn't need to learn anything after eighth grade to pass, and no one needed to stay up all night studying to "express feelings" in English class or "give opinions" in American History. Half the class never read the books and got B's, anyway.

I wasn't expecting anything real big for my birthday—there never had been before. Turning sixteen was about the best present I could have had, anyway.

I trotted home all the same. Mama had told me there'd

be a cake and a gift or two. I did take the time on the way home to swing by and make sure the RX-7 was still there.

Mama had made a cake, chocolate since that was my favorite—something from a mix, she was a lousy cook but could follow directions. There was a new shirt, wrapped, and I put that on.

Daddy had been drinking I guess. He usually had. I have no idea what started it. Like always, it happened too fast.

I was still in the chair, but leaned back on the back legs, my not-quite-finished cake spilled into my lap. His hand was on my shirt and he hit me again, several times, hard, beating my face so that it went numb and soft, as he explained to me that I didn't fucking need a fucking car and it was about fucking time for me to start fucking supporting the family. "Fuckin' kid thinks he's too fucking good to be one of the family," he said, and threw me backwards. The chair flipped out from under me and my tailbone hit a rung.

My head banged on the wall but I wasn't dazed or stupid enough to put my hands up. Once he started one of these, trying to protect yourself just made it worse.

He grabbed me again, dragging me to my feet, tearing my shirt—a new one, a gift I had just put on (why is it I remember every button of a plain blue shirt so clearly?). His thumbs digging into my armpits, he shook me back and forth and said, "We're going to fuckin' start chargin' you rent, boy. It's a good thing you saved up for it."

He cuffed me once more across the back of the head, slapped my face once more and said, with the exaggerated sarcasm of a mean drunk, "Oh, he's not happy. Oh, he's mad. Well, he needs to say 'Thank you, Daddy,' for putting a fuckin' roof over his head, that's what he needs. He's got no fuckin' business being mad, does he. Say 'Thank you, Daddy.' "

I don't know if I was too dazed or too mad. I didn't speak.

He drove his knuckles into my face. "Say 'Thank you, Daddy.' "

I still said nothing. Too numb. Or couldn't think.

He started slapping my face, with his open hand, one blow after another. My left cheek took about ten blows. It was bruised almost black for a week afterwards. Then he threw me on my back and said, "Your rent's due tomorrow, boy. I'll let you know how much." He stood for a moment, breathing hard, and then added, "Here's your cake," and threw the rest at me. Then he laughed a stupid-sounding half-laugh as if he were about to decide whether or not to tell me it was all a joke, or kill me.

I stayed still. After a few seconds his office door slammed. He shouted through the door that he could never get any fucking work done, he fucking had to put up with a lazy free-loading half-nigger and a Commie cunt.

Mama stood by uselessly. Typical. Daddy was crazy, mean, and dangerous. But I hated Mama more. She was useless.

I cleaned myself up, pulled on a sweatshirt, threw what remained of my new shirt in the trash. It didn't seem worthwhile to do anything about the mess in the dining room.

All the clothes I wanted to keep went into two gym bags. I'd never read much and there weren't any books I cared about, but I threw a bunch of tapes and the Walkman in, figuring it might help if I got lonely. It wasn't cold out but I put on my leather jacket.

The passbook for my bank account was in my jeans pocket. Thank god there had never been an ATM card, or he'd already have the cash. I figured the bank opened at 8:30 the next morning and hell if I was going to let the old bastard bully Mama, the co-signer on my account, into getting the money out for him. Probably he'd lost some cash gambling, or wanted to go on a spree with some of his barfly friends, or maybe go hit the whorehouse a couple of times so he could come home and tell Mama about it. Probably he hadn't been able to get the cash out of her because she didn't have it. That would have been all he needed to set him off on this "paying rent" business.

When I got downstairs, I could hear him snoring—he usually passed out in his office, ten minutes after he would go in there, because before he started working he'd have a few off the bottle in his desk.

Mama was trying to get the cake up off the rug by picking up the crumbs one at a time, too scared to turn on the vacuum and wake him up. I didn't bother to say goodbye. She'd figure it out.

But as I opened the back door, I felt her hand in the middle of my back. "You should go to an emergency room," she said. "I can give you some cash for that. What if you have a concussion?"

"I don't," I said, pulling away from her, but she caught my hand and pushed something between my fingers. I looked down. A hundred dollar bill and a house key.

"You know what times he's not in. Come in and take food, clothes, anything you need," she said. "And you know he sleeps real sound. Help yourself. You're entitled."

I nodded and went out the door. I kept the hundred and the key in my hand, inside my pocket, for blocks, just holding them. I knew I would have to part with the hundred soon.

Years later I regretted not having kissed Mama goodbye that night. I guess maybe I figured I'd be back.

The old bastard had locked me out a few times. Never for two nights running, fortunately. But I'd gotten pretty good at knowing how to keep myself out of serious trouble for a night. I knew what places in town would be open at 11 P.M., and would stay open.

So I headed straight to Gwenny's, a diner out toward the edge of town. My face was hurting with every step, and I could feel it swelling. A couple teeth felt loose, but more like I just needed to be careful than like I was going to lose them. My nose was bent and bruised, but probably not broken. Years of drinking had sapped the force of those arms, so the muscles were still big, but they were filled out mostly with lard. He was in pretty shitty shape, and the thought crossed my mind, if I wanted to chance getting killed, maybe I could take him.

Not worth it. So far I didn't have any damage around the eyes, or probably even any broken bones. It would cost something if I got hurt worse. And what would I want to fight him for anyway? The right to leave?

My face pulsed with pain as I crossed the river. The bridge was long and not high, and when I was younger I used to stand on it and look down at the trout behind the pillars. The moon was coming up now, over the willows in their tangled masses, clinging to the sandbars downstream, and I paused for a moment. No longer numb, my face ached pretty badly. I could feel tears and snot streaking over my cheeks and lip, but it seemed like too much bother, just now, to wipe any of that off.

My hand was still in my pocket, digging that old brass house key into my palm like I was trying to drive it into the bone. It wasn't much, but she had defied him more, just now, than she ever had before.

I knew I wouldn't use the key. Sure, I could get in and out and take stuff, but I didn't want liquor. After smelling him all these years I figured I'd never touch it. Anything else I took would just make Mama that much poorer.

The front of my knuckles was brushing something else. I let go of the key, gripped the hard lump I had found, and pulled it out, careful not to lose the key or the hundred.

In the moonlight it shone like magic. The eagle was

worn down, and the ring for clipping it to your belt was gone. I opened the blades and checked; I had kept it sharp.

When I was eleven, every boy in my class became a Scout. Not me. That's not something a Red Diaper does. I also couldn't hang out with the kids who were too cool for it. They were *lumpen.*

So Mama threw her fit, and I gave up on it, like I had on a dog, or a BB gun, or youth hockey. Then one afternoon, early in the spring, Daddy gave me a brand-new Boy Scout knife. Told me to keep it in good shape and it would serve me well. It had never been out of my reach since.

I looked at it. He'd won it at cards or dice. Or maybe he'd been feeling too ill to get a pint, he'd seen it in a pawnshop and been generous in the spontaneous, random way of a nasty drunk. I thought about how a thousand times since I'd heard him tell the story of the knife to his friends, and how they—drunken pigs all—had nodded for the thousandth time and agreed what a great guy Daddy was.

It was the only proof I'd ever had that that man had given a shit whether I lived or died. Not worth carrying the weight.

I was crying harder now—maybe my face hurt more—but I could see plenty well enough to hit the river with that Scout knife. It made a low-pitched reverberating *plonk,* right where I knew there was a deep hole.

The splash made a ring-ripple that drifted downstream maybe a hundred yards before it faded into other disturbances on the water, and the moon wavered and flickered in fragments and bits all over the silver surface. I shuddered and was glad to be wearing the jacket.

Not midnight yet, still my birthday.

I kicked the post a couple times, bounced back and forth. Maybe, once for a second, I thought about flipping over the railing.

Sure. Give the old fuck twenty-two hundred. That'll show him.

I wiped my face on my coat sleeve, pulled out a handkerchief, cleaned up as well as I could without a sink or mirror. I looked once more at the pool of black water where I had thrown the knife, just off the nearest pillar and behind the boulder that always stuck out late in the summer. I sort of thought a goodbye at it, and headed on over the bridge, walking fast to warm up.

Somehow, having done that, I felt lighter on my feet. I cradled the key in my fingers, squeezing it hard until it was warm as my own blood.

There were three reasons I was headed for Gwenny's. One, it was open all night, and Gwenny, the owner, generally took the night shift. I'd been in there some nights when I was locked out, drinking coffee and slowly eating chili, watching the big TV screen in the corner, and she'd been friendly and concerned in a not-pushy way.

Two, she had furnished rooms for rent, or she had had them last week, anyway, and maybe I could talk her into taking the hundred down and the rest in the morning. I had no idea what rent might be but it would sure be less than Daddy would have taken.

The most important thing was that her place was close to the bank. Whether or not I got a place to stay for the night, I needed to be there on the dot at eight-thirty.

Besides Gwenny, her cook Paula, and Verna, the older woman who waited tables, only three other people were in Gwenny's: a couple who sat with their arms around each other looking like they were trying to stay awake, and a guy who talked endlessly to them. That group was in a booth far over to one side, out of sight of everyone else. The rest of the Formica tables and Naugahyde booths waited, napkins, silverware, and cups laid out, for a crowd that there was no sign of. Probably it would fill up more later that night.

"Jesus, Josh, how did you do that to yourself?" Gwenny asked.

"I didn't. My father did," I said, trying to sound tough and failing. Anyone could have heard the tears in my throat.

"Don't look like nothing's broke," Verna said. "But you're gonna look like hell for a while."

"You going to press charges?" Paula asked. She was big on knowing the official way to do everything. "What he did's illegal, you know. He can't be hitting you that way. You're his son."

I shrugged. "Mama would lie for him. He'd get acquitted. And they'd make me go back to live with him. Do you still have furnished rooms, Gwenny?"

She looked at me closely then, a piercing stare that seemed to see farther into me than I had known existed. "Yes," she said slowly, "I do. You know if you rent a room and then move back home next week, the money's gone? And you're going to have to pay for the whole term of the rental agreement, even if you don't stay that long?"

"Yeah, I know all that," I said. "It doesn't matter. I'm not going back there, ever. He'll kill me if I stay there. How much is it?"

"My smallest one's eighty-five a month. If you and what's in those bags is all you're gonna have in it, it might suit. You get two towels and two sets of sheets and things, and keeping them clean's up to you—laundry-mat's round the corner. One shelf in the common fridge, privileges to use the stove, but you got to get your own pans and dishes. Usually I get some student at the university who's really broke to take the deal."

"Well, I'm a student, I guess," I said, "though I'm not sure how safe it'll be for me to go to school. I want that high school diploma for a job. . . ." The world suddenly seemed to reel, and I almost fell.

Gwenny caught me, in her strong arms—she was taller than I was and muscular—and said, "You've just had a pretty awful shock. I think we better get you up to the room, get you settled in, and then in honor of your being a new tenant and all, we might just find you a meal on the house, or some coffee if you're not hungry."

I felt myself blushing all over; I hadn't meant to faint, and now I could feel tears burning down over my cheeks. None of the women seemed to notice. Gwenny guided me back outside, up the exterior steps, and then down the hall to my new home.

In a room about fifteen feet square she had a small bed, two end tables, an old kitchen table, two chairs, and a wardrobe without a door. We got the business of money and keys taken care of, and she told me not to worry about the security deposit. "I'm not worried, Josh, I mean, where would you go?"

Five days later I stopped going to school because I got another job in addition to the one at McDonald's. I was a mechanic's helper at a gas station; at least it meant I could work on cars. Between the two jobs I could afford my car, insurance, and room, with a little extra left over. Mostly I put that extra in my new, me-only bank account. If I wasn't exactly set for life, I had the RX-7 to drive around in.

I kept the brass key Mama had given me in my pocket all the time. I was always pulling it out when I meant to pull out my building key, car key, or room key—but I didn't mind. At night, I put it in a special place on the end table, so that if I woke up I could see the key from my bed, by the light of the diner's sign.

iii

I sit back and look at what I've written. I can't believe how long it took, and it all looks stupid and wrong. I know what story I meant to tell, but all the first paragraph says is "Mama was black, Daddy was white, and he used to hit us both a lot. So I left when I turned sixteen and he said I had to pay rent. I stayed with a woman named Gwenny." There's too much about fixing up the RX-7, and a list of the kinds of bowties Grandpa Couandeau used to wear, and like that. I set down all these details but it doesn't make a story.

And there's just two and a half pages and most of what I remember isn't there. Maybe I write more, this time around, but I sure don't write any better.

I stretch, yawn, feel the way my shoulders cramp. God, I didn't get down a thing about Harris. And I don't know how much of this I'm making up. I suppose the thing to do is to put today's date on what I just finished writing, so I do that. Now at least I'll know I wrote it long after the fact—god, more than a century—and that it's a mix of things I remember, things I think I remember, stuff I figured out from older documents, and god knows what-all.

Maybe tomorrow I'll just talk into the machine. Meanwhile I'm tired and I've had too much coffee. I get up and pace around, wondering if there's any equivalent of TV. If they've got flashchannel or something somewhere, maybe, then I could get caught up on what's going on.

It's also high time for a shower. At least the water seems to be on its first trip through. I use the bathrobe as my towel and spread it out so that it'll dry.

If I were at normal weight the clothes would probably fit pretty well. As it is they hang on me in a loose, baggy way that reminds me of the "gangsta" clothes a lot of kids my age wore, back in the last part of the twentieth century. That makes me laugh, looking at this old man in too-big shirt and sagging pants in the mirror.

Still much too awake and wondering when I'll feel like sleeping, I put the makings of another big meal into the reconstitutor, and then put some more effort into looking for a television, a holobox, or even just a flashchannel reader. Finally I have a vague memory that things aren't separate anymore, and I sit back down at the werp and play around for a minute on the menus.

Sure enough, the werp's also the receiver. I turn it to the "News and Views Basic" channel, since that has no surcharge and I'm not sure who is picking up the bills on any of this, or how much money I have, if any. Then I set the werp a little distance away from me. One thing TV had that these don't, you could take up a whole room with a TV so nobody had to talk and it didn't feel empty. This way leaves you sitting in a lonely little spot, just you and the werp screen a couple of feet apart with the rest of the room empty. Not to mention I have already looked at the werp all day.

The reconstitutor rings, and I get out the meal—goat meatloaf, potatoes, asparagus, beets. Probably healthy as all shit but what do I know? I remember Woody Allen had a movie, a real old one I saw once. A health nut woke up in the future and it turned out all the things like hot fudge, steak, and cigars were what was really good for you.

No hot fudge or steak among the stacked meals in the fridge. No beef at all, in fact. Are cows extinct or am I Hindu?

I dim the room lights and power up the werp. It's almost like TV. Sort of comforting, but I wish the screen were bigger so I could put it farther away.

Well, one thing hasn't changed: whenever you tune in to a news channel the first thing you get is weather from someplace nowhere near you. In this case it's a weather report for North America on Earth. There are no borders. It sounds like whatever runs the Earth is called Resuna. At first I think Resuna is the name of the government, then that maybe everyone on Earth is named Resuna. When they stop talking about it I'm more confused than when they started. A lot of what the voices are talking about is storms blowing in off "Hudson Glacier" menacing the "Floridas." That makes me take a second glance, and now I see that there's a splash of big islands where the peninsula used to be. To judge from the square shape of some of them, they're probably doing something like the old Dutch dike-and-polder system to get the land rebuilt, and it looks like it must have been going on for a while.

Now that I am looking for changes in the land, I see that the Great Lakes drain through the Ohio and the Hudson; the big white blob at the end of the St. Lawrence must be ice? Pretty clearly Lake Ontario has expanded enough so that Oneida Lake is just a bay, and Chatauqua Lake has been gobbled in the same way by Erie. The main drains must be through the Mohawk and the Beaver.

I wonder when I got to know that area so well, and I have a sudden flash of tents pitched in the snow, of men on skis with rifles. Murphy's Comsat Avengers, that's who I was with. I was in that outfit with Sadi.

I noticed, when I was first browsing through and looking at all the pictures, that there were a few of me from when I was Yuri Frederickson, around 2060-something. I call them up now. The pictures show me grizzled, middle-aged, on skis, wearing a pale blue uniform under an open white parka, rifle in hand.

They switch to a weather report for South America. I don't remember anything about the geography there except that I am pretty sure that the passage between South America and Antarctica wasn't ice-covered when I was growing up, and I don't think there used to be big glaciers in the middle of the continent.

A little box pops up in one corner to say "Option Point" and I reach out and push a key combination on the keyboard before I can think about what the box means or what I might be doing. I sit back, take a big bite of meatloaf, and wonder what my fingers remembered that I didn't.

The screen clears and there's an anchorman sitting there, saying "Hello, Mars. Here's the quick break—"

What follows is much like any smalltown covers-the-county FM station, back in the 1980s. A fire in Red Sands City, inside the main habitat. They had to vent some atmosphere and re-pump to pressure. Olympia reports a rash of petty theft. The Planning Council of Marinerburg announced yesterday that the sea level had risen another 120 cm in the last year and that within ten years the water should be up to the piers. Today local elections are being contested in several places, and the current General Coordinator of Mars is in minor political trouble over some complex financial dealings years back, when she had headed up the Port Authority for Deimos.

I can't tell how long people have been living here, but at least I get some idea where the water and air are coming from. They broadcast a list of times and targets for the next day—scheduled impacts for about a hundred chunks of comets and carbonaceous chondrites.

I have to spend a long minute thinking how I knew what a carbonaceous chondrite is. Despite my best efforts I still have no idea where that knowledge had entered my brain from.

But I do know: it's an asteroid made up of a lot of rocky and tarry stuff, along with the usual bits of iron. They are being used as feedstocks for life on Mars. The Development Corporation's crashing fifty-metric-ton chunks of them, dozens at a time, into the South Pole, to make feeding grounds for the oxyliberators. It also releases vast quantities of planet-warming CO_2 and water. Later in the Martian year, at the equinox, they will switch to the North Pole—they always bombard the pole that's having winter, forcing much of the carbon dioxide and water back into the atmosphere.

I hoped the big meal and a little time watching the news would knock me out, but it hasn't helped. I'm still wide awake, trying to piece together memories, documents, memories of documents, and documents of memories. . . . "History is a dull party at which we struggle to fall asleep," I say, out loud, quoting Sadi, then realize I've thought about him ten times, and I don't know—I ask the werp. "Who's Sadi?"

"Reference document list appears offscreen, want it brought up to front?" the werp asks, in my voice.

"Yes," I say. I didn't know it could do that. Considering it's more than twenty years old and obviously it's used to me, it looks like the memory holes are bigger than ever.

I read the documents it pulls up for me for ten minutes or so. Sadi was my best friend, maybe my only friend, for forty or fifty years at least. The documents are all from the middle of the twenty-first century.

I remember one time Sadi and I got a special mission: the last time we ever talked face to face with Murphy, and one of the few times we had any direct conversation with One True. That was in the War of the Memes.

The thought is so sudden and so unasked-for that I don't quite know what to do with it. I ask myself, "Who is Sadi?" again, and bust right out laughing there in the Marshack, with no one else to see me or share the joke.

Not know Sadi? Might as well ask who was Mama or who is Santa Claus or Ronald McDonald. There's a lot I can't remember, of course, about him, but he was so much—I reach for the memory, and this time, for once, more impressions come, the confusion lifts like fog in the sun, and the story hangs together in my head.

Murphy was the colonel—that was the title he gave himself, anyway—of Murphy's Comsat Avengers, Inc., the private mercenary regiment that Sadi and I were in during the War of the Memes. Instantly my fingers are flying over the werp keys: what's a meme, when did we leave the organization, what's a comsat avenger—

The answers don't make any more sense than they did before, right away, but I have a feeling that a few things from 2064 are falling into place, documents fitting to memories and vice versa. I keep thinking and reading. "Comsat Avengers" because Murphy was an old vag *(vag?)* who had been in a business selling access to comsats before the supras *(supras? just a minute ago I knew what those were)* were built.

Supras put comsats out of business, right. So Murphy, crazy as a syphilitic ferret, started out to destroy the people who built the supras. Gotcha. Complete losing cause. Trying to kill the whole world government. By the late 2040s Murphy was down to fifteen aging nuts like himself, all hiding out in a UN Mandated Wilderness Area, pretending to be Castro or Robin Hood or somebody like that.

Then 2049 rolls around and we're in the War of the Memes. All of a sudden there's money for a guy like Murphy, as long as he'll let someone else tell him what to attack. He goes to work for One True and the Organization orders Sadi and I to join him—

One True. Something about that term made me shudder.

So we worked for One True in the War of the Memes.

That sounds like whatever One True was, it was a meme, whatever a meme was.

I ask the werp, "Do you have a dictionary?"

"Of which languages?"

"English will do fine, I think. Define meme."

"There are over thirty definitions."

"Give me all of 'em—uh, no, hold on—give me the ones that are nouns."

"Meme. Noun. Obsolete meaning coined originally by Richard Dawkins, twentieth century, by analogy to 'gene,' to mean fundamental communicable ideas, such as melodies, pottery patterns, literary forms, taboos, fashions, superstitions, customs, et cetera. Also obsolete: fundamental force opposing gene in Walter Koch's philosophic formulation ELPIS. Also obsolete: compelling musical motif, in neojazz and parahop styles of music. Also obsolete: fixation, addiction, compulsion. Also obsolete—"

"Uh, how about just the meaning in the context of War of the Memes?" I ask.

"Meme. Noun. Any of several thousand very large self-replicating artificial intelligences capable of functional copy transference across operating system boundaries, including but not limited to electronic, optical-switching, biological, and text-record operating systems."

I think about that. "Smart viruses?" I ask. "And does 'biological systems' mean 'human brains'?"

"The term virus is long obsolete in a context applied to computing; in its biological sense it is inapplicable here. Biological systems in this case is not limited to human brains as chimpanzee or dolphin brains theoretically—"

"Close enough," I say. "It's coming back now, thanks."

I remember it now. In what had been upstate New York, in 2064. The War of the Memes was down to about twenty-five competing memes worldwide, and just over half the world population was carrying some dominant meme—some program running in their heads had replaced whatever personality grew there naturally. One True was doing pretty well. It had North America east of the Missouri and north of the Tennessee, plus little scattered bases everywhere else.

It was the best deal going. Because it was so secure, One True had an area it could set aside for R&R for its mercenaries—so we sometimes got a real break. And though most troops had to worry about getting memed by putting themselves under a meme's control, we at least had Murphy, who was crazed and paranoid and did everything to prevent One True from communicating with us directly.

"Oh, I'm glad he does all that," Sadi said. "I mean, I have no desire at all to end up as one more copy of One True, and I don't want to see it happen to you either, bud. But I can't help being a little sorry that we never get to talk to it."

"Why? What do you or I have to say to a meme? 'So why is it you want to run my body?' "

He laughed, leaning back in the sun. God, he was a handsome man even then, past his prime; the white streaks in his brown hair ran along his temples like a comic book hero's, his blue eyes still looked deep into you, and his long, slim body didn't have an extra ounce of fat. "But there's that other side. Memes live forever and have such a variety of experiences. Which isn't a bad way to describe us longtimers."

Longtimers? I think to myself. *I knew what those were a minute ago too.* I get up, stretch, relax my muscles and shake out my body, then stretch out on the bed, trying to daydream the experience back into my body, trying to forget I'm on Mars and reach fifty years into my scrambled, uncertain memories. Where and when did we have that conversation? And since it was pretty much the kind of idle chatter that Sadi and I shared all the time, what made this one stand out? I was thinking something about the only time we talked to Murphy and to One True . . . I relax, shut my eyes, try not to force it, try to just listen inside my head—

We were sitting outside our cabin in Put-in-Bay on a nice June day, a few weeks after the Battle of Minneapolis Ruin, when we'd thrown the forces of Free American back from the edges of One True's territory, pursuing them all the way back to Fargo Dome.

That had been fun; Fargo Dome hadn't been hit significantly before, and the loot was terrific. Not to mention Sadi and I had grabbed one whole sorority house at the University of North Dakota, turned the ugly ones over to One True and spent three days serbing the pretty ones before Murphy called the unit back in and we had to hang all of them. Not the way we'd have done it—Sadi always said that when you played with someone like that for a while the least you could do was give them an individual death and then remember it forever. Not really esthetic or special, but still there was something about doing them all in an hour, in one mass hanging, chick after chick hoisted kicking into the air, all of them naked, the ones yet to be done cowering in the corner, bruised, bloody, crying for their mothers—I still got stiff thinking about it.

I fall back out of the memory, sick to my stomach, thinking at first it was some hideous nightmare, but no, I'm quite sure we did that. I want to say Sadi did it but the fact is I was right there with him and I loved it too. Even now, when I think of those terrified kids and how long it went on—high as we were on a triple dose of gressors we didn't sleep or leave them alone for three days. And that last hour—the tall girl with the brown hair that started to pray—

I sit up, breathing deeply, wishing for a pill to make it all go away, thinking of putting on the pressure suit and going out and pitching that werp with all its pictures and sounds into the water, think of—

How good it would be to have Sadi here. He always knew what to do when I was upset. He was much more use to me than Mama or Daddy ever was.

The memory crawls back now, not of Minneapolis but of the R&R camp in the Erie Islands. Nice day, we were sitting outside. I had been going through You-4 withdrawal—a little, the way I did after every big battle—so I'd had two days of dreadful depression, but then I'd woken up that morning feeling fine. Sadi never seemed to be affected the way I was; he took at least as many drugs as I did but he shook them off easier, and he rarely took them to get over the things he'd done. Good thing, too, because when I woke up sobbing or screaming he could be right there to take care of me.

"You just have to get your balance, bud," he'd say. "You had a rough childhood or something. You have a hard time remembering that when it's happening to them, it's not happening to you. Freud said that, you know. What makes a thing funny is when it happens to someone else and not to you. And de Sade pointed that out, as long as you get bothered by hitting other people's noses you'll never really have the freedom to enjoy swinging your fist."

I was sitting there listening to him, a big mug of coffee and a slice of fresh hot bread at hand. Made by Sadi. Naturally. The man could cook. Not like a fag or anything, he could just *cook.* At least as well as he could talk, and I loved to hear him talk.

So I sat and listened; no point interrupting something I was enjoying. Between bites of bread I practiced passes with the white knight. The only worthwhile thing I ever learned from Daddy, something he'd done in prison, practiced all this stuff from *Everyone's Big Book of Magic,* all the ways to make things appear and disappear out of your hand. That little plastic white knight from a chess set had been dancing around between my fingers a long time, going away here and popping back there. I almost always did that while I listened to Sadi.

"Look, Josh," he was saying, "it's the simplest thing in the world. People make a big deal about the War of the Memes as some big tragedy. The only tragedy is someday a meme will win, and then we won't have our freedom anymore. But you listen to Hobbes. What he said was that the state of nature was the war of each against all. In other words we're just doing what's natural, you got that? It's all that old repression and stuff that makes you feel bad, not what you did."

"I don't feel bad now," I pointed out.

"Yeah, but you know what's going to happen, bud. Another mission's going to come up, and we'll have a good old time serbing somebody One True wants serbed, but then after we've laughed ourselves sick on it, you'll start crying and babbling about some German bitch you serbed fifty years ago, or about your Mama, or something, and I'll have to nurse you out of it. And I don't mind taking care of you—hell, you've taken care of me more times than I count. We depend on each other and we're friends and that's what that's all about. But I just wish it didn't put you in so much pain. I worry about you."

I shrugged. "Not much to be done about that, I guess. I don't think I'll get over it, but I manage in spite of it. And it could be worse—if Murphy had signed on with Free American or Unreconstructed Catholic, we'd just be fighting all the time. Neither of those memes will let you hurt a prisoner, let alone serb the civilians. At least One True lets us do the fun part."

A runner came up to us, a kid who didn't look much more than twelve years old, with a note saying that Aristophanes Jones and Euripides Frederickson were wanted at

HQ, in person. We glanced at each other—because it was getting so dangerous, we hadn't actually met our CO in more than a year, even though he controlled most of the buddy teams individually. The runner himself was a sign of how bad it was getting; no electronic or fiber optic could be completely trusted anymore.

A few minutes later we walked into HQ, past all kinds of guards and technicians. Through the pulser to fry any electronics we might be carrying. Finger and iris scans to make sure it was us. Getting to be a suspicious world. Finally they showed us in to Murphy.

He hadn't improved in the last year. He still had a square head with tightly cropped gray hair, and a lot of wrinkles running through his deep tan. And he still had the same mad stare. The Organization had not chosen to back people like this because we thought they were good; we picked them in hopes of keeping things stirred up, of not letting any one meme win, by making sure that all of them had a few units like MCA: competent enough but hopelessly crazy.

Murphy grunted. "Here's the deal. We finally located the source of the Freecybers, and you're not going to believe it. Right back in our home territory, near Oneida. And part of the reason we couldn't find it was that it was never any kind of organization at all. Two freelancers, a husband and wife, working back channels off an old bounce antenna pointed at Supra New York. We finally busted the encryption on it. Well, I didn't, but One True did." He giggled, hard, and looked around to see if either of us got the joke. We stared back at him. "I can never remember which one of you I made a special ops captain and which one I made his body guard."

First either of us had heard of it. "Him," Sadi said, his face perfectly straight.

Murphy wasn't the type to ask for clarification, so he

nodded. Then he giggled again. "See, the stupid thing is that they'd have been fine and had my protection if they'd just worked through the old comsat system. If they weren't doing this through an antenna on one of those fucking supras, those giant peckers of the one world government sticking into the planet, shit, no problem, I really approve of them fighting off the memes since those are all agents of the one world government. But they had to go and use that antenna and give themselves away as just one more representative—"

He went on like that for a long time, which was usual. The longer he talked the more he'd remember whatever his goofy principles were. Finally, though, he gave us our transport pass, specific orders, and directions for finding the house. "And there's one more little surprise. One True thinks this is so important that it wants to talk to you directly."

"No," Sadi said.

"Unh-unh," I added.

"Tape delay. Thirty seconds," Murphy said. "And I understand the fear, I really do. But remember we've worked for One True for a long time and it's got no reason to sell us out."

Sadi's fists clenching and unclenching, feet scuffling, angry, drawing the attention of Murphy's bodyguard—"I'm afraid I'll end up running a copy of One True. I don't want my personality replaced with another copy of that program."

"It just wants to talk to you," Murphy said reasonably. "And you know that the reason it hires us is because we *aren't* copies of it; the shit we do is stuff it doesn't want to remember or have copies experiencing. The other thing you can do, both of you, is turn it on and off, so you discuss your replies to One True each time. So you can interrupt the interaction—and that should keep you safe. Remember it has to have a dialogue with you, with nobody else present, to get into your mind."

I tried real hard not to think about the arguments about whether that was true or not. Most people believed it, anyway.

I thought we were going to walk right out; Sadi and I kept arguing. But the bonus for the operation was huge, with a strong hint that if we didn't want to do it he just might have us shot in order to stay on One True's good side, and usually the longer you talked to Murphy the crazier and the more arbitrary he got so that prolonging a conversation was always a risk, and besides I had to admit I was a little curious and Sadi was very curious. Finally Sadi figured that as long as we were careful to talk to each other and pass notes while One True talked to us, we might be okay. Upshot, we agreed.

The face that popped up on the vid was the first surprise: One True, for some strange reason, had decided to look like Dan Rather, or like Harrison Ford—then I realized it was probably an intermediate morph of the two. Kind of like what everyone wanted an American president to look like back when there had been American presidents. Lots of signs of having lived and thought and felt, none of which it had done really, if you were a hardcore humanist, which is what I was trying to be while I talked to the thing.

Chitchat at us for a while. Missions and all that. Sadi talked a lot about killing and inflicting pain, I think because he was mad at One True for not wanting to have memories of that kind of its own.

Out of no place, One True said, "I haven't seen weather like this since I was a kid in Ohio."

I froze; it felt like my guts were tied in a knot.

Sadi's foot lashed out at the wall plug connected to the terminal, tearing out the connectors. The screen went blank as he lunged forward and pressed a set of keys, dumping the program out of memory—

The place filled up with guards and they marched us off. I didn't care if they shot us right then, though. "Thanks," I whispered to Sadi.

"You'd'a done it for me," he muttered back.

There were at least two bad things about this. One, One True not only knew that I was Organization, but had penetrated far enough to get my Organization password. Two, clearly because I had it memorized so deeply—one of the few things I could count on coming through each transit with—

Transit, I think, getting up off the bed to pace. *That's what just happened to me, I've transitted again.* I throw the curtains open and stare out at the dark face of Mars, lighted by the one tiny brilliant moon that never moves. God, I need sleep. Maybe I got a lot in the last few months or something. Maybe I shouldn't have had the fourth pot of coffee. Maybe I'm afraid I'll dream, now that I know what's in memory. Maybe this is all a hallucination while Sadi and me wait to be shot.

Well, we weren't. Though I don't know how or why we weren't. Memes don't have a trace of sentiment so it wasn't that.

Still, if One True knew a deep memory to touch, who knew what it might have done next? From that deep memory it could well have proliferated and taken me over. Not the first time Sadi saved me, wouldn't be the last, and he was right, I had done it for him and would again.

Still don't know. Did One True just let it all go? Did Murphy talk it into letting us live? Or what? My next memory is of the mission itself, gliding over snow weeks later. Fell early in those days, by August on the south shore of Ontario. Glaciers were growing.

Four in the morning, moon high in the sky, gliding over the snow on skis silent as owls, Sadi's lean racer's body shooting along ahead of me. The house was only three miles away but we couldn't be sure what protection they'd have. Maybe none; electronics were now so detectable that some people relied entirely on concealment.

Sadi was carrying our gear. As we topped the last ridge, he gestured for me to crouch low and follow him. We swung into a clump of pines, running the risk of hitting something in the dark. "Totally fibered system," he said. "Probably optical switching and all. No signature worth talking about but as we got closer, One True's monitoring spotted a slowdown in communication between Free-cybers—which means the machines here were paying more and more attention to us."

"So what does One True say we do?"

"It's going to stage some kind of diversion, then an outright attack, and we go in while they're busy dealing with the attack."

"Attack through the net, right, not something physical coming in?"

"Right. We're supposed to wait till—" He had his hand on his earpiece. "Okay, One True's put their system in an uproar. That happens several times a day, their security won't even bother to wake them up if they're asleep. We should move up to just below the crest of the ridge."

We herringboned up; it occurred to me that right now, with our skis pointed at this ridiculous angle, would be a really bad time to have someone step over the ridge. Unaccountably, I shuddered, as if it had actually happened somehow, or as if I remembered getting shot here.

Sadi waited a few long breaths and said, "Okay, the virus attacks are underway; One True is barging in the logical door, we go in the physical. Time for fun, bud."

Just before an op started I always got a sinking feeling in

my stomach, and then a wild, crazy whoop of joy in my soul. I don't know where either one came from; either I was going to get hit or I wasn't, and with modern weapons there really wasn't any such thing as "wounded"—you barely had time to notice you were dead. So the thing to do was keep going until you won or the lights went out.

They didn't go out this time, either. We skimmed down the ridge, dodging among the trees, and onto the lawn of the big house, one of those huge white sprawling places that was all gingerbread and frouf and was supposed to remind people of the old days, a century before any of them had lived.

As soon as we were on level ground we put a push on, skating to build up speed, then crouching low to shoot up toward the window where One True was telling Sadi we could get in. One True called that one right, anyway—not a shot was fired at us as we zoomed up to the space under that window.

We dropped skis. Sadi nodded hard at me, once, and I scooted up close with the charge. I slapped it against the corner of the window frame, and we backed off around the corner of the house. Thumb on button; boom before thumb touched bottom; back around, hole in house, burst in, shooting.

They had trusted their security system so well that they hadn't even set it to wake them; they first knew that One True had penetrated and we were coming in when the explosion tore a hole in their wall, and the wife was wounded by a stray round while still getting out of bed.

Their weapons cache in the bedroom wasn't much, either; the old guy was bending over his wife when we caved in the door, and still trying to pull the shotgun up to where it could do some good when Sadi kicked his feet out from under him. I grabbed the shotgun and that was that.

Long pause. He breathed hard. Finally he said, "I didn't

get a good look at her wound. She may be bleeding seriously—"

"Good. I'd hate to have her putting us on," Sadi said.

He could always make me laugh.

I checked her out, though; no point in killing them, at least not until we knew what they were good for. The round had been spent by passing through walls; it had hit her over the kidney but had only penetrated the muscle, not even all the way into the abdominal cavity. I dug it out with forceps from the first-aid kit, making a messy job of it so that she jumped and moaned a couple of times.

Once we'd sealed the wound we got down to business with them. "You're going to talk to One True," I said. "Who's first?"

For a long time neither spoke; then the man said "No."

I looked at him closely. Ring of white hair around a pink domed head, squashed features, sort of a goatee; looked like a parody of an old-time professor. Just sort of experimentally, I hit him a few times, enough to get some blood flowing from his nose and lips, and then asked if he was ready to talk to One True.

He said "No" again, so I slapped his wife around some. He still said "No."

So Sadi pulled the nice cop bit—he was always better at it than I was because he could think of things to say—and sent me out of the room "to cool down." I sat just out of sight so I could listen.

"So are you the nice cop?" the old guy asked, sneering.

"Unhhunh. So I'll just cut trying to get sympathy and so forth from you, and making you feel like I'm your friend, because I can see you know the routine," Sadi said. His favorite opening. "What we can do is talk about what the deal is, what you will and won't do under your own power and what I can and can't offer you. Then if there's a common ground in there we can do that, and if there's not, well, then no doubt you've figured out that we're authorized to kill you and to do anything else we like before, so at that point I'll give you to Yuri and he'll get to do what he does. I mean, it's not an accident that he's the tough cop and I'm the nice one; this is all just a job to me, but he really enjoys it. Okay?"

Long silence.

"Is that all right?" Sadi asked.

The old guy said, "As far as I can see we're already dead, whether you kill us or feed us to One True."

Sadi said later that one rocked him back a minute; he realized only then that these two weren't carrying any memes, that though they had been making and running Freecybers they were as much themselves as any mercenaries, ops, or elrefs. But he at least had the old guy talking. "So you'd rather just die? I mean, I can do that for you if that's what you'd rather. I can always just say we demanded that you talk to One True and you wouldn't."

"Can you be quick about it?" the woman asked.

"I can but I won't. My own ass is in the sling if I don't make a decent effort. It's you or it's me, so since I have the gun and you're tied up, it's you. Should I just bring Yuri back and get started? We won't ask again if it offends you, we'll just work until there's a good scene for the follow-up team."

"Not yet," the old man said. This was the point where Sadi usually got them; we'd gotten a bishop this way, and a couple of politicals. It was one thing to be tortured to make you talk, and try not to talk; it was another thing to be tortured to death without any ability to stop it. Sometimes they got up the nerve but usually they wanted to delay a few more minutes. That was what was happening to these people. "Not yet," he said again. "I—can we talk—"

"About anything you like," Sadi said. "I just need to

look like I'm trying to persuade you. If you want to delay a while to tell me about why you won't cooperate, then delay. Tell me about your fucking childhood if you want."

He was in, I thought. It never occurred to them, once they saw that Sadi was unmemed, that he'd be carrying a microphone so that One True could listen in. And the only way to take over a system, be it mind or meme (how much difference was there, now, anyway?) was to know it well. They were about to give themselves up, know it or not.

The old man sighed. "I don't suppose you'll understand this, but in a certain sense I'm on your side. Not on One True's, but I can tell, you're a mercenary, right, from one of the free companies? Mind if I know which one?"

Sadi would have had a big grin as he said, "Murphy's Comsat Avengers. Great unit, fucking-A."

"Bet it is. I've heard of you all. Well, you all know that you could retire any time by deciding to start running One True. And One True takes pretty good care of the people who run copies of it; you'd be comfortable."

"I might do that someday," Sadi said.

"You might but you probably won't. Mostly people like you live free for a few years and then die. That's the choice you all make, isn't it?"

That bothered me a little, as I sat listening in the next room. Close to what Sadi and I had been saying to each other. I had a sudden intuition that this old guy was much more dangerous than he seemed to be.

The old guy went on. "Well, I can understand why a lot of people choose to run a meme, to invite it into their existence. Really, I do; there are plenty of people out there whose own personalities will never allow them any happiness, who tie themselves in one knot after another, people for whom the biggest curse in the world is freedom of choice because they're programmed to keep choosing wrong and blaming themselves for it. There's no meme out there that's as cruel to the people running it as their own personalities would be. They should have the choice to pick up one, even though that's the last choice they can ever make.

"But you and I—or you and this Yuri, if that's really his name, and Monica, and me, probably your Murphy if he's still alive, all of us—for some reason we're fussy. We want to make those choices. The thought of not making them makes us even more unhappy than our own failures. We can't help it, we only want happiness we can get for ourselves, as ourselves, by our own efforts and choices. And if it's not possible we'll go right on being mean and miserable rather than accept a meme to alter us. Do we all have that in common?"

"I'm listening," Sadi said.

"Well, that's what the Freecybers are about. They're memes that respect individuality, personhood, the soul, whatever. Memes against memes, or liberator memes, or whatever you call them. You get a Freecyber, and if you aren't already memed, it won't invade; if you are, it attacks the one you have and tries to put you back together. If you don't like it you can always get back into contact with the one you had. Freedom for the mind . . ."

"Now I understand," Sadi said. One strange crunching noise. Two low *spat!*s. He had shot them.

Rushed in too late. Sadi was a deadly shot, and this was point blank with the target tied up.

He had crushed the microphone in his pocket; that had been the crunching noise. Then he had put the pistol to their heads and pulled the trigger. They hadn't cried out or anything; they looked peaceful. "Think they understood?" Sadi asked. Tears running down his cheeks. I'd never seen that before.

"I'm not sure I did."

"They won the argument," he said. "Though I bet One

True got everything it needed already, anyway. But it didn't get them and that's something."

"We work for it," I reminded him.

"We work for us," he said. "At least I hope so. Come on."

As we skied away, the sun was just rising. Early September, but the snow on the ground was already a month old. Someday soon this would all be under a glacier.

Low boom behind us. We turned to see the walls falling in and fresh flames lashing up from the wreckage; we'd spent some care and effort in planting charges.

Tears, still, trickling from under his goggles. "It was a whole house full of books and comfortable places to read," he said. "And it, and they, are out of the world. But One True didn't get them. That's something."

"Was what they said about Freecybers true?"

"I doubt it. Everything out there in the noosphere mutates pretty fast. Whatever they started out to do, I think the Freecybers are probably just like any other memes now, replicating because they can, spreading out any old way, taking over and running things, no doubt believing themselves to have the best of intentions. But those two people in that big house, surrounded by all that civilization, sitting in there trying to keep some of us free . . . well, I think *they* believed it. That's the other reason we had to kill them. Not just that One True would have taken them over, but that they'd have found out they were wrong, and I wanted them to believe right to the end." He sighed and wiped his eyes.

We didn't usually touch much; Sadi got weird about it. But I reached forward and started to rub his back, and he leaned back against me. There's hardly anything more awkward than embracing on skis, but we managed. He sobbed a long time, and I held him, still not really understanding, watching the burning wreckage of the house behind me, the leaping flares lighting the snow in oranges and reds against the pale indigo glow that clean snow gets at dawn. I wondered if all those books were in flames yet, and that made me think of Mama and Grandpa Couandeau and their houses full of books, and damn if I wasn't crying myself.

I'm sitting here looking at the wall, into space, into the empty spot in front of my eyes, at any old thing; tears are running down my face and I've been sitting in one position so long that my rump is stiff and I feel cold, though the Marshack seems to have perfect temperature regulation. I get up, stretch, put up with the cramping, stinging annoyance of a leg gone to sleep. "To sleep, perchance to dream, aye there's the rub," I say out loud. Sadi used to say that when I would get afraid of falling asleep because I knew I would have nightmares. And then he'd rub my back. It's a quote from something I think.

Since I can't sleep, I brew more coffee, and ask the werp, "Help request, uh, how do I record audiovisual?"

"Turn me sideways so my camera points at you," the werp says. I wonder if they all talk like their owners, or if they imitate whatever voice they hear, or what.

"Okay," I say, "Record this as an AV document. Put a date, time, and place on it."

"Ready to record, no editing," the machine says, in my voice. I swallow the first hot sip of coffee and begin.

iv

I had been living over Gwenny's for some months and it wasn't the worst deal in the world. By now I had three jobs, or four depending on what you counted. The garage was full-time, but I still worked at McDonald's three evenings a week, and in the morning before I went to work, I did some mopping and scrubbing at Gwenny's, getting things ready for the breakfast shift. She gave me breakfast and a few off on the rent for that, and the cash piled up higher in my bank account.

The fourth job wasn't exactly a job, but if a job is work and work is doing something you wouldn't usually do, to get things you want, it was a job. A couple nights a week Gwenny would come up to my room; we would say nothing about it, before, during, or after, but she would undress, stretch out on the bed beside me, undo my pants, and then finger herself while she sucked my penis. Sometimes I'd stroke her breasts or put a finger inside her, but usually I just lay back and thought about girls I knew from school or ones I knew from hanging out at the mall. It took my mind off Gwenny's fat old stretch-marked body, badly done makeup, and graying hair. She never asked me to do anything, though I would have if she had.

Sometimes, when she'd done as much as she wanted, she'd finish me with her hand, and her other hand would rest on my cheek. Then she'd usually tell me I was a "beautiful, beautiful boy." Just like that. Always "beautiful" twice.

If I wasn't feeling well or said I was tired, she'd kiss my cheek and go away without doing anything. But I rarely turned her away. It felt good and she seemed to like it. I never did know what she was getting out of the experience, except that she called me a "beautiful, beautiful boy." She wasn't jealous—I had girls up in my room now and then, the kind that are impressed with a boy their own age who has a car, money, and place of his own. That never made Gwenny jealous or anything.

I don't think she was sentimental, either, though sometimes when I got in late from a McDonald's shift, and there were no customers in the diner, the two of us would just sit in a booth and watch CNN, her hand resting on my thigh and her head leaned on my shoulder. Verna and Paula never said a thing about that.

Not love, but I liked Gwenny better than I liked anyone else on Earth.

One night we'd just finished, and she was pushing her heavy, soft breasts into place in her too-small bra, sitting on my bed. My hand was still wet with having gotten her off, and I had just tucked in and zipped up. I knew I smelled of her scent, and would need to take a shower tonight; I was considering whether to go down to the diner with Gwenny and catch the news and some coffee first. About as normal as nights were in that little room, with the light from the diner sign coming in through the thin yellow curtain bright as day.

I got up, switched on the light, stuffed my shirt down into my pants. Gwenny was struggling around getting her bulky sweatshirt back on over her head.

A knock at the door.

We glanced at each other. I opened the door a crack and found Harris—the guy who traveled for the CP, the one that Mama and Grandpa were so impressed with. "Hi," he said.

"Hi, I'm not dressed," I answered, improvising.

"Okay. I've got a proposition for you, something you might want to think about. Meet you downstairs in the diner in a few?"

"Sure," I said, figuring I needed to get the door closed and this would get him away.

"What's good there? You eaten yet this evening?"

"I've eaten, but I'll take coffee when I join you," I said. "Try the pizzaburger. See you in a few." I closed the door.

Footsteps thudded down the short hallway, then the scraping of him padding down the steep stairway on the thick lumpy carpet. "Who's he?" Gwenny asked.

"Friend of my mother's. He travels in business," I said. "I don't even know how he knew I was living here."

"Oh, your mom knows," Gwenny said. "She was pretty frantic until she found out you were here and had a place to live and so on."

"How'd she find out?"

"I called her and told her, silly. I just thought, if I had a beautiful, beautiful son like you, no matter how estranged we got, I'd want to know he was all right. She doesn't know much more than that you're here and you have a job. Maybe this guy Harris will have some work for you?"

"Very likely," I said. I hadn't thought about it till then. Once I left home I'd dropped everything connected with the Communist Party. Now, if I wanted to, I could let the Party go completely. They couldn't make me do anything; if I wanted to leave the Party forever, I could just listen politely to Harris and send him on his way. I resolved to keep that in mind as I talked to him. "But I've got three jobs already, and I'm not hurting for money. It would have to be something worthwhile."

Gwenny nodded. "He's not a fag, is he?"

"I don't think so."

She smiled. "Good. I don't mind telling you, I hate fags. They do things to young boys, ones that aren't queer, I mean, so that they're never quite the same again. The money can't be worth it."

"It wouldn't be that kind of thing. He's a very old friend of my mom and my grandpa."

She nodded, obviously relieved, and got up, giving me a quick hug on her way out the door. I followed her out, locked my door, and crossed over to the common bathroom to wash.

When I got down there, Harris had ordered a pot of coffee for the table and two cups. He was taking small, neat bites off his pizzaburger.

He wore an old but good suit, the kind that shows just a

little bit of wear for a long time before it stops being presentable, dark blue with pin stripes. His tie was bright red, which wasn't exactly a signal any more, but it wasn't *not* a signal to the older members of the Party, and by that point in "the development of the historical situation," the Party was mostly old people. For some reason, I noticed that his black wingtips were older, but well-cared-for, polished mirror-bright, and obviously expensive. I took a seat across from him.

"Your mom asked me to look in on you," he said. I suppose that might have been true, but I also knew that in the little world they both lived in, Harris was too important to do something iike that just for niceness or as a favor. And I'd always thought he seemed like a pretty cold fish.

"I'm fine," I said. "Probably about time I did this anyway. Life's a lot better since I'm out of that place."

"I think your mom would agree with you," Harris said, "but she couldn't help worrying. It's good to know that you're all right." He took another couple of bites of the pizzaburger and chewed systematically. "I guess you've got a job, or maybe more than one?"

"Three," I said. "Two of them are just part-time."

"Still in school?"

"Nah. No time and I wasn't good at it. I figure I'll wait a while and then get a GED or something, maybe after that do some time at a community college. For right now it's more important to get established so I don't have to go back to that place."

Harris nodded. "Your mother and grandfather seem to agree with you about that. Some of the other members have been trying to persuade your mother to do something more permanent about her situation."

"Like get a divorce?"

"Just exactly like that." He took another bite, chewed

and swallowed it, and then delicately lifted a couple of french fries to his mouth. "There are those of us who have been telling her that for years."

"She won't leave him," I said, glancing around the diner. "I wish to god she would but she won't." Gwenny was back at the cash register, conspicuously a long way from being able to hear us. No one else around. Probably Verna had been warned off. "Nobody will hear us if you say anything," I said quietly, "and it will be a lot less conspicuous than if you go up to my room."

Harris nodded. "Good thought. All right, here's what you might want to consider. Legally your whole existence would get a lot easier if you were two years older. You could get a chauffeur's license and drive a cab or limo for a living, you could take the GED right away for a high school diploma, in general it would be a better deal. And with your technical aptitude, there's something you could consider doing for us. I don't need to mention that we're generous to our friends, but let me add that if it works out right, there'd be very few ties to us and not much chance anyone would ever know. It's money and a good start in the world if you want it."

I shrugged. "What do I have to do?"

"If you say yes, about two weeks from now you'll get a big package in the mail. None of it's classified stuff for anyone. In fact you'll also find there are a couple of math and science books in the package so you can look things up as needed. You're going to master a lot of stuff about radar. Since you'll be studying more, you might want to drop one job—we'll be glad to replace whatever you were making there, with double the pay, cash, so no taxes get taken out.

"Learn the stuff in the package thoroughly. A couple of months after you get the package, you'll meet a man named Brian who wants to sell you fake i.d., as if it were just for getting into bars. You can recommend Brian to a friend or two if you like.

"The trick is, that i.d.'s going to be a lot more solid than a normal get-into-bars one. You're going to be exactly two years older, which means you'll be eligible to do what we want you to do—enlist in the Army."

I half-laughed; it certainly wasn't what I'd been expecting.

He smiled too. "You're going to ace all kinds of aptitude tests, thanks to the studying," he added, "and thus you will end up, sooner or later, in one of the Stealth programs. Money will quietly trickle into a couple of accounts we'll set up for you. And then one day we'll ask you for some things, which you will provide."

"Got it," I said. "How long do I have to think?"

"I'll be back by here in about a week," Harris said. "If you're interested, talk to me then."

We shook hands, and he paid for the food and left. "Was it any kind of offer?" Gwenny asked.

"Something Mama set up for me," I explained. "I don't think I'll take it—a lot of travel and stuff. I'm sure I'll be around here a few more months at least."

"I'm kinda glad. I'd miss you," Gwenny said.

I had decided to take Harris's offer. But since it would be months before I enlisted, and everything up till then was under wraps, I figured I might as well preserve the deal I had. "It would involve a lot of traveling," I said. "Like he does. He'll be coming back in a week with some more details, but I don't think I'll take the deal."

"It's not selling drugs, is it?" Gwenny asked.

"Naw."

That night I lay awake—not long, as I worked hard in those days and it was never much trouble to get to sleep—and let my eyes rest on the key Mama had given me.

I guess regular American guys would have been shocked, but I grew up understanding that the USA had to fall, that it was the center of world capitalism and the target. And then as I got to know Party members, I was exposed to a lot of cynicism too, because by the 1980s the CP was running short on believers and long on opportunists. So I don't think I had much in the way of patriotism, and I'd never had it, and I knew perfectly well that if Harris said the CP would do it, you'd have to go to the Mafia for a better guarantee.

Figure a few years in electronics as an enlisted man; after that, well, if the CP wanted me to stay in the Army, of course I would, and money would keep piling up till I retired at half pay—and with the age jump I was getting out of this, I'd be thirty-six and well-off. Lots of time to do more stuff. Or if Harris's bosses only wanted some specific things, they might cut me loose, at which point I could use some GI Bill dollars to go through college in a lot of comfort—there would be a fat, untouched, hidden bank account out there.

In just the weeks I had been on my own, I was already realizing how much I liked piling up money. Shit, if I'd known how much I was going to like being out of my parents' house, I'd have been *planning* to run away.

Good deal all around. Some risk, but I didn't have much to lose. When Harris came through the next week, he took me out to a business-type steak house, one of those Fakey Olde Englande places, and as I tucked in a twenty-ounce slab of beef, I told him yes. I came back and told Gwenny that I had said no.

That night she asked me to undress all the way, and spent a long time kissing and touching my body all over, working herself furiously with both hands before she finally took my penis into her mouth. I stroked her breasts; they were saggy and covered with stretch marks, and the nipples were too big and too red, but I liked their soft, baggy weight in my hands. When she finished, she curled up beside me and we slept next to each other that night, the only time we ever did. I woke up with her scratchy old gray hair in my face, some of her drool on my chest. Though she was asleep, her hand was already stroking my morning erection.

V

I finally finish talking. It's been three hours. At last I'm sleepy, though my throat's dry. I toss out the last of the cold coffee and reconstitute an orange juice. Food for a month here, if I want.

I talk to the werp. "Give me a table of contents or whatever it's called nowadays."

It shows me a list of about seventy topics, each with anywhere from a dozen to a hundred channels in it. I look over the list, and say, "Give me the ads, just the ones for Mars, and make it a general random browse."

For half an hour I find out what bread costs, what jobs are hiring, what the housing options are. Then I get an urge and say, "Show me the personal ads. What are the categories?"

The list is long, but it's almost all subdivisions under "Sexual Partners—No Emotional Connections Expected" and "Long-Run Relationships with Sex and Emotional Connection." At least it's gotten easier to find what interests you.

"Connections and Memories" is the last category: a bulletin board, mainly, for locating relations and friends, because what with the Die-Off, Eurowar, Diaspora One, War of the Memes, and Diaspora Two, humanity has gotten pretty scattered and there are a lot of cousins out there who have never met, heirs who couldn't be located, friends who haven't seen each other in twenty years. "Can we plug into that?" I ask the werp. "Are we online here?"

"Yes, we've got a new account in your new i.d.," the werp says. "It's intended to be perfectly secure."

"Okay, then scan for any ad seeking any member of the Quare or Couandeau families, or referencing any of my prior aliases."

"Shall I prioritize your criterial parameters, and do you want aggregate score order?"

"Uh, define terms."

"Specify terms to be defined."

I end up spending another half hour, while I get tireder and tireder, before the machine can make it clear to me that what it means is that it wants to know how it's supposed to compare indices to decide which ad to give me first.

Once I understand that, I sit and think for a minute, and then finally, tossing my empty orange juice glass into the trash, I say, "Uh, how many people are there on Mars right now?"

"Three million one hundred fifty-four thousand eight hundred twenty-two as of one hour ago. Crews may have departed on spacecraft and there has almost certainly been a birth or two, and perhaps a death, in the interval. Should non-citizen personnel on Deimos and Phobos be counted as well?"

"That's an adequate approximation already, thank you." Once they start picking nits, nothing picks nits like an AI.

I doubt that I have thousands of doppelgangers, first cousins, or people using my old aliases anywhere on a planet with a small population of mostly younger people. "Just 'OR' all the conditions together, no priorities, and give me everything you get."

"Very well. Stop if I hit what number?"

"If you hit one hundred, I guess."

So after all of the trouble it has put me through, it pulls up a total of six ads. Two Quares, no apparent connection. One Ulysses Grant, ditto. One ad for a Couandeau, but it looks like the family came to Mars from France via the Vermont Reloc Camp.

And one that is just a phone number, followed by, "Joshua Ali Quare—when you get to Red Sands City, call this number. I haven't seen weather like this since I was a kid in Ohio."

I remember exactly where and when I learned that phrase. I don't even need the help of the werp to pull it up.

That phrase, always part of always losing always finding Sadi. Our identities changed: full-fledged deep-cover ones changed at every transit, temporary ones constantly. But our Organization passwords never changed because it was the one sure way to find each other.

"When I see places like this I always wish I was back in New Orleans" was Sadi's phrase. In newspapers, on walls, little notes . . . we put them everywhere, and we found each other.

I remember once, sometime in the middle of the Gray Decade when practically everyone was living on dolework, we'd gotten separated the usual way—he'd had a job to go do in science control, and I'd had a straight strong-arm to put on some politician, way out in the sticks around Spokane Dome, a guy named Bizet who was into good government and no corruption and like that, and who needed it explained to him that he could run his own territory as clean as he wanted it but Spokane was going to have prostitution because that was ours. He was one of those progressive good boys that can't believe you can do it; he had called the cops, found out who they really worked for when they wouldn't come out. I beat him pretty good where it wouldn't show, and he seemed to get the idea. Probably if he was like most of them he'd retire real soon now, start drinking or something.

I caught up with Sadi in Boston Dome; maybe 2044 just before holding the ice back got impossible? First I saw of him, I was sitting on a bench and he was going by on the other side of the street, silhouetted briefly, between two buildings, against the wet, white wall of the glacier a couple of miles away. "Hey, did I see you at Mardi Gras?" I yelled. He turned to see who it was and I asked, "Don't you wish you were back in New Orleans?"

He turned and walked toward me. "Naw. I haven't seen weather likes this since I was a kid in Ohio," he said, getting closer. "Jeez, Josh, they really did you up right this time. I'd never have recognized you."

"I think that's the idea," I said. "Figured you must be in town here since I knew the guy you were controlling was at MIT; so I arranged to have the restoration surgery done here so I could catch up with you."

"Well, your timing's perfect. I hadn't quite bought a ticket back to the house in Kansas yet, so we can go back together after your surgery." He looked me up and down. "Cheekbones, lips, hair color . . . looks like they added some weight?"

"Yep. It's a good job this time. But shouldn't take too much to put me back together."

Over lunch in a quiet place we knew, where we could talk without too much risk of listeners, we compared notes. My little escapade with Bizet had been pretty dull, and besides I didn't want to talk about it much because Sadi and I disagreed on tactics a lot. Knocking Bizet around hadn't bothered me much, but that wouldn't have been Sadi's way. Sadi would have noted that Bizet had a wife, a sister, and two teenaged daughters, and would have done things to one or two of them, for fun, in front of Bizet; he thought that always increased the pressure, because there are a lot more men who can stand to risk another stomping but there aren't many who can stand to risk seeing something like that again. Maybe he was right but I didn't like it. I figured the only asshole screwing up the Organization's business was Bizet, and it ought to be him that took the damage.

Call it a point of esthetics or ethics or something. All I knew was, I slept better doing it my way. And I didn't like it that Sadi would sometimes pick on me about that.

So I turned the conversation straight to the job Sadi had done. "How'd it go? Did it get wet?"

"Not very. He's still alive and he'll keep working. This time we had something better than threats to use."

"I thought threats were your favorites," I said, teasing him.

He poured a tall glass of beer and took a long sip. "Now that really depends on how you define favorites. For carrying them out, sure. I like getting turned loose on people, especially civilian dumbfucks. So do you, you know. That's how we ended up staying with the Organization, it wouldn't have been that hard to leave—at least if you believe the retired longtimers like Peter, and I do. So sure, threats are my favorite for fun. But for effect—for getting what you want—give me bribes every time. And I had a great bribe for this guy.

"He was working on CTCs—and you know that's priority one for us to control or suppress."

"Unhhunh. Lucky bastard—what was your bonus on that?"

"Enough so the next vacation's on me, bud. Maybe we'll go up to the Supras and tear things up a little, hunh?"

"Maybe we will," I agreed. For some reason I didn't understand, research into CTCs—closed timelike curves—was just about the biggest deal going for Organization bonuses. They didn't want anyone to be working on them unless that person was in the Organization.

The trouble was that as research piled up they were becoming easier and easier, and they were fascinating. A CTC was a loop forward into time; that is, you did something or other to make a "singularity," and it created a little loop of time sitting right next to our timeline, with one end of the loop at the moment the singularity was created, and the far end of the loop somewhere out in the future. It didn't provide us with a way to reach the past—the loop could not be thrown in that direction. What it did provide was a way for the future to reach us; within the time loop, you could move on the forward leg of the loop toward the future, at a faster speed than normal time went, then follow the loop till it bent around, traveling rapidly back in time, all the way to the singularity. At the singularity, you got off the loop, into your own timeline—and your own timeline split, into a new one that contained both you and your original self, and an old one in which you vanished the moment you got into the loop.

Right now it was mostly theory, but the year before the Joule Box—the big collider particle accelerator on the back side of the moon, which could put a full joule of energy on each particle—had managed to make a subatomic singularity. I wasn't real sure what that was except that the flashchannel kept saying they had put "a billion uranium atoms into a cubic fermi." Sadi said a fermi was a unit of measure, which helped make a little more sense than the picture I had produced in my head, but I didn't have any idea how small except "real tiny." Anyway, they had thrown about one hundred electrons into the three-second time loop which that opened up. Ninety thousand electrons had popped out of the singularity, *before* the hundred went in—meaning that we had somehow captured nine hundred universes' worth of that set of 100 electrons.

That was the basis for Sadi's theory about why the Organization was so interested in CTCs: he said the Organization wanted to have a system where they could send in a few diamonds, chunks of plutonium, or kilos of You-4 tomorrow, causing tons of them to appear today. In theory, he pointed out, you could even use the ones you got back today as your starter.

My theory was that they wanted to own the first singularity, because it would give them a monopoly on the farthest travel back in time possible (since you couldn't travel to any time before a singularity had been created).

Either way, CTCs were an interesting game. The rules were, nobody got to play except the Organization and the physicists it controlled, and we got paid a lot any time we enforced that rule.

The catch to all that, of course, was that as time went by the science and technology just kept getting better. It didn't look real promising for keeping everyone else behind forever.

"So what did you do?" I asked.

"The Organization told me to offer him a unified theory of something or other, which I had in a notebook. He didn't believe it, of course, right off the bat, but I told him to take the notebook, free, for a few days, copy it if he wanted, and it worked like a charm. Which I think is one of the things it was a theory about. Anyway, he says it will be years just to work out the implications—and while he's working on that, he won't be anywhere near CTCs. Case closed." He held up his beer and I clinked mine against it. "No more science that we don't need."

"Amen," I said. Even if I didn't see much point in the

whole CTC thing, I sure knew I wanted the Organization to keep its monopoly on the longtimer technology.

He grinned at me. "I haven't seen weather like this since I was a kid in Ohio."

Automatically I responded, "When I see places like this I always wish I was back in New Orleans."

"Perfect," he said. "After your restoration surgery, you and I recover in New Orleans and spend this bonus."

And so we did. The 2040s, the Gray Decade, was hard on a lot of people, of course—worst depression since the 1930s—but we had cash and an employer that was never going out of business. When you've got all the money, everyone else is for sale. If I remember New Orleans right, I think we killed somebody.

I have been staring at the werp for several minutes while I thought about that. The ad is still in front of me, still with its phrase. "I haven't seen weather like this since I was a kid in Ohio." I shudder. I'm not sure I want to live that way again, do those things again. It's turning my stomach to remember a lot of it. But I want to see Sadi, if it's Sadi. I have to see him if it's him. I tell my werp to copy the ad but not to respond, and then add, "Set up a queue of documents—everything that includes the phrase 'I haven't seen weather like this since I was a kid in Ohio.' Wake me at . . . what time is it?"

"Nine thirty-four P.M. local."

"Wake me at five A.M. local." I go to bed, and I go to sleep, but I have horrible nightmares and get no rest. The alarm throws me out of bed at five, still tired.

I reconstitute breakfast, sit down, and start talking to the werp. This is how every day starts for four more days.

vi

Some guys say they never forget Basic. I guess I can understand that, if it was your first time away from home, and you weren't used to people abusing you physically and screaming into your face. For me, it was a lot more consistent and friendly than I was used to. My biggest problem was that I could tell the sergeant was actually concerned about us, and I ended up liking him more than I should have. I felt guilty about what I was in the Army for. Not enough to overcome me with guilt and make me turn Harris in.

A few months later I was in a tech school, living off base in an apartment I shared with four other guys, with my RX-7 parked out front. I don't know whatever became of that car, I had it for years, but there's nothing in my werp to tell me when I lost it or how. I feel a little sad about not knowing where and when it went.

The promotions came reasonably fast, and I got security clearances without much trouble. Since I didn't answer letters from my mother, sure enough she complained to her congressman, who relayed it to the Pentagon, and my company commander called me in. When I explained that I was trying to get Communism behind me, my file got all sorts of good things in it.

That was the last time I was ever to hear anything of Mama. Guess I thought there would be time to reconcile, because I didn't know it was "the last time" yet.

Money was building up in my secret accounts, and I liked working on radar. By the time I was really eighteen (and officially twenty), I had a place of my own a couple of miles from the base, and whenever I was off duty I was in civvies and off to Phoenix for fun. I still didn't have to touch the hidden account—I was even saving money out of my military pay. Might've been the best years of my life.

One day in November 1989, when I walked into the base lounge, a bunch of men were glued to the screen. "What's up?"

"They're tearin' down the Berlin Wall, Josh."

"*Who* is?"

"The Germans. Both sides."

I stared at the screen. No trace of a border guard. I remembered that years ago, when they'd told us about the Wall in school, Mama had tried to "straighten me out" about it, pointing out that "oh, sure, some young romantic students that fell for the propaganda are getting killed, and that's a shame, but most of the people defecting from the East waited to finish advanced professional degrees at government expense before they 'fled to the *freedom* of the West.' "

The contempt in Mama's voice when she said that phrase had amazed me, left me without words as she went on, "Get real about it, Josh. If they were suffering so much they'd have run for it when they were sixteen or twenty or something. But they stay there for year after year, getting free tuition and advanced training. Then when it's time for them to start paying back the benefits they received, to be a doctor or engineer for the people who paid to train them, they skip over to the West because the salaries are higher here. The year before they built the Wall, the German Democratic Republic lost practically the whole graduating class of every medical school. Don't try to tell me doctors have some special love for freedom. We know what doctors love, and it ain't that. But what they do love—I mean *money*—oh, there's plenty of that over here. That's what they come for. Because they want to make cash, not make people well."

Something about the thought of the argument with Mama made me think about the kitchen back home, the way it smelled, the rows on rows of books she'd read, and the framed pictures of her father and grandfather. A little lump rose in my throat. No one here was going to notice. Everyone else was getting choked up too.

On the screen a couple of blonde girls were sitting on the Wall, prying off chunks with a crowbar and tossing them down to the crowd. They looked like any two girls you could find in any bar in Phoenix, any weekend. Probably they were just as political.

"That's fucking *it*," one of the soldiers said. "But I bet we all end up unemployed. Three years from now the Army's gonna be half its size."

"You mean *our* Army?" another asked. "Dream on, babe. There's plenty of ragheads out there that still hate us. We'll just be switching who we fight is all. More sun and sand. Kind of a beach Army."

"Shut up, I'm trying to hear," came from a couple corners of the room.

I watched them dancing and waving flags, all the stuff that's now familiar in most people's history lessons, and I kept thinking how much it was like what Mama had told me the Revolution would be like.

I felt sick and sad and sorry. I didn't even know if Grandpa was still alive, and I couldn't quite bring myself to call them and tell them I was sorry. So I never picked up the phone, just went home to my apartment.

It wasn't that big a surprise when a couple of months later, the deposits into the secret account stopped arriving. I didn't let it worry me, much. I could sit on the money I already had, while the trail got colder. Meanwhile I had a good job and I could keep doing that.

By the time of the First Oil War, in 1991, it no longer seemed strange; the USSR was just another nation, more like a big run-down Sweden than anything else. I went over to Saudi, spent some months of boredom at a station that fed data to a Patriot battery, and came back with a good tan and a lot of extra pay. They threw a parade for us.

As I did every quarter, I checked the balance in the secret account, using a bank-by-modem system. This time, there was a new deposit.

I don't think I was surprised, or not surprised. It seemed to imply nothing, other than, perhaps, that the KGB had gotten its act back together. I leaned back and looked over the place; comfortable apartment in a big bland complex, cheap but new furniture, blue Arizona sky outside, framed beer-company prints on the walls (mostly of women who weren't old enough to drink legally, not wearing much). The audio rig was big, new, and expensive, the television huge. I was thinking about buying a house to hold all my stuff. Life was probably not going to get better.

I was watching that big TV a few months later, when all the channels were carrying the news of the Second Revolution (they were still calling it a "coup" that day) in Moscow. The tanks had Parliament surrounded, there were crowds everywhere, and no one knew what was going to happen next.

It happened I was watching at the big moment, and on CBS rather than CNN, so I saw it from the rear view and therefore saw the famous picture of Captain Alexei Nemonynov before I knew that he, and the picture, would be famous.

God knows what Yeltsin was thinking. Probably nothing at all. He was said to be stubborn. But he climbed up on a tank, like he was going to walk right up to Parliament, right over all those massed weapons. He had gotten two steps when Nemonynov climbed up from the other side and stood in his way.

No microphone picked it up, so we have only Nemonynov's word for what they said. He said later he ordered Yeltsin to get down off the tank, go home, and stop making a fool of himself. I've often thought how much better things could have been, for the world and everybody, if Yeltsin had taken that advice.

But he didn't. From the camera behind him, you could see him nod firmly, twice, and then take a step forward, his silver-white hair shining. The pistol in Nemonynov's fist barked, a hard flat sound. Bloody flesh sprayed from Yeltsin's back. He fell backwards, off the tank, to the ground, shot through the guts.

The cameraman must have been so startled that he didn't point the camera down at the dying Yeltsin for a long moment. Instead, I—and millions at the same time, and later almost everyone—saw Captain Alexei Nemonynov calmly put the pistol away, heave a sigh, take two steps forward, and spit twice on Yeltsin's twitching body.

As if that had been the signal, four soldiers rushed up, rifles reversed, and surrounded Yeltsin. Methodically, with the full force of their bodies, the soldiers put their rifle butts to work on him. The rifles rose and fell, rose and fell. The audio channel picked up the thuds on wet flesh. The soldiers' backs blocked the cameras' view—we could only guess from the dull, heavy impacts, and little sprays of blood.

Nemonynov drew his pistol again and pointed it. The CBS camera went dead.

For the next hour, I flicked from channel to channel. Some cameras were still on to show the incendiary shells tearing into Parliament. Even the next morning one guy was still uploading footage to satellite of the bodies strewn all around the streets from Red Square to the Moskva.

I figured my phone would ring sooner or later, but it didn't, though the payments kept right on rolling in, as Bush moved troops into the old Warsaw Pact nations that September. The cash continued to flow when Oil War Two flared and I was temporarily loaned to the ayatollahs to train their technicians for the defense of Teheran. The money kept piling up during the Christmas Crisis when Red Army units started to defect to the various Free Communist governments and Marines went ashore in the Baltics.

On December 19, 1991, one week after getting back stateside from Iran, I parked my RX-7 in longterm storage in Fayetteville, reported at Fort Bragg, and got on the plane for Klaipeda. We were going to be setting up radar pickets for the UN's No-Fly Zone over western Russia, and everybody was figuring war in April.

The Rising might have been inevitable, but it didn't look that way then. It was nearly as big a surprise as everything since the autumn of 1989 had been.

My memories of the big celebrations all over Europe in January are a pleasant blur, but I still remember how amazed I was to realize I would be back in California in plenty of time to vote in the primaries. Not that anyone could work up much concern about the elections. Nobody could have beaten George Bush that year, and Bob Kerry didn't seem to try. It was the first all-state sweep since George Washington's second term. They didn't even interrupt television programming for it much.

And still the money continued to come in, and still no one called me. So I just let myself enjoy fiddling around with radar. Every time clearances were reviewed I got closer to my goal of working on Stealth detection.

Not like I was bored. I had a couple of acquaintances to go for a beer with, and there were lots of movies to rent. And the early nineties were great years for music, all the bands stopped playing boomer shit. I got a lot of new CD's and a great rig to play them on.

Best of all, I was good-looking and didn't mind spending money, at least as long as the girl put out. So I didn't have much trouble getting the kind of girl I was interested in. Generally I'd go out with a girl until I'd fucked her enough times to deaden my curiosity, then drop her—if she hadn't already taken herself out of the picture once it became clear that I didn't talk much, didn't care much what went on in anyone else's life, and was mainly interested in sex. The ones who were looking for someone like me sometimes ended up as semi-friends; the ones who were looking for a "relationship" usually hated me afterwards, like they hated any guy that didn't give them what they wanted.

There was AIDS, but the old, easy-to-prevent kind. I used up a lot of rubbers.

When the visit I had been expecting came at last, I had just gotten Cyssi out of the place that morning—another high school girl, I was getting old for them but they had such perfect little bodies and they were so afraid of acting young that they'd do anything to prove they were grown up. Probably high school kids thought of her as average or even plain, but that's because high school kids are only looking at each other. She had a tiny waist, big tits, a dark tan, and a big pouf of dyed-red hair, and that had been more than good enough for me to overlook the zits and crooked teeth.

I gave her a long kiss at the door, getting another good feel in under her loose, flowing top, and she did one of those pouty little poses. "Call me?"

"Of course," I said, and let a hand slide down over her hip, probing at the cuffs of her cutoffs, stroking her through her black hose. "You're not in any trouble with your folks?"

"Oh, as if. Like they give a shit. Not." She pouted again. "You didn't call till Thursday last week."

"I was working."

"All the time?"

"All right, I'll call." We kissed again and she went out the door, walking quickly away on the concrete walkways that made up the second floor of Park Electra, the complex I lived in—I heard her Doc Martens clomping into the distance.

I had just gotten the dishwasher going and the vacuum out when someone knocked.

Harris, with a man who didn't look like anyone. I opened the door wide for them, and the nondescript man turned to Harris and said, "This is him, right?"

"Right."

"Go wait in the car."

Harris left without saying goodbye, or even hello. I never saw him again.

The nondescript man turned back to me, came in, closed the door and said, "You've got a pretty comfortable life. It's time to start earning it."

I nodded. "You need a drink or coffee or anything?"

"No thank you. I've got a lot of ground to cover today. Let me just fill you in, tell you what's going on, and then go. Feel free to ask questions about any part you don't understand of course."

"Of course."

He gestured for me to sit on my couch, and then sat beside me and opened his brief case. "As you know, things got unsuitable for the organization during the last year. Large parts of our infrastructure had to be sacrificed, not just because our assets were in the USSR and were seized by the New Provisional Government, but also because for security reasons we had to cut traceable connections. But the procedure is complete—we no longer have significant overlaps with the Party, State, or Army. In fact we're no longer even based in Moscow.

"You might say we're doing what Bush wants us to. We're privatizing and moving into being a purely capitalist enterprise. We have a number of clients interested in Stealth, and our penetration is good enough to assure us you will be on one of the detection projects soon. When you are, you will begin to receive brief communiqués, mostly questions, in a brown manila envelope that will be on the upper shelf of your kitchen cabinet. Check that shelf once a day after your promotion comes through. Give me your apartment key for a moment."

I did. He took it off the key ring, dropped it into a box, and pushed a button. A loud beep. He handed me the key back without a sound, and I returned it to its ring. I didn't appreciate them coming in without asking, but I had decided long ago to let them have as much of me as they wanted. After all I had no gripe about the pay.

"When you find a list of questions, write out the answers—in handwriting—and put that in the envelope, along with the list itself. Make no copies of anything. Do not ever use a typewriter or word processor of any kind for this. Answer the questions by the indicated date, but don't compromise yourself to do it. If there's something you can't find out or don't know by the date, include a note to that effect.

"That's it, for that part of the work. Any questions? You'll get a copy of the same instructions in every envelope."

"No questions," I said, and got up to show him to the door—but he caught my wrist.

"There's one other thing," he said, and pulled out something that looked like a ray gun from a cheap sci-fi movie. He saw how startled I looked. I think he smiled. "It's an air-injector," he said. "You're getting a vaccination. Give me your arm."

Figuring that these people could arrange for me to have a life sentence, or maybe a lethal injection, whenever they wanted, I didn't give him a fight, not even an argument. I wonder about that. If I had, would he have said, "Fine, die of mutAIDS?" Probably not, since CDC had not named mutAIDS yet, and besides that wasn't the Organization's term for it. For that matter, I don't remember whether anyone was calling it the Organization officially yet; I think they'd dropped the term KGB since that stood for Committee for State Security, and the Organization was no longer a committee, there was no longer any such state, and it wasn't interested in anybody's security.

Probably I didn't think at all. I just stuck out my arm. He pushed the injector against my bare skin, not roughly, but firmly enough to make sure he had contact. The little gadget made a poofing sound, my arm stung for an instant.

Done. Just like that.

"What's it a vaccination against?" I asked.

"Three things," he said. His infection was flat, and he spoke fast, like he'd said this a lot of times before. "You won't believe me at first, but because you had that shot, you will never come down with AIDS—though within a few months you'll begin to test HIV-positive. Don't worry, it won't kill your job with the secure project—one of your old girlfriends has gotten infected recently, and it will be assumed that's where you got it. But *don't* worry. You couldn't get AIDS now if you tried, nor can you transmit it."

I nodded. "Thank you." At least I could be careless when I felt like it, or when the woman wanted to be.

"Secondly, it's a memory enhancer. You will find for the next several years that you don't forget anything. You'll remember every word you read or hear exactly, and everything you see exactly as it is. You'll still have to study to learn new things, because you have to be able to use the information as well as recall it—but you won't have to memorize anything again. As a side-benefit, you'll be able to learn languages very rapidly."

"You said for several years. Then I need a booster?"

He shook his head. "No. That's the third effect, which is caused by the same stuff that improves your memory. Some years from now—we don't know exactly when—you're going to come down with a bad fever, muscle aches, nausea, the worst case of flu you've ever had. It will last a few months. At the end of that time, your body will have done a fairly complete renewal of itself. You'll have dropped several years in biological age. But you will also have lost most of the memories from the years since this injection. That process will repeat indefinitely—live fifteen years with perfect memory, drop ten, lose all recent memory. So make sure, this time and every time, you keep good records of everything important in your personal life, all the time." He got up to go. "Good luck. Welcome to active duty. Your pay will triple, and we're seeing what we can do about the eighteen months when we didn't pay you."

I thanked him because it made as much sense as anything, and asked, "Where did you get all these things?"

"Which things?"

"In the injector."

He shrugged. "They don't tell me much more than they tell you. My guess would be that it's the results of some of our special research and development work, and we probably got most of that out of the USSR before the Rising. It's not at all perfect, obviously—life extension and memory enhancement is great but the side effects aren't desirable for our purposes, let alone yours. If things had gone better, I'm sure we wouldn't be trying it yet."

He closed his briefcase, got up, and left. A couple of days later I noticed a squib in a newspaper about an unidentified body found in a parking lot, money still in his wallet. The description matched Harris, but I wasn't about to call the morgue and offer to come in and identify him. And maybe I'm remembering a dream about something I was *afraid* happened. After all, Harris was a small fish.

vii

For the rest of it, there's the history books. First reports of a rapidly acting, airborne mutant HIV, December 1993. Riots and panics all over. South Central LA blew up. Then on January 28, 1994, President Bush was found dead in bed. He had been ill for about three weeks before, and probably contagious since July.

There's a principle that most people are only about six contacts away from anyone else in the world, and it's true, but the reason's that few people are more than three contacts away from their national leaders. Think about it; chances are you know some local politician, who knows some national politician, who knows the national leader, and all the national leaders know each other.

My guess is the Organization targeted Bush. Having that on the werp, if they're still around, ought to draw some attention. Why I want their attention, I have no idea, except that fifteen years from now I will be back in this position again. What if I'd just as soon die? Who would be better at killing me than the Organization?

Morbid thought. But that advertisement *could* be the Organization. I have enough memories, and the werp has dragged up enough fragments, to convince me that they're probably still around.

Anyway, when Bush died of mutAIDS, since most of the US was only a few contacts away from him, it meant everyone was infected, from babies to grandmothers, everywhere.

Every schoolchild now learns three things about it: fatalities were concentrated in those over forty years old. MutAIDS confers permanent immunity to AIDS, which is why nowadays they give it to newborn infants deliberately. And in 1994, the year of the Die-Off, Planet Earth lost 10 percent of its citizens between February and August. All that's in the books.

viii

It took a while to get leave. I had not expected how easy it would be to drive across the country—but then most of the people who did things connected with the highways were young enough to survive. Only the major cities had had to use mass graves, and the only places that had really collapsed were ones with a lot of people past forty: Rust Belt cities like Pittsburgh and Detroit, and Sun Belt places like Miami or Phoenix.

For the rest, a couple of backhoe operators and a few people who had already gotten over the disease could toss the bodies in, so that if a town of twenty thousand lost two thousand people in two hundred days, they only had to dig ten extra holes per day. You could even keep the graves marked and allow people to hold graveside services if they wanted them.

I made good time, and when I got to my home town, sure enough, Gwenny, Daddy, and Mama were already gone. I might have figured it would be that way.

I walked over that river bridge one more time, and something gleaming in the stream caught my eye. It seems like a vivid, accurate memory. Just possibly a Boy Scout knife. Just possibly I climbed down the bank, stripped to the waist, and dove for it, bringing that knife up like a trophy only to get chewed out by a policeman, as I stood there in the hot July sun, shivering with the cold of the river.

Just as possibly I saw a Scout knife in a shop, had a fit of sentimentality, and bought it. For that matter maybe I just needed a pen knife and bought a Boy Scout knife without thinking, not even in that town, but a year or two later. I can't trust my memory.

I don't know about the matchbook, either. Maybe I went into Gwenny's, found the diner under new ownership, and picked up an old matchbook, because they were trying to get rid of them. Maybe I had carried one of those matchbooks for all of the ten years since I'd left.

Maybe I left a flower on Mama's grave, but several documents on the werp say I dreamed that, later, a recurring dream that wouldn't leave me alone for weeks and months. Of course you can dream a memory as easily as remember a dream.

I'm pretty sure I didn't creep into the emergency burial ground at night, find the right numbered marker, pull down my pants, and take a crap on my father's grave, a huge, wet, sour-smelling one that left my butt smeared with shit, despite my best efforts with the paper towel I had brought, till I could get back to the hotel and clean it off in the shower.

Pretty sure I didn't.

II

Its Hour Come Round at Last

i

It's the fifth day and I've got all kinds of crap recorded, but when I read it or play it back, it doesn't seem to be what I intended it to be. And I already have a sense that I was at least dimly aware of lying while I was doing it.

I changed the truth. Sometimes I maybe made something up to fill in a gap and forgot to say that's what I was doing, and sometimes I left something embarrassing out. I don't know. It's already getting hard to keep straight and I've only been awake for less than a week.

I guess now I don't blame myself for the mess that was in my werp when I woke up. And I sure as hell wish I'd been able to write as well as Sadi could talk, or something, because I look and I find it took me a whole afternoon to write: "Then the man came out from the KGB with Harris and he said go back to the car so Harris did. He told me about the AIDS vaccination and the memories and the long life, and then he left. I don't know what he looked like, I don't think I ever remembered, I don't think there was much to remember. Later I heard Harris was dead and I kind of wondered." And then the story shows up three more times, different each time I talked it into the werp, and it's not any better in any of those versions. I can already see where in fifteen years there'll be another mess to get through but I don't know how to do any better.

I keep thinking about that ad. "I haven't seen weather like this since I was a kid in Ohio." Password the Organization assigned to me in the first envelope I ever found in that cabinet. I think. Or maybe sent to me on a secure channel scramble. Or something like that. Or something else. But anyway it's definitely my old Organization password.

Somebody knew I'd be waking up on Mars right around now. I checked and the ad started to run two months ago. The documents in my werp don't show that *I* knew so precisely when I would transit. Somebody knows me better than I know myself, but they don't know exactly where I am, and they want me to call them.

Maybe "exactly where I am" is the only information I have that they don't. In that case I shouldn't give that up.

I watch some stories on the werp, drink some orange juice, and read over a lot of what I have written and recorded in the last few days, checking new documents against older documents, fixing them up, which makes them sort of lumpy and awkward, but I don't care about that much, even though some of it might be confusing later.

Later I'm sitting and looking out the window. Maybe today I will figure out the pressure suit and go outside. Seems like a lot of bother just to breathe air that smells stale and too warm. Getting back into city air was always a treat in all my long years as an ecoprospector. Was I one? I check the werp, and yes, I was, for more than twenty years in two different i.d.'s.

I have to assume I did my best to tell the truth to the werp. If I didn't at least do that much, there's no hope.

I am standing by the window. It's a change from sitting.

The waves roll across the water and onto the beach. Air pressure's clear up to eighty-five kilodynes per square centimer, and temperature here on the equator has reached 6 Celsius. The air out there isn't breathable for us—too much carbon dioxide and not enough oxygen—but it's getting there.

A motion catches my eye. I look to see what it is, and the oncoming bug seems to come straight at my face like an arrow. Involuntarily I flinch away, then laugh. Stupid reaction. Thick glass.

The bug flips up sideways, big wings spread wide in the thin air, and air-brakes its way to the window.

It might have started from dragonfly stock, or maybe grasshopper; I'm no expert. For all I know it's a honeybee or a butterfly, heavily genaltered. But the body looks more like a dragonfly's than anything else. The wings are big and gauzy, with a jointed "rib" so they can furl like a bird's, and huge in proportion to the body. I see tissue heaving back and forth inside the big holes that stud its body. A science program on the werp said that Marsform bugs can "scavenge the five percent free oxygen and two percent free methane from the atmosphere comfortably, metabolizing them internally as a primary energy source."

Marsform. That's the word for what this bug is. Adjective or noun, meaning "genaltered Earth organism created as part of the terraformation project." Another part of my memory whispers that there's another word floating around out there, "Moonform." Are they terraforming Earth's moon too, then?

I am fascinated, watching the bug. It sits, breathing-holes heaving and whatever's inside them squirming, on the glass, for long minutes, and I stare at it. I want to move to see if it will react, but the only reaction it could have would be to fly away, and I don't want that. And though its ruby red compound eyes point toward where I stand, a neglected cup of cold coffee in my hand, I have no way of knowing whether or not it sees me, whether the glass is even transparent to it.

Finally it flies away. I check via werp. Yes, Marsform is a word, has been for a long time. Yes, Moonforms are now developing and the first ones are beginning to spread out over the face of Luna, where the first rains have already fallen for a decade or so. The moon is the colonies' major base against Resuna. Yes, Resuna's Earth. No, Resuna's not a new name for Earth. It's all very confusing. Just the name Resuna invites too many puzzles.

I find myself drifting through, thinking about words that came along in all those years. Marsform and Moonform, PSCs and dolebirds, vags and tagrats, supras, One True, MAM . . . I start to ask the werp, and somehow every definition seems to bring up Sadi. What I remember more than anything else is this: my parents were useless. Gwenny was in it for what she could get. The little teenage pussies were useless, and the Army buddies, and the KGB. I had two friends, maybe, this Alice girl that I'm trying to track down in the werp, and Sadi.

So I think about Resuna and I remember when Sadi and I first heard of it. Sadi was scared to death of memes, hated them, every so often he'd start crying about our having killed the Hughsons, the couple that had run the Freecyber movement, because "Honest to Jesus, Josh, Hughson was the last hope maybe we all had, and I shot him. I let One True get his basic ideas. And it's turned the Freecybers that were supposed to protect us and liberate us into Resuna."

So I was always slow, I guess, so I asked him again what it was, and he said, "You know how superfast computers are MPPs, massively parallel processors?"

"I'd forgotten what it stands for, but yeah, I know they work by doing a lot of stuff at the same time. Millions or billions of little computers dividing the problem up between them and pretending to be one big computer."

"Well, years ago they found out that any algorithm a serial computer can do, a massively parallel one can do using cellular automata. You know what those are?"

"Sadi, I do electronics. Or I used to. Sure. All those little computers have a simple program that doesn't do much in just one of them, but by passing results to each other they produce an effect. Like people doing the wave in a stadium; the program is just 'stand up when your neighbor does, and then sit down' but you get these big complex patterns moving through the stadium. Or like ant colonies; the individual ants don't know much, the queen doesn't know much, but the colony pulls in food and fights wars and all. Satisfied? I know this stuff."

"Easy, Paladin," he said. "You'll break your toy."

I looked down to see I was almost crushing the white knight between my fingers. "Guess I'm more upset than I thought I was," I said. "Or maybe I don't want to know what you're explaining. So that's what Resuna is? One identical personality for everyone, human or AI, on Earth, that will add up to One True?"

"You've got it all right," he said. "Every other meme you can at least destroy, locally, by killing a carrier, and every other meme requires a long time to download, you have to get tricked into talking to it for hours in realtime. But Resuna is so simple, it'll spread like a bad cold in an airport. And the more it copies, the bigger and stronger One True gets."

I remember dropping the knight. I had been doing magic tricks and sleights of hand with it for so long, so unconsciously, that I hadn't dropped it or even fumbled it in years. I guess I was realizing how close to the end of it all we were getting. Not long after that the thing in our tent—no, I don't remember the thing in our tent. I check the werp, seeing what's there, and I find two different confessions from Sadi that he killed me, three confessions from me that I killed him.

I sigh, stare at the screen, think that maybe I'll look into that Alice problem next. Who was she, what happened to her, why did she matter to me? I'm sort of hoping that story will have just one ending.

I look at my list of mystery words and I didn't mean to, I was going to do something else, anything else, but I spend the afternoon going through the documents on the werp yet again, and talking into it again, and even typing though I know now that my writing's even worse than my talking. It comes out badly, always badly.

ii

Got back from my long leave. I'd seen enough graves. Things were getting back to normal.

The Pentagon had decided that Russia was still Soviet even if it wasn't Communist anymore, and that the Unaffiliated Republics didn't look as unaffiliated as they first had—especially after the coups that added Afghanistan, Pakistan, and Romania to the Free Soviet Association. Lots of panicking and running around in circles screaming among the brass and at the State Department, I guess. Down at my level, it just meant that we would be moving "forward"—closer to Russia—and that meant the base outside Prague.

Maybe that's when I gave up the RX-7. It was some years old when I bought it back in 1984, and it was a lot older now. I'd given it a lot of loving attention. I loved the weirdness of its Wankel engine, the way it looked. And it had carried my RADARGUY plate a long time.

I maybe figured it wouldn't stay in any kind of condition in storage, and sold it to a guy, or I wrecked it, or it broke down for good. Hell if I can remember. Or rather I remember two different buyers, two different wrecks, and one time a kid torched it on the street.

My stuff went into about ten crates. One of them would have had the key and book of matches, in a little jewelry box with a lock I think. Probably the knife too. Hell if I can remember that either.

"The Central European Union was always a pretty silly idea," Sadi said, years later, just babbling about it while we were getting drunk. The Organization had a line on some guy that wouldn't stop doing longtimer research after plenty of warnings, so they gave him to Sadi and me. We had tied up him and his family, trashed his house, serbed his wife and daughter in front of him and cut up their faces, reminding him it was all his fault, then given him a direct shot of PCP. Probably he'd be raving mad the rest of his life.

We'd also liberated a lot of good wine, and now we were drinking it while we admired those two women's bloody underwear, nailed as trophies to the wall of our house in Kansas.

Whenever Sadi got into the second bottle he would get off on one of his explain-the-world-to-me intellectual tears. "All the CEU was was the re-creation of Austria-Hungary with the capital in a nicer town. And on top of that buying Slovenia from Yugoslavia, and Lithuania from the Free Soviet Association, bankrupted it before it began. It was one of those stupid ideas only politicians could come up with."

I was drunk at the time, and I didn't argue with him. If I had, he'd have made fun of my argument. He always said I argued stupidly, like a kid, always "but I like this" or "but it doesn't look like that" and never used logic. Sometimes we'd shout at each other about that.

So I didn't tell him why I didn't agree, but my reason was true all the same. I *liked* living in the CEU for those five years, and especially I liked living in Prague where the capital was. One of the best places I've ever lived really.

The spirit of the CEU was sort of like old-fashioned American city politics: pave streets, collect garbage, divide spoils, believe nothing. Without the threat of the FSA, they'd never have come together; with it, they just barely did, and got up the guts to ask for American help.

Although officially the Organization no longer existed, it had a lot of fingers deep into the FSA, and just about as many fingers into the CEU leadership. From our standpoint it didn't matter a rat's ass who won. We were in it for ourselves, by ourselves.

That still sounds so much tougher than life was. The CEU, from Poland down to Slovenia, was a place where you could afford about anything you liked if you had hard currency, especially if you could spend your whole paycheck like I did (knowing my Organization pay was piling up). I had a small house in the Nove Mesto, which came complete with Maja, a fat blonde girl who did the dishes and laundry, swept out, tidied up, and stayed the night (for a little extra) whenever I wanted some ass.

In 1996 I barely paid any attention to JFKJr getting elected, just enough to get all the jokes—most servicemen pronounced it "Juh Fuck Jer." Far as I could see he only got elected because who else would anyone recognize that had survived mutAIDS? And maybe it was a lingering effect of Mama and Grandpa's influence, but it sure seemed to me that one white law-school grad in a suit was a lot like another, and it didn't much matter which one was the President. The big event for me that year was deciding to bail from the Army and start being a private contractor, which meant doing the same work for twice the pay and most of the same benefits, not to mention getting access to a lot more material for the Organization since now I could work on all kinds of additional projects.

It also meant I was under a lot less restriction on how I led my life, and so usually any party was at my house. I guaranteed dope, pills, coke, whatever, and plenty of young women, and got people used to the idea that I was always shooting pictures—they were still used to film, it didn't occur to them that a wireless digital camera makes a lot more than one print if you want it to. I would tack up the pictures that rolled out of the printer on the bulletin board right away, and most people forgot to take theirs home, forgot they had ever existed.

Since you never knew who might get promoted, or what might come in handy, every couple of weeks I'd label the pictures stored on my hard disk with who was in them, date, and whatever other information—"That's Captain Gerry Clemson and the girl's fifteen"—and send it off by Internet to an address in Iran.

In the fall of 1999, the election of 2000 was shaping up to be a lot more interesting than the previous one, and that afternoon there was to be a big news special on the Armed Forces Flashchannel, a "Meet the Candidates" thing, where the six Republicans and four Democrats that had announced after Kennedy was indicted would all be talking about themselves. What with mutAIDS and most of the Senate being in their thirties, it was a race between people you'd never heard of, and what with better information tech, the one thing you were sure to know about them was the dirt. I had just bought a flashchannel set and everyone wanted to play with it. So I had a pretty good party over at my place. I expected to get some pictures and get some people talking about stuff they weren't supposed to.

What everyone liked about flashchannel in those early days was that you could call up a commentary in the inset screen, so that you could juxtapose a senator making his pitch with a couple claiming he'd molested their children, or with footage of bands playing and troops marching, depending on how you felt about it. *Later on* people started to claim flashchannel was "better" news or "more complete"—the original sales pitch was "news the way you want to see it."

So it was kind of fun to get some liberals and some right-wingers over, give them a lot of beer, and let them fight it out with four separate remote controls. They were all whooping and hollering in there, and I was out in the kitchen getting Maja and her two friends started on serving the goodies—I had them naked in heels, one each to serve dope, beer, and pills—when the shouting started to sound different, like something was going on.

"You all got that?" I asked Maja. She nodded. I gave her breast a squeeze for luck and walked back into my living room to see if the flashchannel set was on fire or something.

AFFC had broken into the "Meet the Candidates" forum and they had some old gray-haired dick up there looking worried. "What? What?" I said. "Where's the show?"

People made a "shhh" sound, forgetting whose flashchannel set this was. Then I heard what he was saying.

"The fourth major coup in Moscow in the last decade took on a more sinister turn as related coups occurred in Belgrade and Tirana, and German authorities moved to contain anti-government rioting in the former East Germany—"

Someone had clicked up all four inset screens; two of them showed tanks rumbling through streets, one with rocks and bottles ringing off it. Another showed some city—somebody said he thought it was Tallinn—with the scary guys in black with shades marching around looking intimidating. The fourth showed President Kennedy looking worried and answering questions. "Depth it to Kennedy," I said, "maybe he can explain things."

"He can't even explain his check stubs," somebody muttered, but then the inset screen zoomed up, leaving the main screen—the one that showed the newscaster—running in the upper left corner.

"We don't know about that," Kennedy was saying. In the wide-angle screen you could see it was a press conference. "Right now all we can say is that everything looks bad. We're in constant touch with our NATO allies about this, most especially our newest NATO members, Finland, Latvia, and the CEU. We think whatever's going on, there's a lot that needs to be explained, and we call on all sides to remain calm and *not* to try to exploit any opportunities."

One of the reporters in one of the inset screens put his hand up, and his voice came through the main channel. "Mr. President, what can you tell us about the uprisings in Berlin, London, and Rome?"

"I can tell you that they started hours before word of the coups d'état in Moscow, Sofia, Belgrade, Bucharest, and Tirana had reached anyone in the West. We're proceeding on the assumption that they are not coincidental."

"And if they're not, Mr. President, then what—"

"I'm sorry, there's another hand up and I'm not taking follow-ups—"

The black woman who stood up was subcaptioned "People of Color Alliance Radio," and the room groaned, but then they all applauded when her question was, "That's all right, Mr. President, I'll ask the same question. If the uprisings are not coincidence, what are you prepared to do about it?"

"Let me just say this. We have clear evidence that trouble was about to break out in Helsinki and Prague this morning, but fortunately our intelligence service was able to alert local police and matters are in hand. It's now becoming clear that there were large underground organizations in place. We'd have to assume, I think, that if it turns out that those organizations are linked to Moscow, to the uprisings in the West, and to the assassination of Prince Regent

Edward and several Cabinet ministers this morning, we will move hard and fast, because this looks like the first few shots of a war. If that's what anybody has in mind, well, it's a war they'll get. And I call on those who may oppose us to think again. We've been prepared to fight in Europe for more than fifty years now, and we're as ready as ever. I call on those behind the coups, the rioting, and the senseless violence, to think again and back off. Because we will not be frightened. You know my father once said he was a Berliner; I say now, I am a citizen of Europe—and I mean of Riga, and Helsinki, and Prague—and we'll fight for every inch of ground."

"Fuck, here it goes," someone said. Others were babbling about what might have happened in Prague that morning, and did anyone know anything?

"Hold it," I said, "I'll talk to somebody I know in Base Security that can fill me in. After that I gotta call family in the States. And then if we don't all have to run off to get blown up, let's at least make this a party to remember—'cause it's gonna be the last one."

Everyone applauded. I gave a holler: "Maja, bring on the goodies!" and when the three girls came out of the kitchen with the stuff, that was more than enough distraction.

I picked up the phone in the bedroom and dialed a number I had memorized years ago, but never used. "Who is this?" the man's voice at the other end said.

"Hi mom," I said. An easy-to-remember password that you could let people overhear.

"Tomorrow night, go to your regular work period. 'Eagle' is on unless you hear a cancel from us. Acknowledge."

"Sure, mom," I said. "Tomorrow night unless I hear from you."

The man hung up.

We had no operation code-named Eagle, and no message I received over that line was actually an order. The line was intended to be overheard, and to put them off my track.

"Tomorrow night" was the phrase that meant that I could expect arrest at any time; I was to destroy any evidence, do whatever harm I could quickly, and get myself under cover, to one of the safe spots we had pre-arranged. Mostly just filler to confuse the NATO counterintelligence guys; probably there were a hundred more references to "Eagle" scattered through Organization channels.

I dialed another number. "Hiya, Linda. It's me, Josh."

"Oh, *hi,*" she said, her voice getting warm and friendly, "I can't talk right now, things are crazy, and I can't tell you anything about it—"

"That's okay, Hot Ass," I said—figuring I'd at least get something embarrassing into her files; she giggled—"I've had the news on, and I know. I just wanted to make sure I had clearance onto the base—I'd rather come in and work, where I'll be underground in a bunker surrounded by guards, than sit in a wood-frame building in a city where fighting could start any minute. Can you clear me onto the base for that? I'd have been coming in tomorrow, anyway."

"Sure, no problem. Anything else?"

"Just two. One, you might want to have counterintelligence come down and talk to me, I've got something for them. And two, I'm crazy about you."

"You're sweet. Okay, get here as soon as you can, and I'll have someone go down and interview you at your post. That'll give the officers more time to figure out where to use the extra hand, anyway."

"You're an angel, Linda. And you've got the tits to prove it."

She gave another shriek and giggle, said, "Oh, you," and hung up.

I'd been fucking Linda, and then relaying everything

she said about life on the base to an Organization drop. She'd never let anything slip that seemed valuable to me, but I wasn't an analyst. For all I knew what I was getting from her was vital.

I had gotten her drunk enough to compromise herself a couple of times at parties—I had a great shot of her topless, dancing in front of several men—and I'd been commended for maintaining such a good contact.

The two possibilities were that she was unaware, and merely a bad security officer that I was taking advantage of, or that she was counterintelligence herself, and they were on to me. What I had just done was to put them (with luck) off the track no matter what. They might think I'd decided to turn myself in, they might think I was coming in early to get started on whatever "Eagle" was, or they might think nothing at all. In any case, they'd be waiting for me at the base rather than sending a car out to get me.

Back in the living room, everyone was getting high and drunk as fast as they could, except for a couple of nerds and straight arrows who were just leaving, heading back for the base, like they might miss the war or something. I saw those guys out the door as quickly as I could—they would have spoiled what I had in mind next—and then turned back to my other guests. "It's what it sounds like," I said. "According to my inside contact, fucking war for sure. Already starting down in the Balkans, and both sides are moving forces up to the line around Michalovce and Krosno. Lots of violence in the city here. Linda said on your way back, you're authorized to shoot if any civilian does anything even a little bit weird."

"How often you *been* inside that contact, Josh?" somebody shouted.

"Jesus, why do you care? With Linda there's plenty for everybody," I said. That brought a roar of laughter. "The deal is, the way I see it, probably nothing moves till tomorrow night, and they don't want to make the situation worse by moving too fast, if there's any chance the Sovs might back down. So we probably won't be called up till close to regular time. But that's all diplomatic bullshit, and nobody thinks it will work. There's a fucking war on as of tomorrow. So—might as well make this a fucking *party*, hunh?"

Everyone whooped.

"Maja!" I said. "Come here, babe. Set down the tray."

She looked nervous, but she probably felt safer coming to me than she would have trying to get away, especially since she was naked. "I figure," I said, "we're all out of here in a day and nobody's going to come looking for us, so we might as well have some fun." I grabbed Maja by her shoulders and pushed her forward onto all fours. She cried out in fear and I slapped her butt, clutching her head under my arm. "Quiet, piggy. We're going to all get some pork."

The place roared with laughter. Maja tried to stand up. I shoved her ass back down, swinging her around so that her bare bottom was toward the crowd. "Now who wants some?"

One of Maja's girlfriends tried to break for the door, and two men tackled her, spilling the tray she was carrying everywhere, forcing her to the floor. One of them, shouting "Pig, pig, pig," grabbed a beer bottle and shoved it into the girl's ass, making her shriek; already another man was kneeling behind Maja and undoing his pants.

That got it started; the third girl was pulled down onto the floor, crying "Ne! ne! ne!," her heavy breasts shaking as she struggled against the men holding her wrists. She started screaming when two big men pulled her legs apart. I heard my coffee table go crunch as someone climbed over it to get at Maja, and thought, *well, fuck it, I'm not packing the furniture, anyway, and it'll all be gone soon.*

In the other corner they dragged the girl up onto her knees by the hair, the bottle still protruding from her ass, and the men were lining up; one of them was forcing her jaws open. I looked around the room with satisfaction; nobody was watching me, they were either on the women, or watching the others. Left to themselves they'd probably kill one or two of the girls before they were done, but they weren't going to get that much time. I slipped off into the bedroom again, dialed 158 (the equivalent of 911), spoke my address into the phone several times, and then let the phone dangle over the edge of the bed. The screaming in the background ought to get the cops here in a hurry.

The way the men were whooping rhythmically told me they were doing something to one of the women, probably Maja to judge from the steady sobbing and the oinking noises they were making at her. I didn't bother to look out; my bedroom window opened on the alley, and all I needed was my jacket from the closet.

There had been rumblings and rumors all summer, and the last week had been a pretty tense one, so I had my basic "evacuation system" ready to go: a nice, powerful charge in a metal Macintosh case. I opened the slot I had cut in the box, slipped in the single folder that held everything incriminating, and set the detonator for fifteen minutes or whenever someone touched the box, whichever came first. With luck the Czech cops would be in the middle of busting the place when the bomb went off. Make some chaos. Good deal. Get going.

I turned to my closet and slipped on my heavy leather jacket, though it was a warm day outside. Inside pocket: already packed and zipped with all the documents I had to have. Left front pocket: Czech papers for false i.d. Open jewel box on dresser, get out key, Boy Scout knife, and book of matches, zip into right front pocket. Touch pocket once for luck. Check watch, forty-two seconds, better than any rehearsal. I stepped out the window to the alley.

Fifteen minutes later, sitting on a bench in a public park,

I had been hearing sirens for about ten minutes. The distant explosion came right on time, and if the timer had run all the way out, they hadn't been very hot on my trail. If they had been, they'd have conducted a real search, and set the bomb off earlier.

"Do you know what the sirens are about?" an old guy asked me, in Czech.

I said, "American soldiers raping Czech girls. All over the city. This is how they help us. This is their 'democracy.' "

The old man's eyes gleamed crazily. "It was better in the old days. Vanya was a better friend." (Vanya: diminutive of Ivan, equivalent of "Johnny," nickname for Russians anywhere in Eastern Europe.)

"Yes," I said. "I hear too that the Americans have been given one last leave to go out and rape and rob in the city. Some of them are shooting civilians for fun. They gave them all their pay for the year in advance because so many of them won't be coming back. I think I may take a knife tonight and see if I can get some of that."

I watched him toddle off with his cane to spread the gossip. That ought to get some things going and maybe give some people ideas. Meanwhile, I needed to pass the time till dark, so I got up from the bench and took a long, wandering stroll through that beautiful city in the autumn sunlight, staying away from everyone and from all the sounds. Not hard—most people were hiding inside.

Prague was wonderful then, just days before it was wrecked. It had missed being bombed in the two big wars of that century, and in the golden glow of an Indian summer, it was like something out of a picture book. I was there later after the bombings and the fires, when they had put a dome over it, but to me, Prague always remains the beautiful medieval "city of a hundred spires," trees blazing with fall colors, warm with buttery sunlight. I still kind of miss it.

iii

Late. The shadow of my house reaches out toward the beach. No more bugs. I wonder, if I go for a walk tomorrow, if I'll find algae floating in the water, and why the water's not ice—it must get cold enough at night.

I'm not sure whether my memories of the black, dark skies of Mars are projections, or whether I've seen it. I don't know why I'd have been out at night. Or why I visualize an airliner with an open top, like an old twentieth-century convertible. Must have been a dream.

After all, I was an experienced ecoprospector, I knew the back country well, and I wouldn't have been out at night. Though pressure suits are heated and well-insulated, being out at night is not really safe: if anything goes wrong, you're a lot harder to find in the dark, and there are a lot fewer people standing radio watch. So it must have been fairly odd circumstances that had me out at night.

The moon I thought was Deimos has been in exactly the same position each time I've looked for it, so I ask the werp. It turns out that decades ago the two moons were brought into areosynchronous orbits 180° apart, so that each now hangs over a single point on the Martian surface forever, like the old comsats or the supras around Earth. I ask the werp. It says the moon I've been looking at is Deimos, and that Phobos is not quite visible from here—I'd need to go a couple hundred kilometers west before it would hang above the horizon.

While I'm asking questions I find out that the water in front of me is Lake Argyre, and that I could easily walk the two kilometers over to the station—from there the maglev will take me to Red Sands City in only about an hour. Closer than I had thought.

I'm feeling disturbed. I've picked up that brass key and started playing with it again. I guess part of it's the strange way memories get reconstructed; I have four written notes and a couple of verbal accounts of the day I bailed in Prague. I know it was October 1999, anyway, and that fits fine with the start of the Eurowar according to a history summary I called up on the werp. In one of the documents I found an account that had been swiped off a database somewhere, the report of a surviving cop, who said three women had been gang-raped and that they were all down in the ambulance at the time the bomb went off. Three cops and six suspects killed, two cops and four suspects wounded. They were looking for me, and all of the women swore I had raped them as well. I'm pretty sure I didn't.

The funny thing's I feel this urge to apologize. I want to say (to three women who have been dead for at least thirty years, even if they lived to ripe old ages) that it was nothing personal. The Organization needed a public outrage committed by American servicemen, and some dead Czech cops, to add fuel to the fire. The excuse sounds weak in my mind.

I think about that for a while. I wonder what the women thought they were getting into. They knew they'd be waiting on drunken soldiers, stark naked, and for that matter Maja at least was planning to turn a few tricks in the course of the day. Of course that's different, agreeing to do it. Probably I could have handed each of them a couple of hundred and told them to lie down and spread for a gang-bang, and they'd have done it—but that wouldn't have served my purposes. It wouldn't have gotten rioting underway, nor sent the Czech, CEU, and NATO authorities on a wild goose chase.

But I still feel bad about it. I've felt bad about it in the past, too. One of the voice recordings in there seems to have been recorded when I was drunk and weepy about it. That's where I got some of my idea of the things that were done to the women.

Yet it's a long-ago crime done to long-dead people. Apart from my records the only thing left of the crime is a few old police files—and so many of those were wiped or altered during the War of the Memes that they might not be true anyway. No way to verify it against Earth records because they're all controlled by Resuna now. I don't see why I should feel guilty. But I am bothered that I can't stop being bothered.

By now the sun's going down. Tomorrow, if I wanted to, I could get up early, make a trip into Red Sands City, scout around, and come back.

But to do that I would have to go to bed early—I'm still sleeping a long time every night—and I don't. I sit up, zap through records in the werp, drinking coffee and eating an apple pie I reconstituted. Try to pull a story together. The records of five other times I have tried to do this—the earliest in 2080, the most recent just last year—don't agree with each other. Maybe some of them have memories in them that I've now lost, or maybe some are based on documents that I decided were false and threw away. Or is it possible that some of my memories at any given time are not really lost, but just inaccessible?

If I search on "Weather-Kid-Ohio" as a cluster, I turn up too many cases to read and view tonight; yet I don't give up.

"I haven't seen weather like this since I was a kid in Ohio." I can count a good dozen times I heard that expression, just in my memory. The dark outside the window starts to give me the creeps. The glow off Deimos is a funny color, maybe caused by all those lights I see glowing on its gleaming metal skin. I stand up, draw the curtain, reconstitute more coffee, pour a cup, and continue.

iv

"I haven't seen weather like this since I was a kid in Ohio," the man next to me said. "Jesus, this train station's cold."

"Fuck it," I said. "If it gets hot it'll get hot real sudden, and we won't like that either."

Pretty standard remark after so many nukes had gone off, three years or so into the Eurowar. I knew he'd said my password, but I figured I'd make him sweat for the acknowledgment.

"Do you think we'll get more snow?" he hinted. Must be amateur, new recruit, couldn't have much experience. Way he was doing things, wouldn't get much older.

I looked sideways at him. Coat fairly new, outermost sweater almost clean, shoes insulated hightops, shredded by long wear, that were a strange shade of brown-gray from a lot of walking in ashes and muck. They maybe were originally waterproof, but they sure weren't now, not with one dirty black big toenail sticking out of one of them.

"I'm from Ohio, myself, and the sky always looked like that before it snowed," I said, giving the countersign. I had amused myself about as much at his expense as I wanted to, and even after my three years of active duty I didn't know how much fucking around the Organization would tolerate.

He slid an envelope into my pocket. I waited half an hour, got on the first train that seemed to be headed somewhere, hoped a rocket wouldn't hit it for a while, and then went into the bathroom. The first bathroom I picked held a dead conductor. Close that door, walk farther down. Next one was unoccupied. I put a newspaper down on the seat, sat down on it, and opened the note the guy had given me.

A short note like all of them: a British regiment in Amsterdam was showing signs of effectiveness. Go there and kill any two men I thought would do max damage. No more than that. After you bagged two, odds they'd bother to retaliate went up, and we had assets in Amsterdam that they might know about. Just two, preferably in the same incident, could be put down to random sniping or even tourist psychos. Further orders at a specific bench in a public park in Brussels.

On the way, look in on a missing agent who had married a German politician in Essen. Find out why she'd sent no reports in two years. See why he was still alive.

This schedule could easily get me killed—I'd have to stay on the same trains for *hours* to get to the right places at the right times. And every minute a train rolled was a chance for overhead satellites to get a fix and dispatch a deathbird. Usually all one did was stop the train—but now and then a train got wrecked seriously and passengers died, especially from the new Soviet deathbirds that could take out a group of ties just ahead of the train, derailing the works. Besides there were so many tourist psychos out there, playing at being "Resistance Fighters," it seemed like more trains wrecked than not. And you could always worry that someone had virused the train's automated driver. That happened a lot too.

2001 was a year. Nothing worked and 90 percent of the engineers on Earth, probably, were busy figuring out how to keep it from working. Two doctors in Japan announced that they thought they had a way to induce successful immune responses to everything—the "make you well" shot—and the next day one was thrown from a high window and the other was run down, and backed up over, by a dump truck. The physicist in Einstein's old job published a paper about closed timelike curves—limited time travel; most of his family died in a fire, the rest were shot trying to run out of the burning house. The Nobel Prize for Peace was not awarded. This upset half a dozen ayatollahs (who had felt that they had earned it for brokering a peace between

India and Pakistan), so Stockholm was hit with 100 missiles on Christmas morning, seventy-eight people died, and it only made the prime slot on the flashchannel because the *motive* was novel.

The price of teenaged slaves in Benelux fell to 1500 rounds of whatever the seller's weapon took. Police departments couldn't get new applicants for anything less than the pre-war pay of brain surgeons, usually payable in a mix of gold, offshore electronic funds, antibiotics, and food. The file in my Organization-issued palmtop computer, listing what bonuses were paid for different categories of assassinations, was 75 kb long. Good year for money. Bad year for people.

The train bumped past a burned-out column of tanks, big old Abramses that must have been hit in the first week of the war. Not safe to try to clear stuff like that out, so they'd been left where they burned.

I wondered idly if I knew anyone who was rotting in those hulks. Very likely I did. I'd been doing some work on counter-battery-fire control systems, including a system to be installed on the Abrams, at one point, and that meant traveling around and meeting a lot of Abrams crews.

No helping them now. Or any of the hundreds of thousands of unburied dead still lying around Europe.

The First and Second Oil Wars had taught everybody a lot of lessons. Mainly how to write SMOT's, Simulation Modeling Optimizing Targeters, ultrafast programs that ran on microsupers and could make "smart weapons" into "brilliant weapons."

Smart weapon: a munition that hit the target more often than not. Old-fashioned bullets and bombs, the kind you saw in WWII movies, were "dumb"—meaning that it took 10,000 rounds to kill one enemy soldier, and a bomb came down within one kilometer of the target. With dumb weapons, misses outweighed hits by factors of hundreds or more. Smart weapons hit more than 50 percent of the time. The number of shots you have to fire to get the target is 1, divided by the percentage of hits; 50 percent means you get it in two shots, instead of a thousand.

Brilliant weapons: the smart weapon went after the most important thing on the battlefield. A smart artillery round would jump out of a howitzer, look down below it, find a tank, and land on that. But a brilliant artillery round would look down below and pick out the tank that contained a general. Dumb bomb landed somewhere around a power plant, smart bomb went through the roof in the right place to hit a generator, but brilliant bomb hit the generator that was carrying peak load.

Essentially in the split second before the weapon was launched, the SMOT simulated a thousand, or ten thousand, possible hits and consequences of those hits, picked the one whose result was best for its side and worst for the enemy, and reprogrammed the smart weapon to go do that.

Nobody realized *both* sides had SMOTs. The NATO nations had been developing them right along after the First Oil War, confident that they had the only ones. The FSA thought they had invented the idea after studying Western weaponry during the Oil Wars, and had been scrambling to get them working, especially after the new government had come to power and achieved some kind of stability.

Pretty soon the pilots and gunners gave up aiming at anything in particular; the SMOT, with its faster reflexes and better ability to evaluate all the data flowing in, could pick out the preferred target within several square miles. So you'd just pop up, fire, and get out of there, not even really knowing what you were shooting at.

SMOTs got better, and faster, and able to think about more issues at once—tech evolves quickly in wartime, and software evolves faster than other tech. After a while you didn't really need people in the loop at all; you just sent out a drone to carry the SMOT, weapons, and sensors, linked to a a network of SMOTs via encrypted tightbeam, and told it to go make life miserable for the enemy.

One time, in the middle of getting drunk and high together, Sadi said "every big war begins by slaughtering privates to educate generals." The Eurowar was different. We slaughtered generals, and presidents and ministers, corporate executives who knew what they were doing, and lately both sides had been nailing engineering talent.

There were rumors that this new Pope, Paul John Paul, was going to do something for world peace. One of my contacts had laughed and said he must have some divisions no one had heard about. I looked at him blankly, and he tried to explain it was some kind of old joke going back to Stalin. I guess he'd been in the Organization a long time.

The train rocked on through the winter landscape. At least we had heavy cloud cover and only had to worry about radar satellites. Nowadays most trains were carrying jamming rigs, just like the few airliners still flying. Next year they'd probably have those on city buses too.

I looked out the window at land that got flatter and flatter. We'd be crossing the Rhine in little time unless—they used to say Murphy hears you.

I saw it coming—bright silver, like a model airplane with a three-foot wingspan, zigging and bouncing a couple of feet off the snow, skating in toward the train. A deathbird, maybe fired by a mine miles away, dumped in from orbit in a container, or shot out of a robot sub off the North Sea coast. Probably it had started after the train within a few minutes of our starting to move along this line—deathbirds had enormous range but they were not fast, and it might have taken an hour or more on its way, easily.

I had needed to see only that flash of silver and the

strange swirl in the air of the electrostatic propulsion system. I rolled off the seat and down onto the muddy, grimy floor of the railroad carriage.

The jolt was pretty bad—it took out a group of ties—and derailed us. Floor bucked, slammed against me, belly-lurch of weightlessness before things settled out. Then I was sliding on my stomach over the grit and mud of the train floor, several feet face-first toward the door.

As soon as the train carriage came to rest, with the car canted over to the side but the door mercifully on the up side and the little lights indicating the power was still on, I jumped up, scrambled back, got my valise, made for the door.

Only a few people on the train. Safe way to get anywhere nowadays, walk slowly by yourself. So I'd had the carriage to myself.

As I was opening the outside door, the door to the next car slid open, and a man, in a three-piece suit, came in, already reaching inside his coat. Reflexes kicked in. Draw and fire, fire, fire, fire. He fell over backward.

Nice. All four shots in the head and chest.

The man lay sprawled in the up-tilted bank of seats, dead. Something clenched in his hand—his weapon? Might be worth trading up.

A pocket watch. I shrugged. Call it education—he would not make that mistake again.

His pocket held a Boy Scout knife, like the one my father had given me, which I had lost sometime before. I took that. He also had an American passport, which I took for resale, and a Missouri driver's license, worth nothing here so I left it on his body to identify him. The authorities would probably get his body home. Better deal than the conductor was likely to get, since he had looked like a Turk, and they'd probably just cremate him and mail his effects to his relatives.

I wondered if I was the only survivor of this train. Three men got on alive, one got off alive. The story of Europe lately.

I climbed out the door onto the side of the train, then down past the overturned wheels to the ground. No sign of any other passengers, so they were hurt and still on the train, or had already gotten away—either way, none off mine. Or they might be already out of the train, waiting to kill me.

I slid on my butt down into the ditch beside the embankment. Nothing shot at me. I waited a few minutes. Still nothing. Either they had more patience than I or there wasn't any "they."

I climbed back up the embankment and started walking up the track toward the Rhine. Sooner or later I would cross a main road, which would take me to someplace where I could steal a car.

Stealing a car was getting really tough now that most civilians had White Flag transponders—radio gadget that told satellites and mines that this car was promising to be a noncombatant, give aid to neither side, and obey whoever won. Normally a White Flag wasn't abused because if they found you driving something with a White Flag on it, and contraband inside, they hanged you on the spot and relayed the owner's i.d. to everyone, and whoever could do it, on either side, would kill the owner.

That made it tough to steal a car, but not impossible. Civilian protection systems were far, far behind the military stuff that had been developed during the three years of war, and the Organization had the latest from both sides.

Twenty minutes later I walked into a little German village, a quiet, sleepy kind of place that had a couple of gas stations, an old shut-down movie theater, and one tiny Catholic church next to one tiny Lutheran church, all surrounded by about fifty houses.

I needed a car I could work on without being observed. I set the low-energy scanner to look for household protection software it recognized, and my cellular datalink to see what it could find out about security systems purchased here.

Most of these German households were in hock up to the eyeballs with buying all the various security systems, plus enough guns and ammo to back up the alarms. A good, fully trained Doberman nowadays was renting for more than a chemical engineer made.

But since these poor bastards just wanted the war to go home and leave them alone, that was what they had predicated their defense on—protecting each individual house. So I could walk right up the middle of the street, in the middle of the day, and though almost everyone telecommuted now to avoid the weapons targeted on transit, nobody was patrolling the streets; they sat in their individual cocoons and waited for the blow to fall on one of them, even though probably half the houses in the village had picked me up on sensors, and the householders were undoubtedly sitting with their hands on their guns, waiting with sweat staining their armpits. If one of them had just not waited to see what I would do, seen what I was and taken one good shot, it would all have been over. But they lacked the balls. They always did.

The cellular data link spotted my chance a half second ahead of the scanner. Side street not far ahead: integrated home security system with known bug, plus hole in his camera system, angle of approach uncovered.

I checked again—jackpot—systems analyst for the German government. One of those obscure ministries, likely intelligence work. Probably a small fish, but all the same I could expect to collect a bounty on this one. The Organization was currently under contract to the Sovs, just as if it were the old days, so a German who worked in that ministry was bound to be worth something.

He probably had gotten this system cheap, and then never bought upgrades because the old one was still keeping people out. The report said he'd registered a marriage to some girl half his age, address unknown, two years before.

I walked up the path my computer told me to take, and when we were close enough it seized his house's cellular link and dropped in a bunch of tranquilizer viruses. Suddenly the house was as dead as any old building. It wouldn't call the police for help and it would sound no alarms when I broke in. And it would not tell the people inside that its status had changed, either.

Of course he would know what was up when his door caved in. But I knew I was going to shoot at anything that moved. He had to decide. The advantage was still mine.

I didn't have any explosives to do the job with, so I gave the door a good old-fashioned roundhouse kick. The cheap lock broke and it swung open with a ripping, booming noise as the veneer facing on the door tore to shreds and the bolt of the lock cut through the wooden doorframe.

He came out naked. I pulled the trigger and he went over dead, onto his back. They'd have executed him anyway for letting me steal his car. So what the fuck.

In the bedroom his wife trying to load a shotgun; she was cute, a brunette with nice little breasts. Probably she'd been out on the street, a runaway or war orphan turning tricks, and he'd bought her services permanently with his techie salary and nice safe house—though she might even think she loved him now. That was pretty common in those days.

"Put that down," I said in German.

She did, and I said, "Kneel. Open your mouth. Shut your eyes."

She did, again. Tears were running down her face and she was mouthing some word; I told her to shut up.

I wanted her to think this was going to be an oral rape. Most women complied, hoping to survive.

I couldn't let anyone who had seen me live—composite pictures got more accurate with every witness, and, if I let witnesses live, the time would come when an AI checking street camera records would recognize me. But I could make it quick. I shoved the gun into her open mouth, the muzzle forcing her palate back and up, and pulled the trigger. It made a hideous mess, and the sound hurt my ears in that little room.

The girl had had maybe one minute of terror from the time the door caved in, tops. No physical pain other than the instant of the gun thumping on the roof of her mouth. A lot better than most people got nowadays. Still, that made three I'd killed today—more than in the month previous—and that made me feel funny.

That was when I realized the word she had been mouthing was *Kinder*. Children. Shit.

I violated a lot of rules. Stupid stupid stupid. It wasn't like I'd just done them any big favors, I'd just orphaned the little bastards. But the twins looked to be about two. *(Stupid shit. Probably she was pregnant when he took her in, and they weren't even his.)* I didn't think those kids could contribute crap toward identifying me.

And after all we were expected to improvise. So I did. I picked up the phone, called for help, and told the emergency dispatcher that I was monitoring him on datalink (I wasn't—my cellular wouldn't patch through), that I had handcuffed both of the kids to a remote-controlled charge, and that if he fucked with the White Flag on the car I was taking, or tracked the car, or if the cops got there in less than an hour, the kids would be blown to the moon.

Then I took the car from the garage and peeled out for Essen. I figured the dispatcher would behave for an hour, mostly, though I expected cops were tracking the car one way or another. But they wouldn't dare try bombing or blasting the car—too much chance I had a deadman program running. And an hour was all the time it would take me.

Those kids had had it made, I thought, as I shot down the highway, doing top speed because there was nothing else on the road. That little house had been wall-to-wall toys. Father had had a telecommuting station, so both their folks were always there.

Probably they'd even gone outside in the backyard a lot. Dad probably loved the hell out of Mom, because she was so beautiful and he'd never thought he'd get a pretty teenager for a bed partner. Mom probably loved him for taking her in, cleaning her up, giving her a place that was safe and secure. Probably those kids had no idea about a war, thought the world was one big warm friendly.

Well, welcome to reality, dumbfucks.

Still, I hadn't liked the way they'd looked when I'd left them in that house with the bodies of their parents.

Our agent in Essen turned out to be dead—caught and executed the year before. I nailed the politician to collect the bounty. The Amsterdam gig was routine—a good CO with one sharp staff officer. I bombed the car they both were riding in. One of those trips where all the bad stuff happens up front.

The guy who talked about the weather in Ohio with me, in Brussels, gave me a jar of something to pour into the Seine above Paris. A complete milk run, or so I thought at the time.

The first sign that the Eurowar was entering its last and worst phase came on that mission, and it wasn't much just yet. As the bus headed south out of Brussels, I saw long rows of men and women filling sandbags. It was winter, after all, so one might have expected some flooding, but the river wasn't particularly high. And it did seem strange to see so many people risking their lives by being out in the open. I was bored, so I asked.

The bus driver grunted. "The worms, they say."

"The worms?" I asked.

"Eating through dikes and destroying levees, far upstream. They're having to spray poison but the worms don't die easy. They look like ordinary earthworms, you know, but when they get a chance—poof, solid banks of earth become mud overnight. Not a good thing, you know, there aren't many to work on these things with a war on. I don't like being near it myself, I keep thinking what if the worms are somebody's trick to get people into the open. I just can't imagine what will happen next, you know, if this keeps up."

I sighed and said something about the damned war and the politicians. I didn't want to draw too much attention to myself since there were only four people on the bus, and once we reached the city of St. Quentin I was planning to get off the bus and leave a bomb behind me. In an abstract kind of way I admired this man's guts, and anyone who could keep an old pile of rust like this running through three years of a war deserved some respect, but the existence of reliable transportation in an area where we had only sporadic control had to be dealt with. I'd get a substantial bonus for identifying and eliminating this one.

The bus rumbled on south, bumping and slamming over the potholes of three winters without road repairs, as it wove its way through the smaller roads and every little cowpath, never repeating a route, like an ant or bee that knows roughly where it's going but may jog and wander all over the map before getting there.

There were more and more rows of sandbaggers. If the worms were Organization work, we'd done a fine job.

Even then it didn't occur to me, really, just how bad the emergency must be if they were exposing so many civilians to attack. But things changed fast—three months later it was no surprise when the Netherlands and Belgium signed a separate peace to get a chance to evacuate. Another typical dumbfuck move in a war full of dumbfuck moves, mistaking their allies for their friends. All they did was trade FSA deathbirds and mines for NATO deathbirds and mines. They still lost thousands who tried to take buses, trucks, or trains. After the first day, people just moved any way they could. June of 2001 saw the great refugee swarms pouring into Germany and France, walking or cycling to high ground with whatever they could carry or drag, and the beginnings of internecine fighting in NATO as the fleeing populations became too large for the refugee camps.

By that time, though, the Sovs were too busy to exploit the opportunity. Prague and Budapest had to be abandoned within a week after fire-roaches appeared, with their terrible stings and single-minded attraction to anything that smelled of Russian gun-oil. The first tailored potato blight showed up later that fall, across Poland and Ukraine, and simultaneously the other potato blight swept Ireland. First one to jump the Atlantic.

Individual things happened, at first all over Europe, then around the world. No eels here, no robins there, turf that turned to black slime in one place and deer who became inexplicably aggressive and migrated in great destructive herds like lemmings in yet another area.

The flashchannels kept trying to come up with names for it—ecowar, environmental terrorism, all sorts of terms that mostly told us, as usual, that the news people were the last to get what was going on.

After all, it was a logical consequence of having SMOTs plus good remote sensing on satellites. An ecosystem's more complicated than a rail net, electric power grid, or market, but it's the same kind of math, you can study it the same way if you can get enough data, and therefore disrupt it the same way. The only thing that had kept both sides from waging ecowar right from the beginning was the problem of learning how to translate the targeting into DNA. Both sides had raced to get the genetic code up as a piece of general engineering; they had finished so close to each other that from our perspective, in the twenty-second century, with so much history lost, we can't even say which side "won."

The SMOTs running on thousands of microsupers in tiny little labs, a few freshly trained microbiologists in each one, wrote script after script for ecological disaster. Here a new fungus to attack a particular set of roots; there a bacteria that locked up soil phosphorus in an unusable form for a few weeks out of each growing season. Here the super-grasshopper, toxic to birds and especially attractive to them; there beetles that fed only on the leaf buds of trees in the spring. Everywhere, as vegetation lost its grip, mud and slime replaced soil, and the living parts of the continents bled down into the oceans.

Hawaii and Cuba seemed almost in a race to see which could have worse things happen to sugar cane; California, South Africa, and the Crimea all had the same mad proliferation of insects; cabbages died equally well around the Baltic and around the Great Lakes, destroyed by modified loopers.

The final blow, the one that forced all the politicians to sit down and talk straight, came in the West Pacific War, one of a dozen little brushfires that flared up as we got the allies involved. Japan and South Korea had no desire to attack the Soviet Far East and face being turned into another helpless, prostrate Europe. China had been quietly feeding Russia. Neither side felt like getting involved on the home ground.

Hence Indonesia, backed by China, was brought to attack the Philippines, backed by Japan and South Korea. The bio labs were hit with precision munitions on the first day. And what escaped from the two labs was so identical that no one could tell who had "originated" it—not that anyone wanted credit. Tailored Rice Blast was going to wipe half a billion lives from the Earth.

The best brains in the intelligence communities went to work on that. How had labs more than a thousand miles apart, working without any direct knowledge of each other, created two things so identical genetically that they couldn't be told apart? To the analysts that was a lot more interesting than the mere starvation of hundreds of millions, which after all was new only in scale.

The answer they found was painfully simple. The tendency had been noted in the 1970s for public, not secret, labs to move faster and farther. More heads and hands on the problem meant greater speed. Leaked information diverted other researchers toward itself, and multiplied the effect of research in that area. By 2001 the side that won the scientific race was almost always the side that kept fewest secrets—the rewards of getting there first were always outweighed by the dangers of being second.

Once the smart guys figured that out, everyone published nearly everything—so military inventions were appearing on both sides of the conflict at almost exactly the same time. The software you distributed to your troops this morning would be in the other side's hands before nightfall.

The idea that you could attack an ecology using the same algorithms as were used to attack railroad systems, communications nets, or power grids—and tailor organisms to do it—wasn't any one general's idea, or even any one SMOT's. SMOTs had been told to look for systems on the other side that could be disrupted. No one had told them to stick to highways, water pipes, and warehouses. The SMOTs copied each other. Became more alike. Got brighter and more destructive. As if the war itself had become an intelligent being, with purposes all its own, which didn't include human survival.

"By the next spring the people at the top of the warring nations were finding out what any sophomore in college ecology could have told them"—that's how Sadi put it, once, in a file he was filling up with his personal history of the twentieth century. Why was a copy of it on *my* werp? "Release anything in large enough numbers, and not all of it will die on cue. The next spring saw all the bugs and germs spreading back from the infected zones into the places that had launched them, and also revealed the (now obvious) point that what's easy to modify is apt to mutate."

From my standpoint, the summer of 2002 was the summer when I was getting rich. Bonuses were raining into my account, and though collapse was coming on fast, and with it the war's end, if I lasted out this last winter, and if the final collapse came in the spring, then I could live like a king in the aftermath. Plenty of the world's fortunes had gotten started in wars. No reason why mine shouldn't be one of them.

Meanwhile we were busy. Targets we had been trying to hit for years—especially scientists and engineers—were popping out of their protection like pheasants out of a cornfield, as the spreading ecological catastrophe made their hiding places and secure areas uninhabitable.

One night, I met two other Organization agents under a bridge in Germany, to swap data between our computers (the major secure way of trading information by then). We all stuck around to get drunk together, and in the course of talking and bragging, we discovered that every one of us had nailed at least one Nobel Prize winner. The blonde woman whose name I didn't get had bagged three of them, one while in bed with him.

It gave us all a good laugh. But considering how much wine we'd had, almost anything would have.

I was sitting next to the blonde woman, and we were passing the jug back and forth. Peter, the other agent, whom I'd worked with a few times, was passed out on her other side. We had begun to get maudlin, about things like sausage stands and the good beer there used to be, and I was thinking about not having gotten any ass in a while. I sure wasn't going to try with the lady beside me, though. If she didn't like what I was doing, I'd be dead before I knew what hit me.

The damp of the ground was soaking through the seat of my jeans. Mostly I was thinking about what I would do after the war was over. With all the money I could get a big, defensible house somewhere, with servants. There would be a lot of desperate young woman—so I could probably find a pretty one that would do what I wanted for a safe place to sleep and enough to eat. Hell, I could probably keep a harem if I wanted. In a couple of years, I'd be sleeping in a great big warm bed, eating huge hot meals, waited on by naked bitches. . . .

For right now I had a jug of red wine, this spot under the bridge sheltered from the drizzle, and the touch of the blonde woman's leather bomber jacket against my shoulder. It was less lonesome here, in the damp dark, than it had been for a while.

"So, you gentlemen want to show a lady some fun?" she asked.

"You mean sex?" I asked stupidly. God, I was drunk. I just hoped I'd be able to function and remember it afterwards.

"That's the idea, fella. It's been a while since I got the itch scratched just for fun. And I'd like to refresh my memory about what it's like to do it just because I want to."

"Fuck," Peter said.

"Unhhunh," she said, nodding emphatically.

"Fuck," he repeated. "Fucking killing kids and cops and

teachers. Murder the poor bastard firemen. Poison in the wells. Fuck." He fell silent. Passed out again.

We rolled him over on his side so he wouldn't throw up and choke on it—as much privacy as we were going to get. We each had a ground cloth, and that gave us a surface that, if not comfortable, was at least tolerable.

The kissing was the best part; the rest was just relief after getting worked up. When we had finished, and pulled our pants back up, she held me for a long moment, and then whispered, "There's something else I'm supposed to communicate to you. It shouldn't matter that Peter's around, I think he's out. Memorize this—the name is Jason Testor, that's spelled with an 'o,' and here are the account numbers and passwords."

She rattled off some long character strings. By now I was used to my enhanced memory, and not surprised that I could recite it back on the first try. Then I asked, "So who is this guy? Am I supposed to partner up with him, kill him, what?"

She laughed, and folded her fingers around mine. "No, stud, you're going to *be* him."

"It's an alias?"

"Yes. For after you transit."

"After I—"

"You remember a shot you got, just before you went active for the Organization? The one that let you repeat all those twenty-digit numbers back without a hitch, and kept you from dying of mutAIDS?"

"Sure." It came back to me. "I'm going to lose my memory and get ten years younger."

She nodded. "We know a lot more about the special treatment than we did when we first gave it to you. About three months from now you're going to come down with something that feels like the worst flu you've ever had. Then for about six months you'll be pretty helpless, raving with a fever, not aware of your surroundings. You want to be somewhere where people will take care of you—you won't be lucid. At the end of the six months, you'll emerge about ten years younger, biologically, than you are now."

I was thirty-five now; physically I would be twenty-five. "How do you know it will be in ninety days for me?"

"I have orders, you goof. They can figure it to within plus or minus three weeks now, because they've had a lot of experience with it. In fact I'm part of the experience—I was one of the first tests in the field. Believe it or not I'm just over forty years old if you go by the clock." I'd have pegged her thirty at most.

She went on. "Anyway, the important thing to remember is that your appearance will change enough—due to weight loss and youthening—so that you can take on a new identity easily. But make sure you've got everything you need written down, and with you, by the time it hits. Start keeping your records with you right now, if you aren't already. Make sure they contain everything you want to remember—*especially* the account numbers with all your cash in them. And try to make sure you come down sick near a charity hospital, or with a private duty nurse around, or something like that."

"And the Organization will take me back on afterwards?"

"Oh, yeah. You'll be younger and have an airtight false i.d. And your motor skills will stick—you'll still be a good shot. They'll want you. Don't worry."

So I didn't worry. We had more wine, and then tried to have sex again, but I couldn't get it up so we just messed around for a while until she was satisfied. The whole time Peter stayed asleep, as far as we could tell, and when we were done we got a blanket out of his pack and covered him, shook the cold and damp off ourselves, and walked back along the canal to the town, holding hands till we parted company, with a gentle little kiss, in the white-green smear of harsh light under a streetlight. Just as if we had been any other couple, or known each other's names.

▼

I rise and stare out into the dark. My first lifetime wasn't even my worst. In my memories—and many of my notes and text—I seem not to be bothered by it at all. That worries me, or ought to.

I guess.

For right now I just want to get the bare facts down. I find several tearful confessions in here, drunken maudlin babblings where I rave on about how delicate and pretty that very young German housewife was. I talk about her breasts so much that I think she must have been naked to the waist—perhaps they were making love when I burst in?—or something unusual must have happened that involved them.

But in my memory now she's wearing a black sweater and a long skirt. As if maybe I'd kept her alive for a while. Or made her strip and then—

Did I actually serb her? I'm sure I accurately remember killing her. But did I serb her first? If I did I think that was the first time. I'd heard other agents talking about it; the nasty little Fourth Balkan War had given us the word, because it had been the Serbs who had discovered and exploited the same thing everyone had always known, that rape, destroying a person while leaving the body alive, was often more effective than simple killing, just as wounding enemy troops had always cost the opposing general more than killing them. Some Organization people regarded it as a perk, some as a trademark, some as just one more tool. All of them said, "You gotta try it."

Was that the first time I tried it? Am I forgetting that? Surely not. I was in a hurry. I needed that car. I couldn't be completely sure that all the alarms were out. I didn't have a second to spare. Even if I had wanted to, or been the type, surely I wouldn't have, not that one, not then.

But then, how rational was I at that moment?

I can't settle it out. The blonde woman who gave me the information—what was her face like? It tends to blur into Gwenny, into the German housewife, into Sadi if I'm not careful. Sometimes I think she was there, that the two of us tied up the German housewife and I raped her while the blonde woman watched. It's all slipping away from me as I grab at it, and what I write to straighten it out makes it worse.

I seem to remember every document I read or see, now, from my werp, exactly, as if I had a perfect movie with sound for the whole time since I woke up. The memory enhancement must still be working. If I had just, while the memories were perfect, managed to set down some, accurately, for every year since about 1990 . . . well, I didn't.

And I can tell that I don't have the skills to do that this time around, either. The records I am making don't look like my memories, but like all the other records in the werp.

It's late now, and I don't set the clock. When I get up there will be sun. I will make coffee and see if I can get further with my memories.

Tomorrow for sure I will go to bed early, so that I can catch the maglev into Red Sands City. "I haven't seen weather like this since I was a kid in Ohio." The phrase in that personal ad just keeps coming back to me. If I were to pull out of here, move my bank accounts, jump to some other town, and *then* answer the ad . . . would I be safe? From what?

vi

Several of the documents I have on the werp use the same phrase for it: "I missed everything." I suppose you could say that. I went into a Catholic Worker hospital in Madrid in March 2003, war still going. I had ditched all the i.d. except the stuff that was going to go into a locker at the hospital, plus an envelope that I told them was a letter from my mother that I wanted in my bedside table.

Late in September I woke up for the third time I could remember, exhausted, seven kilos lighter.

Ten years younger.

No war.

Two thirds of the beds on the ward were empty. The TV by my bed didn't have any flashchannel controls but it could get the main screen signal for AFFC, CNNFlash, NYTFlash, and ObsrChanl. But they were useless—I had no idea what the Mutual Surrender was, or that there had been a war, or what a Public Services Corporation was, though I got from context that it had something to do with the UN.

More puzzling was the fact that the American President, the Soviet General Commissioner, the Japanese PM, and half a dozen other people were in Rome at a meeting chaired by Pope Paul John Paul (American media loved to call him PJP) and it sounded like fighting—*what* fighting?—had stopped everywhere.

Every Japanese and Korean shipping company that could manage it were putting the few ships that had survived the roving air torpedos—and weren't needed to feed their own people—to the job of getting a couple of million American soldiers home, along with all the millions of refugees who had been invited to help resettle North America. There was a new mutAIDS outbreak in the States, so there was even more room once people were vaccinated.

Lots of reference to "indocoms," to the "Global Habitability Report," and to "the coming Rebound Winter in which we expect to lose millions despite our best efforts." As far as I could figure it, an indocom was an apartment building linked to a mall linked to a factory, where you had to be a member to live and work there; the Ecucatholics, who were apparently Pope PJP's people, were building a lot of them, and it sounded as if, mysteriously, there weren't many other churches anymore, though the few there were didn't like the Ecucatholics much. I wasn't sure who wrote the Global Habitability Report, or who they wrote it for, but it must be highly respected because every politician referred to it at least twice per minute. For some reason it was going to get really cold this winter. That was about all I could get, even though I had nothing to do but lie there, eat soup and bread, and watch the TV.

The Catholic Workers were nice about letting me stay until I recovered more. The "letter from mother" told me why I wanted to get my metal box from hospital storage and look through it. A few days later, I had read everything scribbled into several notebooks, and listened to five audio tapes. I was in shape to move around, so I tried going to the three addresses I was supposed to check in Madrid.

First: empty, door hanging open by a single hinge.

Second: bombed out.

Third: street number that had never existed according to everyone in the neighborhood.

I had ten phone numbers. Tried dialing all of them, all disconnected.

Well, supposedly I had money. I already knew what was likely to happen, but just the same I went to the Estacion Chamartin, the biggest train station in Madrid—they had just restored service to Paris two weeks before—and got into line for an ATM.

When I finally got to the head of the line, I punched in my new codes to access my bank accounts in the name of

Jason Testor, and much to my surprise, the banks *did* have a record of Jason Testor. All the account numbers were valid—but all the accounts came out overdrawn. Besides the valise (two spare shirts, some socks, underwear, the jewelry box with its keepsakes), the clothes I was wearing, and the change in my pockets, I owned *less* than nothing—fourteen thousand dollars in bad checks were out there looking for me.

I did a general query, and it showed that all my accounts had been cleaned out on 9 June 2003 between 5:08 and 5:12 GMT, from an ATM in Stockholm. Four months ago. While I was lying in the hospital, not knowing where I was. Then about twenty checks, all dated 8 June 2003, had come in between 9 June and 11 June. The checks had all been written to Stockholm businesses as well, and the businesses with English names all had names like "Reality Associates," "Information, Incorporated," and "Business Operations, Limited." The blonde woman—or Peter—or anyone in the Organization, who had access to the account numbers, had also had access to the security codes. Somebody had decided they needed that money more than I did.

No good pissing off the growing line behind me. I knew everything I needed to know. I logged off and walked out into the echoing railroad station.

Before the war they'd had card tracers, I recalled vaguely, a system so that if you checked in with a bad card the cops nearest you were immediately alerted. I didn't know whether they still did, or whether the Spanish authorities were even interested in catching debt skippers, but anyway the Jason Testor papers were no use at all, and I still had my old Joshua Quare papers.

You lose almost all the facts, you don't lose motor skills, you don't lose attitude. I went around a corner, pulled out a pencil, and wrote down all the ATM codes in the back of the Jason Testor passport. Then I wandered down a couple of alleys, talked with a few guys on the street, and eventually met Raul, who looked something like me and thus like the picture of Jason Testor on the passport.

After we'd haggled a while, and he'd pawed over the passport thoroughly, I agreed to accept the price of a week's hotel room for it. He asked where I'd gotten it. I told him I'd taken it off an American who was drunk and passed out in an alley.

He asked if I was selling ATM cards, and I said I had been planning to take them to a hack shop, one of those places where they could jack into the net illegally, submit the card code, and then break data security to watch the machine try to check the number—thus getting the access code. Usually at those places they split the proceeds fifty-fifty.

"I will give you triple what I've paid you already," Raul said, "for the cards. I think I have a way to hack them more economically."

He was an amateur; he couldn't help touching the pocket where he'd put the passport.

I let him talk me into the deal. He was off like a bunny to the ATM the minute he'd handed me the cash and I'd handed him the cards.

The cash in hand wouldn't get me to Paris by itself, but it was a dandy start. I figured if I could get to the main American repat center in Paris, with luck, as a civilian in a needed specialty, I could get repatriated within a few months. After I got home, either the Organization would find me again and I'd have an income, or I could take my skills and go make a living—radar and electronics were going to be in demand for decades. For that matter I wasn't a bad hand at software, either, though they said hand-coding was about to die out for good.

For tonight, anyway, and maybe for a couple days following, I'd check into a YMCA or whatever other kind of secure shelter they had—no sense spending cash when I didn't need more than that. Meanwhile I figured I'd take a look around.

I had been walking only a few blocks when I saw the big banner on the side of the building: SALVATION ARMY REORIENTATION LIBRARY. I went inside and discovered the guy at the desk was an American, a wrinkled guy with white hair, thick glasses, and a heavy accent in his Spanish. He seemed relieved to have someone to talk to in English, and he was proud and eager to talk about what they did. "It's really the most useful thing we can do for people right now, since there's not much actual starvation anymore, and with so many dead there's plenty of housing, you know. So we run a temporary shelter around the corner, and we provide this place because so many people were so cut off from their usual information channels by the war that they're having a hard time adjusting."

"Er, I think I'd like to apply for the temporary shelter," I said. "And a hard time adjusting how?"

He shrugged. "The world has changed a lot. Plenty of people were unhooked from the news for long periods of time. They need a place where they can just look up what all happened and read about it."

I grinned at him and said, "I think I've found where I need to be. Can I get set up in the shelter and then come back here?"

"Sure, we're open hours yet. We close at five, dinner at the shelter's at six—"

"Prayer service's at seven," I said. "I can tell some things haven't changed."

His eyes twinkled. "When were you—"

"Oh, my old man used to hit me and lock me out," I explained. "I slept at the Salvation Army some when I was a kid."

His smile was warm and friendly. "Well, we're here if you need us. But I sure hope your luck changes."

"Me too."

I got myself checked in at the refugee shelter, stashed my gear, kept my cash with me, and came back to the Reorientation Library to read. For the next several days I stayed at the shelter, ate thin soup and bread there and food from sidewalk vendors during the day, and spent my time reading in the library. They never even really hassled me about going to prayer service.

One of the ways I had always frustrated my mother and her father was that though I was quick enough at learning, and bright enough, I just never saw anything all that interesting in books. But for those few days, I was a great student. I *had* to know what kind of world I had ended up in, especially since, besides my missing six months due to fever, most of my memories from 1992 forward were gone.

The Reorientation Library was mostly just books and newspapers on CD-ROM, with older issues and books available over the wire. I read pretty fast—a perfect memory helps—and thought pretty hard. And now that I had a better handle on things, I could see that I had been more right than I knew: with my technical skills I was going to do pretty well in the new world that was forming, now that Pope PJP had apparently put some peace together.

I would always be able to get work because you can't operate in space without radar, and humanity was going to space—no choice about it. Even with all the deaths thus far, there were way too many people for the food we could grow, and the various blasts, blights, worms, sterilizers, viruses, and so forth were still mutating rapidly, so no crop of anything was safe on the ground—space offered the only perfect quarantine.

Besides, the American and Soviet weather weapons had

apparently blown a bunch of methane into the atmosphere, caused teratons of carbon dioxide to dissolve in the oceans, moved the jet streams and created some condition they were calling the Super-Niño . . . the list was long and I couldn't follow all of it, but the weather was going to set records for hot and cold, drought and flood, wind and snow and hail, everywhere for the next few decades. You couldn't count on a factory or a power plant on Earth's surface—before it was finished it might be buried under ice, the river that cooled it might dry up, it might not be able to get materials over the sea or via roads.

They were caught in an even deeper bind: the plants they needed would have to be *big*—bigger even than the giant ones in East Asia that had been built in the last few years—and there could be no more giant plants. The total ecology of the Earth was now "thrashing."

I spent a day looking up "thrashing," tracing its meaning from the time I had been in high school forward, and that was an interesting little education all by itself.

The word "thrashing" started out in computer science, migrated into music and fashion, and had now become a stock term in environmental news—which had changed a lot too while I had been unconscious.

Back at the dawn of computers, when they first invented parallel processing and time sharing and all the other ways for a computer to run more than one program at once, they discovered that as the work load got bigger and more complex, the system spent more and more time just moving work in and out of the processors, until eventually you hit the point where system management was taking up so much time and space that the system wasn't doing any work anymore. That was called "thrashing."

Kids with skateboards and guitars in Silicon Valley picked it up from their nerdy fathers and used it to mean "going out of control"—especially going out of control by switching off the outside world, and just banging to the rhythm in your own head. For them it was a *good* thing. When I was in Army tech school, I used to say that some of the programs we had to work on were headbangers—you could tell because instead of doing any useful work, they'd rather thrash.

"Thrashing" had become a bad thing again while I had been lying in the hospital. Just as a computer system, when it was working right, used some power and processing space to keep itself running, but mostly processed outside stuff, Planet Earth, when it was working right, used some of its energy to keep nutrients and vital materials moving around, but plowed most energy back into binding more energy and making more life. Wild, natural ecosystems, left to themselves, ran sizable surpluses of bound energy, which became essential to other ecosystems.

Not now. Huge flows of heat and chemical energy, almost none bound in the biosphere. Like a computer that couldn't decide what to do next, frantically busy while nothing got done, the Earth as a whole was thrashing. "Thrashing" was about every tenth word in the *International Herald-Tribune* environmental news section.

"Environmental news" was another measure of how much things had changed. It had started as a back-page thing in newspapers, read mostly by kids, and now was the thickest part of the paper. At a corner newsstand one day I saw an issue of *El País* with front-page news that four whales had been spotted in the South Atlantic and that the USS *Rickover* was on its way there—the world's biggest submersible carrier to save four animals. The same front page also featured a long, complicated story about bottom temperatures and dissolved oxygen in the Mediterranean.

The world had awakened to the environment beyond the dreams of the Earthies I could remember from ten years ago. We could hardly help it—because taken by itself, the environmental news was a death sentence. The four and a half billion people left alive after mutAIDS and the Eurowar couldn't afford large-scale agriculture or industrial facilities anymore, at least not as we had known them in the past. Zero surplus production from Earth's environment anywhere anymore. Anything we did might make the situation worse. No risking big industry or big agriculture.

But we had way too many people to just turn into hunter-gatherers and survive. In fact, because they needed more land, energy, and minerals per pound of stuff produced, the Third World was much more expensive to operate, in *per capita* environmental terms, than the First World. If we wanted to live, somehow we had to achieve a living standard far above that of Japan or pre-war Germany, for everyone on Earth, without building industrial facilities anywhere on Earth—and as fast as possible.

That was the loophole: "anywhere on Earth." Everything we needed—energy and raw materials—was available in space. Apparently people at NASA and a lot of other space agencies had been studying that since 1975, and they knew it would work. As I was sitting in that library, the leaders of the Earth were meeting in Rome to figure out how to do it. Fast.

A couple of new gadgets that had come out of the war would make it easier—the protonic/lithium reactor, which didn't emit neutrons and therefore didn't make materials around it radioactive, meant at least we could build nonpolluting power plants on Earth to drive the launchers, which would give us a temporary (but risky) way to keep the lights on while we moved everything into space.

The other thing, which reporters were making a huge deal about, was that we were close to "phase reversal MAM." I had to hop around flashchannel recordings a lot to find out what MAM was, but it turned out that some bright guy at Tsukuba University had finally explained why surplus power was coming out of the old "cold fusion" experiments; in just the right electromagnetic field, the quantum numbers of a proton could become indeterminate enough so that some protons would flip over to being anti-protons. It didn't take many of those to get something hot.

The scientist who had figured that out had been "killed by a prostitute still at large." I had a sudden memory of my friend under the bridge, and a moment of admiration; she'd bagged a *big* one. Then I spent half an hour that day looking through my notes in my werp, to make sense of the memory. All I really figured out was that if she'd ripped me off, at least the person I was looking for was one hot piece.

The hope was they would have MAM working as a practical technology within five years. At least the surviving best brains in physics were on the job, and money was being thrown at the problem like there was no tomorrow. Of course if they didn't solve the problem, there wasn't.

Meanwhile, whether or not they'd have MAM to power it, they were going to be putting up space stations, and huge spaceships, and starting to colonize Mars and the Moon.

So with all that going on, a guy who had a pretty good background in radar and electronics ought to do fine, even if the Organization no longer existed or didn't want me. I just had to get back to the States, where it would be easy to get hired.

After a few days of reading and studying, I thanked the nice old guy behind the counter at the library, checked out of the shelter, and went for a long walk. Around noon I had lunch and stashed the valise in a coin locker (using the last of my coins to do it), and started wandering around in the back streets near the Calle San Jeronimo, where if there were any tourists, they would be likely to be drifting around. Sure enough, there were a couple of kids, a man and a woman in their early twenties, wandering along in the narrow streets. I let myself shadow them for a while, listening in.

I don't know exactly what tipped me off that the guy had been a tourist psycho. One of the most bizarre features of the Eurowar: rich American kids who dodged the draft through any of the wide variety of legal means, then got themselves over to Europe, armed to the teeth with all kinds of weapons they'd bought privately, and wandered around attacking things and people in the areas controlled by whichever side they didn't like.

Weirder still to me was the fact that so many of the tourist psychos were Japanese, South Koreans, well-off Arabs, or Brazilians—people whose nations were not in the war at all.

The favorite explanation seemed to be that entertainment had been so violent for so long that these kids thought an opportunity to go somewhere and commit random mayhem was better than Disneyland. Everyone denounced them but because almost all of them were anti-Sov and doing a lot of random damage in the Soviet-controlled areas, the West had done little to curb them. They were a great deal for their home governments: volunteer soldiers who paid their own way and who could be abandoned with a clear conscience if they were taken prisoner.

Of course from reading through my notes I knew I had been no angel, but still, I had been professional; civilians I had killed were "collateral damage"—I hadn't gone out of my way to kill them, their killing had just been incidental to my mission.

I suppose I hated tourist psychos the way a call girl looks down on a streetwalker. Especially tourist psychos who were now walking around, hand in hand with the pretty girl from back home, showing her where they murdered Communist labor organizers and shot people they thought were Soviet agents. And most especially when the tourist psycho and his girlfriend were obviously carrying wads of hard cash.

Late in the day. They still hadn't noticed me. That might have been because they had each had a liter of wine in a café. I was hungry, I'd heard more sweet little nicknames for "Margaret" than I ever needed to hear again in my life, and finally they were taking a turn into a dim alley.

He probably wasn't armed now. Even if he was, he was drunk, and he'd more than proved he was unaware. Still, no sense taking chances. I came quietly up behind him, and at just that moment he stumbled.

The note said I'd keep my motor skills, and that's when I found out what they were. I sidekicked him a hard one, right into one kidney, as he was still catching his balance. He went down without a cry, probably too startled, maybe already in shock, and I gave him another hard kick, with everything I had, on the point of his chin.

Little Princess Maggie Margie-pie Meggy Meggums turned around in a swirl of sharply styled red hair, her black-lipsticked mouth gaping to see him, knocked flat and still, with blood running out of his mouth. I grabbed the mass of big dangling earrings in one of her ears with my left hand, yanked her head toward me as hard as I could, and drove the heel of my right hand into her face. The earrings tore out and her mouth gushed blood. I closed in while she was still staring, not believing what had happened, and put her out with a solar plexus punch. She fell to the ground like a sack of wet sand.

I got both their wallets and her purse; one of his loafers was lying by his foot, and I saw the money in it. More in his undershorts. These were the kind of people who put it everywhere.

Sure enough. Two hundred dollars in Amex Universals—those traveler's checks you could redeem for gold—tucked into her bra. Three little "microingots," the pea-sized chunks of gold carried by nervous travelers these days, in her panties.

I looked them over. His pants down to his thighs, her clothing pulled aside and ripped. Both still breathing, but I figured I'd concussed them good. Days at least before they woke up lucid.

I drew my Boy Scout knife and slashed her clothes apart, flung her legs wide open, took his limp hand and scratched the nails all over her thighs and belly. I pulled his passport, city visitor permit, and i.d. papers from his inside jacket pocket, taking them with me. I dropped the bloody tangled mass of earrings into his open palm and folded his limp fingers around it.

On my way back to the train station, I phoned the 091 emergency number, claimed I'd foiled a rape in progress and the girl was unconscious, told them where the two of them were, and left the phone dangling.

I walked away whistling. As long as the cops got there before either of them woke up, she'd go to a regular hospital for treatment, and he'd go to a police hospital for interrogation. It could well be days before she was coherent enough to say anything about what had happened and get him out of there. Meanwhile the Spanish cops might kill him while questioning him, without anyone ever finding out who he was. By the time she woke up he might already be in a hidden, anonymous grave. I loved it.

Maybe he had only been pretending, making up stories about his exploits. A lot of tourist psychos had gotten over to Europe, found out they had no balls, and spent their time in hotels or wandering the streets within a few safe blocks of home.

Better still. If he wanted to pretend to the role, what could be better than his having to pay the price for it? And on the other hand, if he really had been a tourist psycho, we were well rid of him. I decided the same policy covered girls who dated tourist psychos, especially girls who encouraged them to brag about it.

After cleaning out the money, I pitched the wallet and purse down any old alley that didn't have anyone in it; I figured they wouldn't stay there long—someone would see them and move them. His i.d. went down a storm sewer grate.

I got my bags out of the coin locker, changed the cash, black-marketed the gold behind the station to get some more cash, bought a ticket, and was on my way to Paris with a stake in my pocket. I splurged for a compartment all to myself, so that I could sleep on the way.

The next morning I was at the USA Repatriation Office, seeing if I could swing a berth to the US. I figured that given how fast they were going to be moving into space, a radar whiz would be high priority.

Apparently a lot of people were in my spot, or a similar one, to judge by the long line for "critical specialties—no papers."

I got in that line, told them my name was Ron Richards—such an ordinary name they'd never notice it—and half an hour later they parked me in front of a terminal to talk to the AI that would check me out on radar and electronics.

Ever have that nightmare about knowing you studied for a test and not being able to remember anything? I knew everything up to when I'd had the injection. After that, maybe I knew and usually I didn't.

And when there's been a major war, tech development has gone far and fast in ten years. Suppose you'd been an airplane mechanic in 1937, gone to sleep for ten years, and then tried to get hired in 1947.

I might as well have come in qualified to shoe horses, run a keypunch, or troubleshoot tube radios for all the good it could do me. The AI administering the test noted that I had a lot of aptitude, and said that whenever I got my clearance to come over, I'd sure be welcome to take the test again, and even if they couldn't use me just as I was, they'd be happy to train. But—(and I could swear that I heard regret in the artificial voice)—the need was for existing skills with state of the art equipment, and humma humma humma. Out the door, kid, and come back when you know some stuff.

I had told it Ron Richards was twenty-five years old, so I was surprised that it didn't bother to ask how I knew so much about radar from the years between my ages of six and fifteen, but it didn't. Apparently they hadn't yet asked the testing AIs to look for anomalies. This might be useful to remember.

I wandered out into the bright daylight of Paris—a city that was already working hard. The French hadn't bothered to worry about how they were going to pay for Reconstruction, so they'd just started rebuilding, because to them it was obvious that Paris needed to be a great city rather than a great ruin. Most of the workers were getting paid in scrip that could be redeemed somehow, sooner or later, in the sweet bye and bye, in theory. What the hell, the French always liked theory better than reality.

The only place you could spend scrip was in the tent cities, or for soup and bread at the kitchens.

It would at least conserve my cash. I was swinging a pick within the hour, helping to clear rubble from a caved-in Metro entrance.

By the end of the day my hands were pretty sore—it cost me more scrip to get a pair of gloves from the little store at the camp, for the next day—but I had a bed in out of the rain, all mine, and food enough.

The French don't trust banks. Or at least they don't trust French banks, and who can blame them? Paris has more safes, lockups, private storages, and so forth than any other city I've ever seen. I spent more scrip to lock up my cash and the jewelbox of keepsakes in a rented strongbox at the camp's central office.

I worked all fall, got into great shape. I wasn't going anywhere, and meanwhile I got fed. When the first hard snow came in October, we all started to find out that they hadn't been kidding about Rebound Winter. The Northern Hemisphere was about to start growing glaciers again.

They moved our tents down into the Metro, but it was still cold. There was a new protonic power plant running outside the city, so they could afford to power space heaters for us. When they had space heaters. Different tents got them on different nights for a while, usually every other night but now and then your turn would come for two nights without heat in a row, which was bad. They were promising that by March there would be a heater in every tent.

On nights when your tent had no heater, your choices were to lay out more scrip and rent additional blankets or towels (if you got there early enough), or huddle up with everybody and watch television together on the big screens they'd set up in the Metro stations. The trains roared through all night, but we were used to that; a lot of times I fell asleep wedged in between half a dozen other people. It beat freezing your ass off in the tent.

The trouble was you could get shoved to the outside of the huddle, and then it was really cold. Usually I was big enough and aggressive enough so that that didn't happen, but when I got in late, there I'd be, butt on the cold concrete, back to the windy tunnel, huddled up and trying to press into the people in front of me.

One night in February when that happened, my second night without heat, I finally gave up in disgust. I decided to go do something, anything, that I might enjoy. So I got some cash from the strongbox, and got on a Metro to the Place de la République. If you wanted anything people didn't approve of—alcohol, drugs, pussy, violence, whatever your action was—you went to République.

Fairly bright, outside the station. With so much power available, they had all the streetlights on. Far below freezing, but no wind, a crisp night. For a little while I just walked around the big, open space; the Place de la République is one of those places Paris is made out of where several major boulevards converge around a pillar with a statue. Before the war it had been kind of upscale. Now it was where several long corridors of rubble and a few choked streets emptied into a squatter's encampment surrounding a shattered pedestal, the statue long gone, and *the* place for contraband.

Around one corner I had to wait for a long convoy of trucks to pass. Their tires ground on the icy grit, plumes of exhaust roiled in their headlights.

I thought of waving but probably only the lead truck was driven by a human. So many surplus robot vehicle controllers around after the war, price down to almost nothing, usually only the lead truck was driven by a person, the rest just programmed to follow it.

When they had rumbled by, a girl, thin, with stringy black hair, wearing a cheap plastic raincoat over a bunch of sweaters, stood under the light across the street. I crossed the street. As I passed her at the corner (keeping a wary distance in case she had a gun or something) she said, "Wanna get high? Get laid? Get some travel i.d.?"

I looked at her closely. She couldn't have been more than nine. "Uh, you're pretty young to be selling any of that stuff," I said.

"You're telling me. Wish you'd tell it to Pop," she said, in English. Obviously she'd recognized my accent.

"He doesn't make you—"

"He doesn't make me have sex," she said. "And I don't

handle the dope, either, or the i.d. I just bring guys in for him, okay? And don't think you *can* do anything with me, either, he's got you covered right now. Make a wrong move and you'll see a laser designator spot on your chest; keep moving if you want to see a bunch of holes." Her chin was up and her lower lip stuck out a little.

I didn't believe her, but I was curious. It beat wandering around and getting colder, and there were a lot of ways to kill time that I didn't like as much as I liked getting high or laid.

"So how do I meet this solid citizen and president of the Chamber of Commerce?" I asked.

"Don't make fun of me just because I'm a kid and my old man's a crook," she said.

"I wouldn't dream of it."

"He's over there in the shadows," she said, pointing into a crooked alley. "Talk to him. He deals everything. Good prices, fair prices, he doesn't care as long as you pay him something he can spend. But he discounts scrip ninety percent."

That was the normal street discount, easy to figure and the traffic would bear it. My scrip would count for one tenth of its face value.

I followed the kid into an alley. If someone cracked my head, right now, I would probably lie in the alley and freeze to death, but they'd be wasting their arm strength on the job—I was carrying about enough cash for a round-the-world with one of the young girls who sold themselves over by the statueless pedestal, or for enough synthak—receptor-addressed coke—to be extremely happy for five or six hours. Enough for an evening's fun, not enough for anything else.

The man who squatted on his heels at the end of the alley turned on a rechargeable lantern between his knees. The blue-gray light, washing over his face from beneath, made him eerie the way a kid's face in a school fair "haunted house" is—that is, you could tell he was trying to give you the creeps and not succeeding. Probably forty-five, definitely overweight, and he'd be strung out on a bunch of shit for sure. I stopped well out of arm's reach, but near enough to see both his hands clearly, and said, "Your daughter here said you got some merchandise."

"Yeah," he said, wiping a blob of snot from his nose. Something glinted at his neck in the dim light. I wasn't sure of what it was, but it looked familiar. "I deal a lot of stuff, man, you just gotta say what it is you need. If I ain't got it, for a finder fee I can put you on to a man that does, someplace. The little chick will take you wherever I tell her to, to whatever your thing is, and bring your finder fee back as long as you're satisfied. So there's like no risk if you want something I don't got. But I got most anything."

He talked like an old boomer, though the real born-in-the-1940s boomers were almost all dead. He looked like something that would grow gradually, over years, in this corner—or in any other dank, cold place, if there were enough dirt.

"What's your specialty?" I asked. "Just now I happen to be bored and cold. I want to be warm and amused."

Face wrenched sideways in an angry smile, he coughed like a sick dog. Definitely coming down off synthak. "How about a fucking cup of hot chocolate, a fireplace, and a nice storybook to read to the little chick?" The sneer in his voice was thick and loud; the attitude said synthak, the way he was just blurting it out said screamies. Bad mixture—coming down off them together made people paranoid and extremely horny. One very screwed-up staff sergeant I had known back in Prague got himself arrested on that mix, fortunately not too near any party I had thrown, and had tried to hump the cops' legs. We all thought that was pretty funny. "You can read her *Alice in Wonderland,* and you can both have chocolate and marshmallows, and then you can make her eat your mushroom."

"She says you don't sell her," I said.

"Does she? She's a liar *and* a whore. If she's what you want, I'll take your money and give you a place to do her, but I ain't holding her down for you."

"Is she what's on special?" I said. "I think that poor kid's all you've got, and I don't buy children."

"Ha," he said. Probably in daylight his teeth were brown and yellow, but in this light his mouth just opened and closed like a hole. The tips of the stubble of his beard glinted silver. What the hell did he have around his neck? Quite a chain it was on—something he wanted to make sure he kept. His mouth gaped wide at me in a grin that I think was meant to let me know we were getting down to serious business. "I got a bunch of goodies. You want synthak, you want screamies, you want hemp, you want Big Angel or Little Angel or even old-fashioned heroin . . . it's all here. Just say the word and I'll say the price. Screamies cheap enough so you can hire a chick to relieve you on the down side—that's pretty special."

"I'm thrilled," I said.

"Got these," he added, and his arm stuck out as far as he could comfortably reach; something clinked and tinkled at the end of it, in the shadows. "No picking but I'll give you whatever's closest to a match."

He brought his hand nearer to the lantern. Seven DoD-issue dog tags hung from his hand; I was looking at a fortune—it would get most people to North America and into their new lives at least two years early.

"Real?" I asked.

"Real enough," he said. "Twenty kay in pre-war francs, or one hundred gold dollars, Amex same as hard stuff."

I was carrying thirty kay of pre-war. "Fakes," I said, bluntly. "The real thing's worth sixty times that, and you know it."

"Can't fault an old dealer for trying," he said smugly, his hand still holding out the glistening tags. Probably they were solder copies—the cheapest way to make a fake tag was to press a real one in a wet flour and salt mixture, then pour liquid solder into the image. You could put an ordinary black shirt button on the back for the readout.

It wouldn't fool anyone who saw it in good light—but that wasn't what you had here. These were to be sold to some poor bastard who was so high that he was throwing money around at random; he'd buy the tag, have a grand dream that as soon as he came down he could go to a repat camp for a comfy bed, good food, and a ride to the States . . . and then wake up hung over, minus his money, with a chunk of solder glued to a button. "The special on screamies is real," the man said, "and I got a little hooch here where you can wrap up in some blankets to stay warm. Go for a nice ride on a screamie, ten kay, and on the down side, the little chick's not bad—and she's just eight kay."

"Let me see the fake tags again," I said. "I might want to deal some of them myself if you can cut me a wholesale price."

"Twenty per cent discount," he said, "if you take them all." He extended his arm, holding them out to me.

I grabbed his wrist and yanked as hard as I could, whirling to drive my knee hard in the face. His nose and lips made a wet squash against my knee cap.

He cried out, and when I stomped down in the blanket by his side, his hand was already on something heavy and hard. But I'd hit him hard enough so that he didn't have much of a grip, my foot had smashed his fingers, and in a second I'd reached under the blanket and wrestled the heavy thing out of his hand. I gave him a couple more kicks and ordered him to lay quiet and keep his hands stretched out in front of him in the light.

Just putting my hand under that blanket had made my fingers smell bad. My knee stung. For nothing. Of all the useless things, the weapon he'd been concealing was a NATO 9mm, at least ten years of no maintenance, clip empty, corrosion visible in the light of the lantern. He tried to pull a hand back. I ground my heel on it. He sobbed and said, "Please."

I told him to behave.

Well, this was a fiasco. I'd hoped to get a usable weapon out of this, which would have been the first step to getting out of the tents. I felt like using the useless thing to club him senseless, especially because something about the way he was treating his little helper pissed me off.

A thought grabbed me. I reached down and under his collar, took a grip, and yanked hard, pulling the loop of thin steel chain over his head. Probably I scraped his lips, ears, and nose with it.

"Give that back," he whispered quietly, "please give that back."

"What did you do to get it?" I asked. "Kill some GI? You don't look like you've got the nerve, unless you killed him while he was sleeping. You a tagrat, shit-boy?"

"No, no, I . . . I just found it."

"Found it on a body, I bet," I said.

"Yeah, that's it—"

"A body that just happened to be in a casket you dug up, by any chance? A casket that just happened to be at Chartres?" I asked. Part of the fun of this was that he had no idea what was really affecting me—which meant he didn't know what answer might make me pissed off enough to stomp him to death.

The joke was, I didn't give a shit, except for the pleasure I was taking in his terror. He could be killing and eating GIs for all I cared, or strangling them in alleys to get their ears for trophies. I'd killed them myself, during the war, for worse reasons.

And it looked like I had guessed right about him. The one place for getting a tag that was easy, no matter how gutless you were—as long as you weren't also squeamish—was in Chartres. Close to where four thousand American paratroops had all been hit in midair with Soviet body-temperature-seeking bullets was a big burial ground that the French had thrown together in a hurry, using the least possible money and effort, after the bodies had lain out for a couple of years. Being French, or busy, or just bureaucrats, they had ignored the request from USDoD to return all the tags. They'd crammed the bodies into pine boxes, stacked those five deep, and bulldozed a lot of broken concrete over the whole thing. There would be a lot of campaign mileage made off that in the States, for sure.

Anyone who wanted a tag only had to throw concrete chunks aside for a while, then start breaking open boxes. Somewhere amid the remains in there, there very likely was a precious dog tag. Sometimes more than one. Our heroic French ally hadn't been too careful about getting it one boy to a box.

If that tag matched you well enough, and your English could pass, presto, a ticket to the land of opportunity.

"That's what I make my living with," he said. "Please."

"You've still got six fakes to sell," I said, "if I didn't break them. They'll be lying around in the alley someplace. And all those drugs, and the girl."

"Fuck," he said. I could hear tears in his voice.

"Ain't life a bitch," I said, and walked off a couple of steps, just in time to turn around and kick him hard in the ribs as he went to get to his feet. He rolled over and bellowed, "Ow! What was that for?"

"For fun," I said. "I just like having you know I did that,

and you never got even. You never even had the guts to *think* about it. Remember that. Think about it when you get around to jumping from that high window or opening your wrists—and be sure you go ahead. I'm keeping the gun, too, I'm afraid you'll bruise yourself with it."

I strode out of the alley, and heaved the gun in a high arc into the dark. Likely it would land on a roof. Chances were the tag wouldn't match me, but I could sell it to a dealer for good money.

It had been a great evening. Besides getting the tag, I had come out looking for excitement, I had found it, and I hadn't spent a dime. I enjoyed making him think I wasn't afraid of him, but of course what I was dealing with here was a cornered rat, and I could just as easily have gotten myself killed fucking with him like that, especially if he had been carrying a weapon that worked.

That was the whole appeal; if I'd picked the wrong guy I'd have gotten shot. My ears were ringing from adrenaline and I thought maybe now I would go find something to get high on, or maybe a whore.

I was aware of the girl just when she came up beside me. "You really did him right."

"Not much of a way to talk about your father," I said.

"Him? Shit."

"He's not your father?"

"Naw. Dad was GI, or that's what Mom said. She was a college student over here, and she got pregnant. Too ashamed to marry the guy or maybe she never knew which one it was." She said it so firmly that I was sure it was a lie; probably her mother was one of those "students" who just lived in Europe on parental money for several years, not bothering to enroll anywhere, let alone study. That used to be fairly cheap. "Spent all her time getting high and listening to music. She never went out or learned a word of French. Mom didn't last long in the war."

"How long have you been on your own?" I asked.

"Mom died in the first missile raid on Paris. But I'm never on my own. I always find somebody I can work for."

"Did that old bastard really—"

"He'd take the money, then we'd both run and split up. I got caught a couple times. But it's not like I *did* it for the money. Just a couple times someone paid him, and then caught me. It wasn't like he *meant* to sell me."

We came up on a streetlight, and I turned and lifted her bony little chin. She might be eleven. Go hungry long enough and puberty gets delayed. Maybe even twelve. I bet she didn't know, either, by now. Her American English was pretty good, so I figured her mother probably was what she described. I just didn't think her father was; probably her mother told her that to give her another claim to American citizenship.

Yeah, that was a mother for you—anything you needed, as long as it was a lie that didn't cost anything.

There were a lot of kids like this scrawny brat in front of me, kids nobody kept track of, who either found some adult that was nice to them, or just died.

I turned away from the girl and looked down at the tag. I could manage to match it—at least this guy John Childs had my blood type. I pressed the little dot for a read, and projected it on the snow in front of me, shading the image with my body. I could match Childs for height, weight, and age, near enough. If they checked prints or DNA of course I was dead but I heard they were loading ships pretty fast.

And then I saw the dependent list. He had a daughter; his wife in the States was an unfit mother, and he had sole custody. "Hey kid," I said, but then I looked around and she was nowhere in sight. "Hey kid," I said again, louder in case she was walking away. "I need a little girl to be named Alice."

Long silence.

I thought, *fuck me, I'm going to have to find another kid,* but then she reappeared in the glare of the streetlight beside me. "Are you gonna do father bullshit?"

"You mean like make you clean your room?"

"Like that. Do I *get* a room? All my own?"

"Possibly," I said. "I wasn't planning to have a daughter. But you know, you're going to die if you stay over here. It's a miracle you've lasted this long. And the food and bunks will be better in the repat camps."

She thought for a moment, and then took my hand. Unselfconsciously—probably no one had ever told her not to—she put her other thumb into her mouth. We walked some way before she said, "Yeah, I would like to be named Alice."

III

Slouches Toward Bethlehem

i

Did I really get Childs's tag that way? It makes sense, but I seem to remember what he looked like. Wait. Pull up the file on the werp. The read button on that tag has long since gone dead, but somewhere back there I copied the image onto the werp. Sure enough, the face and expression I remember is the one in the werp. Probably I was talking to the image from the button, the two times that I have recordings where it sounds like I was talking to him.

I'd rather not have been a target. And besides, GIs learned early to avoid being alone with anyone who looked like them.

It's the seventh day I've been awake and able to remember. I'm up early again. After probing around in the werp, I find myself thinking I'd rather get moving. The werp shows that I have a good pile of cash, enough to live on a year or more if I have to, even in comfort.

But Martians, like most space people, despise idle wealth, so I probably won't do that. Never make yourself too noticeable to the neighbors. So off to find my funds and then find a place for me to be and a thing for me to do. Eco-prospecting, maybe, that wasn't so bad the last time.

I don't know if I will come back here or not, so I run all the clothes through the fresher in the corner and pack them in my valise. Then I put all the mementos back in the space allocation box. I seem to know the list of them without trouble as I check them off. Matchbook, key, knife, picture, dog-tag, chess piece, napkin. I look over them one more time, close the space allocation box, and slide it into the valise. Still plenty of room in there, so I slide in the werp also. The valise has a shoulder strap and I can carry the whole works without difficulty—it masses only about twelve kilos or so, which means it weighs only as much as five kilos does on earth.

I will leave nothing of mine behind except the Marshack itself and the food in the fridge. Maybe I'll be back—free food and a free place to stay, just a short ride away on the maglev, and the fact that nobody's here yet means no one has found this hideout. But more likely I won't come back. It's not a good habit to come back to where you've been. I have no trouble remembering that, either.

I'm pulling on the pressure suit as the sun comes up. I go through the written checklist carefully, even though my hands are executing all the moves faster than I can read them and think them.

When I open the outer airlock door, the first rays of the sun are glowing on the boulders, and a few little patches of shore grass are twitching in the light breeze. The sky's pale pink. I walk farther and crank up the helmet's outside mike so I can hear. Wind in the grass, slap and splash of waves, wind whistling around the little shack by the shore. Like the beach at home, if Earth's home anymore. If my records are right I haven't been there in about forty years, not since One True went cellular and massively parallel, converting itself to Resuna.

I wonder if that little girl in the hologram's Alice. I think so but why didn't I write it down?

I think that at other times, when I had a slightly different set of memories and more of them were about her, I missed her terribly. By now, of course, she's long dead of old age—I have a short note from the day I heard that she died, in 2095, or 2096—why is there a discrepancy? Anyway, she was a hundred two years old.

The trail hasn't been used in months but there's so little growing stuff that it doesn't matter—it's only wind and the occasional rainstorm that erases the passage of people, so far, on Mars. There would have been a time when it was only the wind. . . . I wonder idly, remembering the one time I visited the Apollo 11 site, if they're doing anything to preserve that from the moon's new wind and water (in fact, it was on low ground . . . might it end up at the bottom of a lake or something?).

Jesus, I think, I was one year old when that happened. I was born when no one on Earth had set foot on another world. Can't be many of us left. A few physical freaks, a few plutocks who got the very earliest life-extension treatments, a few Organization longtimers. Maybe they should just let the Apollo 11 site sink beneath the waves. Would it matter to anyone?

The trail climbs at a gentle angle over a high ridge. Loose gravel and stone around. Not much on the path. I have a vague memory of a machine, something called a "thumper," that you use to make these paths.

I sit down on a boulder by the path, reach into the valise, pull out the connector, jack it into the werp and then into the data port on the pressure suit. Zip up the valise, pull it onto my shoulder, get going again. Now I can talk to my werp if I want to.

Encyclopedia search shows that yes, there's a gadget called a thumper—it looks like a lawnmower and slams the dirt hard enough to compact it. So much of the Martian surface can be mistaken for other parts that even though it's firm enough in its native state to walk or drive on, it's important to have a pathway to follow. I look down at the trail and see that every few feet there's a little number "166704 1842" fused right into the sand, probably burned in with a laser.

It makes sense—that way if paths cross you know which are yours.

It's only going to be about fifteen minutes to the station, then half an hour or so to wait there, supposedly, and finally just about an hour's ride into Red Sands City. Plenty of time to think and remember.

I tell the werp to read me some more about Alice.

ii

"Yeah, *college,* why the fuck not?" I said to her.

"You're not my Dad."

"You tell me that all the time, but I notice you don't mind it when I buy you school clothes and groceries, you don't object when I pick up the whole rent, and—"

"Oh, fuck off, Josh." Alice sounded tired. "I've told you before I want to get a full-time job, and split expenses." She extended her hand and studied the nail silvering; it looked perfect to me, but I suppose the real point was that she didn't have to look at me.

Alice hadn't grown up beautiful, but I doubt she cared. She'd learned how to get boys with the body she had. And she liked what anyone likes at her age—frying out brain cells, fucking around, and sneering at everybody that isn't young and good-looking.

She was wearing her hair in a NeoFormal, which is what I could have told her was known as "Big Hair" when I was her age. Her lips were painted vivid pink, her eyelids almost black, and she had just set a streak of Confoam over her breasts and snugged on a pair of gauzy pink oddy pants, dressing for a typical Saturday night in the foreigner section of Quito.

I'd never complained about how she handled her life. I remembered being in my teens, and how much I liked getting into pointless trouble. The clothes and makeup were coming out of what she made at her after-school job, serving booze in a topless bar near the cablehead. I covered necessities but they didn't come to much. I had just asked that she not make too much noise in her room, and keep most of the trash in there.

Hell, we were just roommates—it had been a long time since she'd wanted an adult to pay any attention to her. I was tough on only one point: I expected her to go to school and I expected her to do her homework. Naturally that was what she got herself into a snarl about all the time. Well, in another three weeks she would graduate, and then we'd have to find something else to fight about.

I sighed. "Okay, okay. I know. I didn't go. And there are lots of good jobs now that don't require college, or even a high school diploma. That's what happens when you kill everybody over forty, and then ten years later you kill the best-educated people. It's a big world full of opportunity. But there are still more opportunities with the degree than without, and kid, I like you, for god knows what reason. And the situation won't last—colleges are reopening and those diplomas will start to matter again. All I said was I'd pay, not that I'd make you go. Hell, I *can't* make you go."

She nodded. "That's sweet. But I've got a job that pays plenty."

"Showing men your tits."

"Yeah. Is that why you come in there with your friends all the time?"

"Point to you, Alice."

"Shit, you know where you found me. You never tried to make me behave myself. I hope you don't think I'm blushing and fainting about it all." She faced the mirror and fluffed her dark curls, then put in the little static-electricity clip that would keep it all inflated for the night. "Josh, you made a kind and generous offer. I said no. If you want to know why not, it's because I'm not going to fit in there or be comfortable. I know I'm an okay student in high school, I know I *could* do college if I wanted to work at it, and I *don't* want to work at it. I want to do my own stuff. I love you, you know, and I owe you my life, but I've got things of my own to get done, you know?"

"Yeah," I said glumly. "Well, it's okay, I mean I'm not just saying that—but the offer's open as long as I've got the money."

"I know," she said. "Look, uh—friends?"

"Always."

She hugged me—I was always afraid the foam would end up stuck on my clothes, but that never happened—and said, "Okay."

She was out the door a couple minutes later. I quit worrying about it and got into the shower.

Scrubbing in the hot shower, I told myself that I was thinking too much about the fact that in just under six years, I would slip into another six blank months. I had never told Alice about all that, and for some reason I didn't want to.

We had had to stay together for several years, because INS was a bunch of suspicious bastards. By the time I had gotten the job on the hang crew for the Quito Geosync Cable, and we were down in Ecuador where nobody would have paid much attention, we were used to each other.

Well, all right, I would miss her. If I paid for her schooling she might leave earlier but she'd stay in touch for longer afterwards. And I just plain wanted to know what was up with her. Sentimental dork, I know, but might as well admit it.

Then too, if she'd take my offer, she could be two years into a good job—an engineer or something—by the next time I was going to transit. Maybe by then I could tell her. That way I'd have somebody to take care of me through transit and help me recover memories afterward. That would be good. That would be the *best*.

I turned off the shower. Supposedly next year, when Quito Geosync Cable was built, they'd be moving a lot of us on to build Kilimanjaro, and from there on to Singapore. A few guys were going to be shipped up to space to build Supra New York and the transfer ships, and a few others would be moved over to the Deepstar Project.

There was more work in the world than there were people to do it, but we still had millions living in refugee camps because there weren't enough people to teach them the needed skills, or enough transport to get them to where they were needed. Still, every month you met guys fresh from the camps, and they said that though life was hard there, there was plenty of hope—they needed people so badly that everyone's number would come up sooner or later.

Funny thing. World full of crime and violence. A lot of people had lost everything. Civilization wrecked. Ecosystem still thrashing. And more hope now than at any time in my life before. Hope is weird.

I pulled on my own gear. Physically I was thirty-five, and the work on the cable was keeping me in great shape. We had finished the steel up into the stratosphere earlier the year before—the great truss like a six-legged, hex-shaped Eiffel Tower that thrust nineteen miles into the sky, clutching Mount Cotopaxi like a huge talon.

If the world had had the time and resources, the way to do this would have been to design the special equipment and the robots, and only then begin building. But we didn't have the time, so we built it anyway, climbing around on that crazy spiderweb of girders in our heavy, awkward pressure suits. The project killed workers now and then—suit leaks, falling stuff, squashed between moving members, every so often the Long Dive. But I never heard of anybody quitting because of that.

All of us got to be muscled like apes because there weren't machines to do the special jobs. And if you were thirty-five, single, ready to party till it killed you, and had great muscles, Quito in 2012 was the place to be. The Ecuadorean government knew a pile of loot when they saw it, and NihonAmerica, Global Hydrogen, and the other big PSCs had bought everybody right down to beat cops and garbage collectors. If we did anything that endangered the project, provoked mob violence, or was just too big to ignore, they could throw us in jail forever or just have us shot behind the barracks. But if it wasn't anything big, it wasn't anything at all.

Saturday nights were the nights when you could buy anything if you had the money, and anything short of a major civil insurrection was regarded as blowing off some steam.

So my little squabble with Alice was nothing, really, as far as I was concerned. I wanted her to have the best things that could be managed, but I knew she could look out for herself—she was smart and would work. That was all it took during Reconstruction.

I suppose I still miss those times. What I remember of them. At least the documents from the werp seem that way.

I pulled on my going-out clothes: big white Cavalier shirt, tight black ringmaster coat, plush burgundy clingpants that started about as low as was practical for trousers, and spiked black boots. I put in a couple of big hoop earrings and checked myself in the mirror, pushing back the black hair falling in loose curls around my face. "Arrrrgh," I said, grinning at my own image—a crazed pirate.

I wondered idly for a second if the Organization was really gone, or if it had just lost track of me somehow. That reminded me of my looted account from nine years before, but it was only a shadow of a resentment—I was comfortable and well off now, and I had time to get more socked away before another transit.

Well, time to go out and strut my stuff again. I took the air injector and gave myself a power dose of my personal mix: Immunobooster so that I could fend off any new strains of AIDS or syph, of which there were still plenty. Wake-me-up shot of gressor. Slow-acting alcohol metabolizer so I could get drunk and not wake up hung over. Performance lifter because I knew that even in great shape, I wasn't necessarily able to keep up with some of the younger girls. To-the-limit dose of You-4, which was just coming in that decade and was already the Big New Drug Menace.

One good thing the war had done was that not only had it caused molecular tailoring develop a long way, it had forced the technology to disperse into millions of garage labs, and nothing and no one had been able to shut them down since. Labs that had been making ecoweapons in 2003 and 2004, getting cash from any of a dozen governments, were still in business—but now they had moved over to the private sector. There were still drug laws, and people who took the old shit, but the only reason for either was tradition.

I swallowed a candy bar in two bites to give the shot something to run on, rinsed my mouth, and headed out.

Everyone knew Spanish by then, but the language of the Calley Alley had stayed English. Plenty going on—a lot of girls, standing around waiting to get money spent on them. A few of them might actually be whoring, but most were just out for fun and didn't see any reason why they should need to carry money when so many nice men would buy them everything.

A lot of guys dressed like me checking them out.

Gaggles of new workers just down from Norty or up from Argentina, still in their issue coveralls because they hadn't yet gotten out to spend the wages in the shopping district, wandering around with their eyes and wallets wide open.

The BFH Lesbian Brigade were out in their cammies, holding hands or clutching their bats, but so cheerful about it all that you'd have to be pretty stupid to be afraid of them. Sure, if you tried raping some poor girl around them, you'd wake up with a fractured skull, but it would serve you right.

One of them I knew from my crew waved and dashed over to say hello. "So what's the news, Josh?"

"Flat zil so far. I just got out. You check the posting for next week? The crew's all the way topside."

"Yuck," she said firmly, running her hand over her shaved head. "Extra half hour commuting each way."

"Positive-definite," I said. "We've gotta lean on Joe Schwartz about that portal-to-portal thing—what kind of a shop steward is he, anyway? And I think since we've gotta suit up at the bottom we should get the pressure suit wage for it."

"Yep. Joe will whine, you know—he's always trying to be reasonable with the PSCs, as if."

"Hey, Syd!" one of the Brigade yelled.

"Gotta run!" she said, and scooted back to her group with a wave of her bat.

I waved after her and turned back to look over the Alley. Right on the equator, the sun goes down bang at 6:00 P.M. and comes back up bang at 6:00 A.M., every day, all year round. So the sky was already dark, the narrow strip I could see of it, anyway. The street glowed in the red and yellow glare from the long rows of advertising signs. I'd already had a good blast from the injector, so I wasn't up for either of the chem bars I was facing; the next shop over was a restaurant but I wasn't planning to eat just yet, either. A couple drinks might be nice. . . .

The You-4, starting to hit, made all the women dead solid gorgeous. Not that they needed any help. Those were great years if you had the body to get any—besides Confoam, there were oddy pants, those wonderful little poufs of gauze that went from just above the crack of the butt to an inch or two down the thighs and swished like poetry, and great thigh-high cling boots, and everything else you could think of. It was also one of those great periods when there's no VD they can't treat, and everyone has the time and the money.

Four girls, classmates of Alice I think, all waved at me as they went by, and although objectively they looked about like any other teenagers, under the You-4 they were the four hottest pieces I'd ever seen in my life. I drifted into the bar—the most wonderful bar, filled with terrific people who I was dying to meet—and ordered a marvelous bottle of Bud from the bartender. He brought it right away—so fast! the man was a saint!—and the first sip told me that this was the best bottle old Augie Busch had ever made.

The You-4 hit harder. I worked hard not to start giggling. I loved this stuff but I didn't want other people laughing at me. I sat down on the bar stool, which caressed my bottom like the firm hands of a trained Thai masseuse, and let the Bud soak into me and blur out the acute edges of pleasure.

Great to be alive. After a while, the band started up, and my Bud was about gone, so I decided to dance; those were the years of the Boink, so everyone had an oversized belt loop on each side of their clingpants or oddy, to give your partner something to hang on to. And if you were on You-4, so that sensations were enhanced hundreds of times, the Boink was the best dance ever invented.

I spent an hour or so floating from partner to partner, watching as the women got themselves off on me, sometimes feeling the little surge of a pseudorgasm—one of You-4's better side effects—hit me as well.

About the time I was thinking seriously that I was hot and wanted another beer, this girl Myndi, a school friend of Alice's, came up to me and asked me to Boink. They were starting kind of a long number, and I was tired and hot—but on the other hand, Myndi was a nice-looking redhead, one of the tall, rangy, horsey kind, with big floppy tits on a totally fatless body. So I said yes.

She really pushed hard into the grinds. I might have wondered what someone that young wanted with someone like me, but between You-4 and gressor, I couldn't imagine, just then, that any woman didn't.

She came on me a couple of times when the music hit crescendos, and at the end she wrapped her arms around me and jammed her tongue into my mouth. My hands slipped under the cuffs of her oddy pants, caressing her butt, and she pressed closer.

So after that it was natural to get her a drink—Myndi was seventeen, a year younger than Alice, but there wasn't much concern about age along Calley Alley, for drinking or anything else. And then after she'd put down a couple of pink things with little paper umbrellas, and I'd had another couple of Buds, it seemed pretty natural to go back to my place. We staggered in trying to be quieter than usual, because even though Alice and I sure knew the other person was having sex, I wasn't sure how she'd feel about my nailing one of her school friends.

It was one great fuck, and it lasted a long time. The enhancer let me manage two more times before I settled into kneeling between her legs and licking until she finally said she was satisfied. By the time she said that, I was sore and tired like I'd spent the night boxing bare-knuckled—and losing—and I didn't care if I never saw that devil's-mouth tattoo that she had in her crotch again.

I woke up late the next morning, to discover that I was being had again; she had climbed aboard while I was asleep. This time I wasn't on all the drugs, and I could see that she was young, but also that she didn't seem to be involved with *me*, just pumping away (though she certainly seemed to be enjoying it). I came in a minute or so. She went down on me to clean it up. When she came up she kissed me and started to get dressed.

"That was great," she said, as she sprayed a fairly modest Confoam top on, "I thought I was doing Alice a big favor but that was pretty nice. I guess older guys do know more. Maybe sometime again, hunh?"

"Uh, wait a sec," I said, trying to figure it out, but she had already given me a little wave and gone out the bedroom door. I grabbed a pair of sweat pants and yanked them on, but by the time I got out of the bedroom she was gone. I stood there for a stupid second before I recalled that she had said she thought she was doing Alice a favor, which meant Alice had asked her to—

I turned and looked around the apartment. Light was coming in from the three big windows, and sunlight was splashing in from the kitchen window, so it must be past 3:00 P.M.

No spill of makeup bottles across the coffee table. No laundry basket full of filmy nothings. I knocked on her door—an odd, hollow sound. When I looked inside the bed was made for the first time since I had stopped cleaning in there. Closet open and empty. Plenty of dust and stain on the end tables and dresser, but nothing else.

The note on the bed said she was going to be staying

with Joe Schwartz, the union guy for my section. I looked at that and started to laugh.

Syd had been right. I'd have to talk to him. Well, I could hardly fault his taste—let alone that after all, he was only ten years older than she was, and considering how much older than Myndi I was, I was hardly in a position to pick on Joe about it. I wondered if Alice had set Myndi on me as a going-away present, or a diversion? She'd certainly been diverting.

It bothered me that she hadn't told me what she was up to. But then, being Alice, she was probably afraid she'd get my blessing.

iii

I am sitting on this bench at the maglev stop, just thinking and letting my eyes roam around the red sand hills of Mars, with dark brown streaks from which a thousand tiny stars glint and glitter. The bioextractors are replacing oxygen with sulfur and creating surface deposits of pyrites wherever the dust is deep enough. A lot of Mars will glitter for a few years, until the wind and rain spread soil over it, and then those cracks and pits where the dust used to lie will become the permeable beds through which groundwater will rise and fall. At least that's what the werp tells me.

I wonder whether, a thousand years from now, when the glittering pyrite beds are being covered up, there will be people who will miss them. Right now, this century, it's pretty.

The sun's warm through the bubble helmet. Suit temp control's good, I'm not really sweaty. Where was this back when I was doing space rigging? Oh, well, that's the nature of things. As long as it was just working stiffs, nobody was going to bother making suits comfortable.

I wonder about what to do with what's in the werp. One part of me argues that I ought to wipe the works, write ten short paragraphs, and bury the werp and the space allocation box someplace. Next time around start clean—after all, the poor bastard, whoever I have become, will be sixty-five physically. I know he could live a long time after that, but why not just let him live comfortably confused, troubled only by the occasional nightmare or haunting dream?

I can't bear to part with the space allocation box, or with the tangle of stuff in the werp. It might have been different if I had never known it existed, but now that I do it seems like it's the one thing that absolutely has to go on.

Once my life gets back underway, then I'll be less hung up on this, I'm sure. Part of the problem was having nothing to do but this. It must have been even worse that first time, when I just had the paper notes and had to fake my way through the hospital without knowing what was going on. I think I remember I was afraid and upset, but of course that vague memory could be nothing more than my making it up. It seems convincing, but maybe I just know myself well enough to know what details will make it convincing to me. After a long life, even with six memory erases, you know what a hospital smells like (bad) and how doctors and nurses treat people without money (like frozen shit on a stick).

The notes say the Catholic Workers were pretty good to me, but I don't really believe it. I've been around too many handout windows to believe anybody gives you decent treatment unless they're going to make cash off you. It isn't the poor they buy off, but their own oversensitive consciences. Probably I was just too young to notice them being condescending.

The maglev arrives almost silently, even with my outside microphones amped up. A shimmer of white above the trough-shaped metal track, far off in the distance. Something flashes bright white in the sun. Breaking out of the distant hills, there it is, slithering to the station at high speed. A voice in my earphones says, "Please acknowledge that you are the passenger who requested a train stop. You have twenty seconds to acknowledge. Twenty. Nineteen. Eighteen . . ."

"I acknowledge," I said.

"Number of people in your party?"

"One."

"Number of bags you are carrying, and will you need extra time for loading?"

"One shoulder bag," I said, "and once I'm aboard you can start again."

"Thank you, sir. Please stay behind the blue line until the train comes to a complete stop."

I walk up to where a blue line appears on the ground, as if it had been painted there very precisely. The train keeps coming. I take a moment to kneel and lift a pebble from the blue line. It turns red-brown as soon as I pick it up; I throw another pebble onto the line and see it turn blue instantly.

Oh, well, I wasn't planning to work as an engineer this trip around. I only need to know what things do, not how they do it.

The train comes to a stop with a low hiss, making less noise than the brakes on some cars I've owned. It's huge—at least forty foot wide by a hundred long. At first, coming in at such speed, it looked pure white, but now I see it's smeared with fine dust.

One of the last cars stops in front of me, and the whole train sinks a few inches as the pedestals settle silently onto the track. "You may board now. Please board quickly. Thank you," the voice of the train says in my ears.

I walk forward and enter the car's airlock; the door

snugs tight behind me. There's a thud I feel through my feet as the train shoots air into the lock, and then the inner door opens. I walk through, unlocking and lifting my helmet.

My cabin's the third one on the right. It's supposed to be for up to four people, so it has two fold-down beds, a long bench seat attached to the wall facing the windows, a small washstand, shower, and toilet, and a table that folds into the wall. I pull down the table and unfold the seats.

Red Sands City is a few hundred kilometers away, I would judge, since it takes something more than an hour to get there. The maglev pulls up inside the enclosure, so I won't need the pressure suit there; I strip the suit off, shower, and dress, which kills half an hour of the journey.

By the time that I'm clean and dressed, we are passing a lot of "ranches"—the word doesn't mean exactly what it would on Earth, because these people don't raise things to sell, they tend the genetically tailored wildlife that is slowly populating Mars. They get a salary for that.

My memory twinges. On Earth, for most of my life, "ranchers" were guys who looked after whichever buffalo happened to wander across their land. The older meaning's nearly gone except in books and movies.

I order soup and a sandwich. About the time I toss the napkin aside and drop the tray into the return slot, the enclosure of Red Sands City is dancing in the heat rising from the plain ahead. I straighten things up, get the pressure suit into its bag, and wait for the warning bell that means we're decelerating into the city. I get off onto a wide platform, no different from any other train platform, looking out over the treetops inside the enclosure, from which hard white spires and steeples occasionally poke up, to the blackened sky, much of the harsh daylight screened out, where the city enclosure arches.

iv

"It took us a long time to find you," she explained. "By the time we did you were about ready to transit again."

"Transit?"

"The age reversal thing. So anyway, we just watched you to see what you set up, and here we were, waiting for you. You have a heap of back pay and interest coming."

"I'll say." I took a long sip of coffee and a bite of doughnut. The first time I had come out of transit starving and broke, this time I was rich. At least if I took this deal.

I had awakened facing the blonde woman I had met under the bridge years before. She looked maybe five years older than she had then, and I looked five years younger. Aging at different times and in different directions. Confusing.

Now, a week after waking up, here I was, spending May 2017 in a big, comfortable hotel room, eating like an ox on an unlimited room-service tab. The Organization had found me again.

While I was unconscious they had moved me here and done the coverage on "Brandon Smith," the new i.d. I had established for myself, so that the i.d. was a lot more airtight than what I'd done.

I still had not learned this woman's name. From what I could read of my past experiences in the pile of letters, still photos, holos, and scrap paper, I had never known her name. Apparently I had thought she was "the bitch who ran off with everything I owned," except when I thought it was somebody named Peter, except when I thought it was the Organization itself.

"Not that I don't want to work for the Organization," I said. "I'm confused because looking me up to give me the money that was owed to me, and then taking care of me during recovery, doesn't sound a lot like the Organization in my notes, or what I remember from back when we were the KGB. I mean, we *used* to be the KGB, but here you are acting like the Salvation Army."

She smiled. "We haven't been the KGB for a long time, and we absorbed a bunch of other outfits, so we don't really have a single origin anymore. When your home country joined the Pope's Global Concord in 2008, we picked up a lot of good people, sometimes whole offices, from several of their agencies. In other places there were existing groups that merged with us."

"Like the Mafia?"

"Yes, and national liberation movements that had lost their mass base but not their cadres and weapons. Smugglers with no borders. Mercenaries with no rogue governments to hire them. The world was full of people who still had means but no ends, Joshua—I guess we should practice calling you Brandon."

I was sure she had pretended to slip and use my real name so that it would seem more like we were old friends. Or had I—seen her with her head shaved, in coveralls—I wasn't sure what that memory was.

"So I know you can't *prove* that I should trust you, but make me a case," I said.

She fluffed up her thick blonde hair. Who'd have thought that style would keep coming back? "All right, I'll tell you the whole story. It happens I was there for a lot of it, so you can believe me—but if you'd rather not, well . . ."

"Let's hear it."

Something flew by the window—a big private car, somebody with a license to fly inside Manhattan Dome, I figured—and I glanced sideways at it, watching it descend to land on the roof of the old World Trade Center, a kilometer below. When I looked up, the blonde woman was staring off into space, toward the translucent wall of the Dome some miles away. Two thirds of the way up one of the central pillars, we could see a long way in all directions, but since vags tended to cluster by the dome wall, people looking out tended to stare into the distance, the way you'd put on a thousand-yard stare when you passed a beggar on the street, when I was a kid.

"Well," she said, "the Organization, capitalized, works a lot like any other organization, not capitalized. So we favored seniority, and like the military outfits, we tended to value combat time, and of course people with more energy and vigor . . . so longtimers, people like you and I tended to do better."

"Makes sense," I agreed, "except that our experience all goes away every fifteen years."

"Not all of it. We have each other. We can be each other's memories. Do you remember a quiet little guy that traveled under the name Peter?"

"I have notes about him in my own records." *As you goddamn well know.*

"Well, he made station chief for Paris, right when the old people up at the top were getting to be afraid of us. They were looting accounts and erasing i.d.'s while longtimers transited, hoping to slowly eliminate us. They thought if they killed us it would leave more trail than if we just vanished, the way a lot of agents were vanishing voluntarily and going to work for the Reconstruction." She sighed, turned her head, stretched like a yawning kitten—sexy as all shit and intended to be. "So . . . Peter and a few others he could find made their move. Peter pulled a coup about two years after you were cut loose. And then we started the long, difficult process of finding all the other longtimers who had been thrown away."

"It just went from 'them' to 'we,' " I pointed out. "You're with the longtimers?"

"Oh, pos-def." Kidslang. It made sense for her to use it—she must be past fifty but she was clearly vain and playing at being young. "To the lim."

Trying to needle her, I asked, "Uh, just how old are you right now?"

She grinned. "Chronologically I'm fifty-eight. Just went through another transition two years ago. Not bad, hunh?"

"Not bad at all. So the longtimers are in charge now?"

"Pos-def, and we're slowly adding more of us, both by recruiting new young people and by finding our lost ones. We want every single longtimer to come in with us, and we're prepared to offer a lot."

"This is probably stupid of me to ask," I said, "but just what happens if you get one that won't come in for any reason at all?"

"I don't know."

"It hasn't happened?"

Shrug. "It has. When it does I report it and go on my way."

"The old Organization, the one I knew, would have killed them," I said. I had about made my mind up to throw in with them, but I wanted to *know* the worst thing they might do.

She nodded. "No question. The old Organization would. And I don't suppose you remember Peter, but I worked a couple cases with him, and I shudder when I think about things he did. He didn't get to be a longtimer till he was past forty, so he spent a lot of time in the old KGB, back before it was the Organization. I can't imagine he's changed that much. But I don't really know. What they tell me, and tell me to tell you, is that the last thing they want to do is draw attention to their existence, and so the next best thing to a longtimer that works for them is a longtimer who goes quietly through life without raising any eyebrows. Mysterious murders of people who have only recently established i.d.'s would trigger all kinds of investigation. We don't want that. So supposedly we leave them alone, keep tabs on them, wait fifteen years or so, and try again when they're waking up again."

I thought about that. It might even be true. When the truth works just as well as a lie, sometimes people tell you the truth. It made me wonder—"Did you contact me after my last transit, and did I say no?"

"Everyone asks that. No, we didn't find you until about a year and a half before this transit. By that time you were working construction on Supra Tokyo, and we don't have many ins up there. We were trying to figure out how to get to you when you conveniently came back down to Singapore and established a new i.d.—damn good job for working all by yourself, by the way, the trick with setting up credit card records for your fake father was brilliant. We only cracked it because we were watching you. We figured we owed you a decent room, at least, so we moved you here—and here we are."

I would never know if that story was false, or true. Just one more thing to take on faith. You wake up ten years older, with a few scraps of evidence for a thirty-year life you don't remember, and here you are. Over and over, if this was all to be believed.

She stayed the night. I suppose it was standard practice; she told me that I was a lot better in bed than I'd been under a bridge. I had only remembered that we'd talked.

I took the job.

Two weeks later, early in the morning, I was on a high-speed diskster to Atlanta Dome. First-class compartment. The disksters were new—I didn't remember them, but I might never have ridden one, since I had mostly been up at Supra Tokyo for a couple of years.

A diskster was an electrostatic aircraft that took advantage of ground effect, and looked a lot like a flying saucer.

The little MAM power plant in them—about the size of the engine in my old RX-7—could put out more power than all the engines of three 747s, and the radar and AI pilot let the diskster move along at close to 300 mph on the old freeways, since it could dodge obstructions faster than any human driver, run over river surfaces, fly short distances, and at last resort brush things like deer aside. They were a great ride—the kind of luxury that had last existed on the old ocean liners.

As we cruised out the 57th Street Door (I turned around like any tourist to gawk at the five-story-high door rolling back down like the garage doors of my childhood) and across the river into Weehawken Ruin, I saw a flash off to the side. I turned to look and saw men running for cover. A moment later, a rocket, probably out of a patrolling helicopter, had blasted the place where their mortar was set up. The diskster, meanwhile, stepped sideways hard, sloshing the coffee on my tray and making the tray itself slide along the polished wood table, so that I had to catch it. I didn't see the shell splash—I think it landed behind us.

I muttered "Nice shot, guys," and went back to my breakfast. Vags were making the best efforts they could, which wasn't much.

I sat back to enjoy the ride. At first we ran down the Hudson, close to the Jersey side to avoid the rougher water out in the bay, but shortly we were rounding the Statue of Liberty, what was left of her after the blast that had hit Jersey City just after the war—no one ever seemed to settle whether a smuggled bomb, a delayed long-range cruise missile, or just a whoopsie with a piece of surplus hardware had converted Miss Liberty into twentieth-century art. You could tell what the shape was supposed to be, but rusting steel stuck out here and there, the surface was strangely mottled where parts had melted and run, and the skeleton had twisted hard as the statue lost its torch, so that now it looked more like she was doing a dance of mourning over New Jersey.

We zipped up the earth ramp onto the old Jersey Turnpike and we were on our way south. I poured more coffee from the little pot they provided, and settled back to read with my new toy, a brand-new Reconstruction Standard Issue Werp.

My previous life, apparently, I'd concentrated on having fun. I had gotten on to Reconstruction work early, and adopted a daughter for some reason I couldn't fathom, though it looked like we'd been out of touch for a while. She was listed as Mrs. Joe Schwartz, Supra Berlin, though the last note I had from her, four years before, said she was planning to get a divorce because apparently Schwartz had decided to accept a permanent post on the *Flying Dutchman*, and besides she'd found "a new guy, a really nice guy, I mean Joe's kind and he works hard but this is so different from anything I've known." She'd had to give up her visiting rights to her kid, who I'd never seen. Reading between the lines, it sounded like the nice guy was a plutock, and I figured I'd done a good job of raising Alice. Given a choice between a five-year-old son and a rich husband, she'd made the choice that made sense. That was sort of a relief since I remembered her as kind of sentimental.

With an inward groan I turned back to review the material for my mission. I already knew it thoroughly but I kept hoping it would look better. The job was so bizarre—an Organization guy in charge of getting a bunch of libertarian bandits to join a new religion—that the better I understood it, the more confusing it got.

The reason we'd gotten into this business was that Reconstruction was going too far too fast. We had no problem with rich people—they make better customers or better victims, take your pick. But the refugee camps and the indocoms, where our power base was, were shrinking rapidly as the main economy began to absorb people faster and faster, and we were having very little luck with keeping our low-level people once they moved into the domes or up to the supras.

And we couldn't seem to get a toehold outside Earth orbit. There'd been a genuine lynching at Ceres Base the year before. The locals had pushed nine of our organizers naked out the airlock. Worse still, our reprisal strike against EuroNihon had been caught before it accomplished anything and the whole team was now in jail.

Behind the whole disaster that Reconstruction was turning into was PJP, Pope Paul John Paul. He'd gotten his prestige by brokering the peace settlement that ended the Eurowar, which is to say, he'd started out by costing us plenty. But the Ecucatholic Movement he had launched at the same time was the kicker.

The policy documents frankly admitted the Organization had misread Ecucatholicism. They had thought it was mere PR, or a recruiting method. By the time the Organization learned how much more it was, it was too late for shooting the Pope to solve the problem.

By canonizing practically every Protestant leader since the Reformation, and then establishing the principle of "surface forms and deep forms," whatever that was (apparently a lot of theologians were turning out book after book explaining it), PJP had somehow gotten millions of Protestants to come back under the Roman umbrella. Realizing that there was now a Saint Brigham Young and a Saint Mary Baker Eddy gave me an idea of how far things had gone.

The result was what everyone else was calling a "new moral force." The Organization didn't concern itself with that kind of crap. What we knew was that UNRRA-2, Global Hydrogen, NihonAmerica, EuroNihon, Americ-Euro, and all the other Reconstruction PSCs shut us out no matter what we tried to do. From the top down everyone insisted on squeaky-clean operations. There were more stool pigeons and straight arrows than the world had ever seen before, and those dumbfucks were ruining it for everyone else.

We still had a finger in the indocoms, the old factory/mall/apartment complex setups that had emerged right after the war, but the ones that couldn't afford to get domed were shutting down, and most of them were losing people into the domes anyway.

So we were left recruiting where we could and not where we chose. That meant the vags—pissed-off people in the woods, many of them useless lunatics, thugs, and cranks of course. Most were people who had had a comfortable life before the Eurowar, wanted compensation, and weren't coming in till they got it.

They were usefully stupid. Driven by their "right" to their old houses, businesses, jobs, prestige, whatever, they would fight to the death rather than accept that all that was gone, united by the conviction that the Reconstruction authorities had cheated them of their "freedom." You take your malcontents where you can find them.

The other force in the mix was cybertao, the only religious movement that looked like it might challenge Ecucatholicism. Of course nobody knew who the author of *Forks in Time* had been—the cybertaoists believed it had somehow grown in the net itself, like primitive life forming in the primordial soup—but it had spread rapidly among Western agnostics and atheists, and seemed to be absorbing (or being absorbed by) Buddhism and Taoism in the Far East.

Even when it began to recruit some Christians, mostly Protestants who had lapsed after their churches re-merged with Rome, Pope PJP had been careful not to condemn it too harshly, apparently not wanting to start any new religious wars, and the cybertaoists referred to Ecucatholicism as "special case literalism," meaning as far as I could tell that the viewpoint was okay with them, if narrow. Unfortunately all that tolerance meant that thus far there had been no overt clashes, just some garden-variety bigotry.

Even the appearance of a second cybertao text, accepted at once by virtually all cybertaoists as authentic, last year, had not led to any further clashes. *Surfaces in Opposition* was just as tolerant in spirit as *Forks in Time.*

In the briefing I was reading, the Organization admitted neither group was much to work with. Most of the vags could have been richer now than they had been before the war (assuming they were all telling the truth, a pretty big assumption) if they had been willing to go to work for the PSCs. They were genuine losers, misfits who couldn't forget that they had once thought of themselves as superior. And the cybertaoists were highly principled and at least as pacifistic as the old Quakers. (Who, of course, were all Ecucatholic now.)

But if the two could be put together, so vag rage and cybertao influence could somehow merge, maybe we could get something going again. As a program it wasn't a boil on Bolshevism's butt, but it was a better bet than anything else.

Something thudded off the diskster window; I looked up from my reading. Might have been a duck, passing through, or might have been a rock, thrown by some vag. No trace of it now. Might as well not have happened.

The view out the window was dizzying at 300 mph, but I sat and watched it roll by a long time. Everywhere, empty crumbling buildings. Twice, smoke, from campfires perhaps. Once a diskster going the other way. The world had gotten empty, outside the domes.

A month later I was squatting in a field with five of the most unpleasant people I've ever met. And I'm not fussy, either. But for me to hate you more than I hated these guys, you'd have to be my blood kin.

I was giving them a one-more-time-through on the drill. The Condor would come in from the south, like they always did, gliding gently down to its landing field. Most of the Condor pilots took pride in landing with the tanks full; the engines were only supposed to be auxiliary.

Karen, a squat, dark-haired woman, wanted to argue that the Condors didn't have to come from the south and might not come from the south—after all they were really just space shuttles, space shuttles the Japanese had stolen the plans for from us, and space shuttles flew out of Cape Canaveral, didn't they? Which way was Cape Canaveral from here?

"South," I said firmly. "And it's not coming from Canaveral. It's taking off from the drop station attached to the Quito Geosync Cable, about a hundred miles above Quito, Ecuador. Which is also south. So it will come from the south."

"Are you sure?" Karen asked. "That doesn't sound right. I think I learned different in school. They've changed everything in school nowadays but that doesn't make false true."

"Quite sure," I said. "Okay, now, James, when do you lock onto it?"

"When he starts final approach. When his landing gear are all the way down."

"Why not sooner?"

"Because they'll get a fix on me and we'll all get blown up, Brandon. Everybody knows that."

I doubted it but didn't say so. "And then what?"

"Put the rocket through the landing gear, so that the shrapnel will probably get a control surface too. Then when it undershoots the field and crashes, because the pilot didn't pull out, we run forward and get stuff."

"What kind of stuff?" I demanded of the others.

"Gold, silver, hard currency, hostages if any are alive," they all recited. The hard part. I didn't have much faith it would come out right.

Our lookout, in the tree above us, whistled. He'd seen the bright flash in the blue sky that meant a Condor was coming in.

The part of the plan that was up to James went perfectly. He snapped his rocket launcher to his shoulder, sighted, locked the radar on, squeezed the trigger, and dove for the ground as soon as the rocket got off. The little rocket, no bigger than a paper-towel tube, zipped out to the Condor, now just spreading its wings to their widest position, and nailed the landing gear. Fragments streaked in all directions. Suddenly the big ship flipped over on its back and fell out of the sky, its tail section whirling off toward the landing field. The vags got up and ran to the crushed, broken body of the plane, more than a mile away, getting strung out and separated. Didn't matter much since there was no one to shoot at us.

Then it all turned to shit. Too much loot of the kind they really wanted, the things they thought were theirs by right—so instead of going after the hard stuff, the jewelry, safe deposit boxes, or even wedding bands and gold teeth, they swarmed into that shattered fuselage, kicking the dead and the dying aside in order to grab Italian shoes, Rolexes, pre-war hats, anything at all that stood for the vanished world.

When Karen ran out the door with dozens of shoes, I shot her. Even that didn't restore discipline; they weren't paying enough attention to notice.

I walked back to camp. I'd be in trouble with the Organization if I shot my whole cadre, but if I stayed I'd have to.

Three months later I helped them lug a four-hundred-pound rocket up a godforsaken hillside to launch into a fortified village full of corporados and their kids. We scored a direct hit on the duck pond. I'm sure it was a crushing defeat from the ducks' point of view.

We blew a couple of disksters off the road, and they got back on again, unhurt. Since a diskster was not in contact with the ground, the impact got used up moving the diskster, not crushing it. Probably we spilled some people's dinners.

At the end of eight months we had murdered about two hundred people—most of them on the two Condors we had brought down—and blown up or otherwise destroyed a hundred million dollars of property. And they still weren't bothering to send the Army after us, since the Georgia state troopers already had us mostly licked.

I used some of that initiative we were supposed to use, slipped away in the middle of the night, and dropped a self-repeating message into the net that would circle around the world a few times (to lose its connection to me) and then pop up in the Georgia Patrol's in box and tell them where to get my particular group of vags. Total achievement, as I reported to the Organization, was some pointless pain and suffering (not even fun to inflict), some trivial robbery, and a precipitate drop in the Georgian vag population.

I spent another pointless year around Louisville Ruin, trying to be a cybertao prophet and get a Stochastic Jihad going. Lots of luck; it seemed to be difficult, within cybertao, to say much in favor of hurting people.

I wish I remember when I hooked up with Sadi in all that time. I don't think he was with me at the first but I'm sure he was around by the next time I transitted. He was another longtimer with the Organization, brown-haired, blue-eyed, tall and slender, an elegant sort of guy, the kind we all wished we were when we were sixteen. He had seven thousand books on his werp, all from the Everyman's Library, and had read about half of them, in cliffotated editions. He looked sort of like an old Nazi poster.

He had read more books and knew more facts than anyone I'd ever spent any time around, but I don't know that he could do more than dredge up stuff he'd read. He tended to remember one or two sentences about everything; I had a feeling that things were probably more complicated than that.

I do know he was there more than once when I woke up after transiting. I saw him transit, more than once, too. I don't know if you'd call that love, but when I think how much it would have helped to have Sadi or someone like him this past transit, waking up here on Mars, I think being friends all those years with Sadi might have been the closest to love I ever got. Him or Alice. Fuck if I know.

▼

No time at all to get my accounts moved and recoded—could have done it over the wire, didn't want to take chances; in person means you can code fingerprints and DNA, nail it down every possible way.

I'm rich, this time, but I have no friends.

I could reply to that ad. If I wanted. But what would I be getting into? I call up an AI and start asking questions.

When I think about it, personals are surprisingly *scarce.* So much of the human race has vanished one way or another, and so much of it didn't exactly exist in the first place (figuring there must be a lot of false i.d.'s in there). Why aren't more of us looking for each other? There should be *zillions* of personals.

Finally I find out why not. There are several references

to the Copy Transference Recovery Database. Since "copy transference" is a cybertao term for what happens when you die but your ideas live on (like Jesus or Elvis), or for what happens in a religious service when people "get the spirit"—I'm not sure which—my first thought is that it's a religious thing, but it's showing up as a government function.

The Copy Transference Recovery Database turns out to be what I was looking for—a giant database with all the data known about every human being who ever lived, compiled as a chronological list of facts with the inconsistencies noted. Access is free to anyone.

I play around at first. Find somebody there have been thousands of biographies of—Hitler. There's a huge, almost day-to-day account, tons of film, all flat and almost all black and white. Zeus shows up with a note that not all the stories fit together and he probably is entirely mythical. Holden Caulfield, who I remember from some book in school, is in there with the note that he's known to be fictional, though the name has been used as an alias at least eighteen times. Well, at least they seem to be getting things straight enough.

I grit my teeth and try JOSHUA ALI QUARE.

My service record includes a note that I was suspected of having killed those men in Prague, a further note that I was believed to be KGB/Organization, and a final note that I might have been the Josh Quare that turned up in Quito, but if so I was unusually well preserved. No notes about my possibly being Brandon Smith or the later lives; instead it just notes that I checked into private care, that a woman named Katrina Triste checked me out and moved me to some place unknown, and that I vanished. One cop dropped in a memo titled "Speculative Note." He thought the Organization found and killed me.

Katrina Triste. So that was her name. Then. If she's still

alive, she's older than me, but only by about ten years on the average. At worst she's had to make it through a couple of years of being eighty-five.

I check the other aliases and sure enough, a lot of it agrees with at least some of the stuff in my werp. I download it all to the werp and set up an automatic cross-reference. It only takes four minutes and next time after transit will be that much easier.

I check out Alice Schwartz, back up to find her as Alice Childs and Alice Quare. I had no idea about the number of times she'd been arrested while living with me, always for something she could pay a fine for (mostly selling a feel to a vice cop). Looks like she stayed married to Schwartz for a few years, just like in my notes. So good to confirm *anything*.

Then there's a period when she's married to Hutchins Dyen, one of the Dyen MicroIntelligence family, a family of Supra Berlin plutocks. She has twins by him, the marriage lasts awhile. He gets rid of her and keeps the twins. Probably losing her looks, not the breeder she was, getting into the bottle too often.

The record notes that she disappeared during the War of the Memes, like a lot of people and records. But I'm ahead of the records on that—she departed on the *Flying Dutchman*. I drop the note in and after a moment it says the records do link up validly, and thanks me.

Of course. Sadi. I type Edward Sadi Trichin. Then all the aliases that my records show he ever used. Then I search by every incident I know Sadi was involved in where cops or soldiers got called in. Zil every time. Nobody and nothing can vanish that completely. Can it? But Sadi, who is all through my records from about 2020 to just before 2078—a man who lived for decades, spent money, committed crimes, made contracts, forged i.d.'s, enlisted in armies (even voted a few times, god knows why)—Sadi is gone.

vi

"Hey, buddy, every time you transit, somebody either stops a war or starts one," Sadi was saying. We were sitting out on a back porch on the little house he had built way out in one of the bison ranges. Hard to believe all this had ever been farmland. Now they tracked the bison from orbit, and robots harvested them.

The land-use regs said your house couldn't be right on a migration route and had to be at least a mile from all other human structures. We'd had good-sized herds passing by all fall. Maybe the bison had changed their migration route without telling the government.

"Yeah, I suppose." I pulled down another beer. Notre Dame was playing OSU in low grav—with the new hose-line systems it only took a day to go to the moon, and the forty-three-man lunar version of the game was a lot more exciting since it allowed for real aerial work, leaping over the opposing line, and the pop-up QB. "I don't know, though, Sadi. How long have we both been with the Organization? And people I knew back when are chiefs now. We're still a couple of dumb field grunts. The money's not bad, the life's not bad, I'm not complaining. I just wish they'd ask me, once, for the hell of it, just to make me think they care what I think, before they threw a war. Especially since I don't get what this one's going to be about."

He reached for the chessboard. "Okay, let me see if I can show you what's going on."

"You don't know how to play chess," I pointed out.

"I'm just going to use the pieces to show you."

I shrugged. "Okay. But you still don't know how to play chess."

"I'm just going to use the pieces to show you. Then if you want to play chess, you can play with yourself. You've been playing with yourself a lot lately, bud, and so have I, so after I get this explained to you about the war, let's talk about what we do about getting laid. Talk about violence, gotta talk about sex to balance."

Late October, 2048. I was due for transit in three weeks. I had been living under the name Ulysses Grant, which was a small joke for me, and since the USA was long defunct and anyway Ulysses was such a popular men's name in the late 1990s (which people would have judged to have been when I was born), not many people noticed. The occasional history buff was about it.

This transit was going to be the same old drill: Sadi would check me through a bunch of phony aliases and hospitals for six months, then help me get restarted once I recovered. We'd have eight years till Sadi transited, and then I'd do the same for him.

The only complication this time was that it was about time to relocate. I hated giving up the house out here on the Plains—we'd been coming back to it for more than twenty years, by switching ownership between our i.d.'s—and I hated, more than that, to see things coming to an end, but according to the Organization, it was just as inevitable as the Eurowar, Long Boom, Great Crash, and Gray Decade had been. They had a team of experts some place that figured out what was inevitable, I suppose.

Sadi and I had bought this place early in the Long Boom, shortly after the Organization re-found me and we partnered up. When the Crash of 2032 had hit, the house was paid for and most of our money was in cash, the ideal way to go through a depression.

"The thing to remember is that in a deep depression, the prices will fall to historic lows," Sadi had often said. I'm sure he'd read that in a book someplace. He always made it sound like he was my investment counselor or something, and his foresight was why so much of what we owned was cash in safes in secure places. When the real reason was to keep cops and tax guys off us.

Well, whatever the reason, all that cash would buy eleven times as much in 2048 as it had in 2031. At least we'd had some fun during the Gray Decade even if no one else had. It had made us richer than ever, and who's going to argue with that?

"Did you ever pass through here in the old days?" Sadi asked, "back when there were still interstates and McDonald's and little towns and that? When you could get your kicks on Route 66?"

"You didn't either," I said. "We looked it up, remember? Route 66 was all gone before either of us was born."

"Ahhh." He drained his beer most of the way, grabbed a You-4, popped it under his tongue, dissolved it in the beer still held in his mouth, and swallowed it in a gulp. "You still want me to show you why the war's going to come, just like the Organization says, just like those worried-looking buroniki on the flashchannel keep threatening?"

"Do I really get a choice?" I asked. "Shitmaryjesus, look at that."

The holo we were pulling off flashchannel was projected right in front of the porch, lifescale. Looked like six meters in front of the steps was the fifty yard line of the game being played on the moon—see right through it if you just unfocused your eyes. One September afternoon we had watched a herd of bison charge through a porno movie, their hooves shaking the earth and their thick, hairy hides brushing against the walls of the house as all around them fifty-foot women with tits the size of automobiles sucked on seven-foot dicks. It had been a sight to see, especially on a lot of You-4, gressors, and beer.

What was happening now was almost as much fun; a

kick line of OSU cheerleaders right there, a bunch of sweet little honeys with perfect bodies.

We whooped and cheered and had another beer each, and I thought that had gotten rid of the stupid subject of the war, but as soon as the holo went back to the game, he was setting up that chessboard again.

"Okay, now pretend this tall white one with the cross on top of it's the Pope—"

"It's the king," I said.

"In this game, it's the Pope. Now the one we've got's pretty talented and pretty tricky and all that, but he just *isn't* PJP. He doesn't have the moves. So all these little guys—"

"Bishops. And the sides go by colors—"

"Not in this game, and bishops is perfect. All these guys are trying to get their own corners and run that, you see, exclude everyone else. See, four corners and four bishops. But they can't sell their ideas for shit. Which didn't used to be a problem, because old Paul John Paul kept them in line so they didn't need to have any ideas, and *he* did the selling. They're finding out that while they've just been taking orders and processing the bodies that PJP brought in, the cybertaos"—he pulled out the queens and rooks—"have been getting fucking good at recruiting." He put the rooks and queens around the center of the board and dragged the pawns into piles around them.

"So they don't stand a prayer. *Unless.* You see, unless? Unless they can enlist the cybertaos to go in with them. And the cybertaos would just love that, because any idea that gets too *close* to cybertao ends up *being* cybertao, which is why the Jews and Muslims and Hindus have all gotten so paranoid about cybertao—because they've all lost millions of believers overnight. The poor fucking Buddhists and Taoists just disappeared entirely, you know?"

"I lived in this century too, Sadi, and right now I remember more of it than you do. So what's your point? Yeah, everyone knows that the Ecucatholics are ripe to splinter, there's a lot of bishops ready to break with Rome, and when they do they'll ask the cybertaos in to help them move their brand of EC. So what the fuck?" I handed him another beer. "I know we'll get into it, buddy, the Organization's always there when shit goes down."

He laughed. " 'When shit goes down.' Talk about blowing your longtimer cover!"

I laughed too. "Well, yeah, but in such a groovy way." That cracked him up, and then we had the bands out for halftime with some majorettes, so we walked out into the holo and followed their butts up close, talking about them (of course they couldn't hear us or see us, they were just holos, but it was fun anyway), and that time I thought for sure he was off the kick.

No such thing, pos-def no way, unh-unh. The game started again and there he was fumbling around with the knights. "Well, see, here's the thing. You can do a lot with psychorrects and shit, and a lot with combined CSL tactics and all, but when you come right down to it, if you don't want a brain to think the wrong thoughts, the surest way is to put a hole in it. You can do all you like with intelligences that aren't in bodies, but it's the ones that *are* that call the shots. If you shoot those bodies, that settles the question. And who's got the expertise in shooting? Us horses."

"Knights."

"Even better. Samurai." He tossed me another beer and I took a long gulp of it. "See, the struggle isn't going to stay diplomatic and religious forever. It can't. It won't. And then there'll be a real market for us. Not just around the edge like dealing You-4 and shit. Not just loans and construction and running hos. Real work. Kick some butt. Make some bucks. And fun too. Remember what it was like to have a woman all by herself, no cops, and do whatever you wanted, kill her right in the middle if you wanted?"

I almost choked on my beer, and then I started to tell him about that little German girl I'd murdered, the one that was living with the computer nerd ten years older than she was, she was bare-naked and sobbing over the nerd's body, how I'd made her eat the gun to the trigger guard, pulled her black sweater up around her neck, how small and perfect her breasts had been as I stroked them just before I pulled the trigger and how her head had gone apart. It made me feel so bad that I just lay there crying and sobbing while Sadi tried to get me out of it.

The comedown off You-4 can be like that, and once it starts, a diskster load of them won't get you back up. You get crying and you can't stop.

I thought the little German girl's name was Alice, and that was the name I was calling in my sleep all that night, according to Sadi, but when I checked my werp I had no record of her name. I was sure I had seen it on the marriage certificate on her wall. Anyway, the next morning I was feeling better, having sobbed it all off in my sleep. Besides it was pretty hard not to feel better when Sadi fixed one of his monster breakfasts.

"Just the same," Sadi said, "we know what's coming, bud. Time to start the disappearing process and get you under wraps. You got an i.d. even started?"

I yanked out my werp and grinned at him. "Here we go," I said, and pulled up the master for it.

He looked over my shoulder. "Fred Engels? You're on a history kick. No more of those after this one. You don't want to get a pattern going, you know."

"Tell me about it, Joseph Andrews. Who was Tom Jones before?" Sure, he'd had to explain it to *me*, but who said a *cop* couldn't be an English major?

He shrugged. "Well, I won't call myself 'David Copperfield' next time. So is yours all in order, bud? Can you give me a file to take care of?"

"Jack the werps together and I'll do it for you right now," I said. "Now, you were saying—"

"Well, I thought maybe we'd take some of the throw-away cash and go throw some of it away up at one of the supras. It'll just go to waste otherwise." We had hit on the tactic, when it was time for one of our i.d.'s to disappear, of establishing a pattern of wild spending just before, leaving a substantial wad in the bank to just lie there, and scattering a few blank checks and credit numbers around to insure there'd be withdrawals after we disappeared. It made the exact date of disappearance hard to identify and also made it look like the fake i.d. had been killed and robbed, by the time it came to any police AI's attention. That made a nice, cold confusing trail to nowhere for anyone trying to follow us.

"You're right," I admitted. "We need to make Ulysses Grant look like he's off on a spree."

"You know I'm right," he said, and put through a signal for a robot cab. "One spree coming up. Got your keeper box and other junk in order?"

"Always. Ready to jump to the next life when you are. What kind of spree did you have in mind?"

"Well, the supras are expensive, and lots of vice is legal there. I was thinking Supra New York. We can get it onto your debit accounts that you're gambling and losing, and maybe have a serious ho habit and a tendency to gobble You-4 like popcorn. Which you do of course. That should make you look like a small-time hood who got careless on a spree."

"*'Louie Miller disappeared dear/After drawing out all his cash . . .'*" I sang.

"What's the matter, Lassie, is Timmy caught in the fence again?" He poured another large mug of coffee and plunked it down in front of me. "Drink that and let's get some more potatos and bacon into you. You're not as young as you used to be and we need to get some extra weight on you before you transit. But yeah, in fact, I had another idea, we can maybe help each other out on this. Suppose it looks like maybe I looted your accounts—a couple of them, missing several others—shortly after you vanish. Make the AI suspicious."

"And then what? Getting yourself watched by the cops isn't exactly—"

"That's the beauty. If they just *think* maybe I did you, I go into the back-burner file as the guy to arrest whenever they find Ulysses Grant's body or other evidence he's dead. True?"

"If you say so. We can hack Interpol's system, scan a bunch of files, and see if that's true."

"Way ahead of you, I've already done it. Answer is, they like to solve murders with minimum effort, especially when it's social scum like us, bud, because us killing each other is a *low* priority. So as long as it just looks like one of us doing the other, they leave it to the AI to remind them, once there's a body."

"Hmmph. So . . . I *get* it! When the 'suspected murderer' disappears, it makes it look like they can close the case on the 'victim,' right? Every time one of us transits the last police records of the other go inactive. Slick. How long before they notice that chain of victims?"

"Length of four or so I guess. Thirty-plus years. A lot can happen in that time. Why worry?"

"Unhhunh." I gulped coffee and shoved in a mouthful of the scrambled eggs he'd plopped down in front of me. It was never fancy but Sadi could cook. I thought about our plans some more. "Yeah, a spree in Supra New York, I think. Then we make it look like our boy Tom Jones did something rash."

The biggest advantage of losing your memory every fifteen years is that there's a limit to how sentimental you can get about anywhere or anything. I took just the bags for a vacation (clothes and my werp), plus my space allocation box. On my way out the door, Sadi turned and picked something up. "See if I'm not right, bud. Try to remember it for the next trip around, and note it in your werp."

I switched on the recorder and said, "What have you got there?"

He walked in front of the werp's camera eye, and said, "Okay, official prophecy from Sadi, currently Tom Jones, and your old buddy. When you wake up in 2049, I'll buy you a steak dinner if there's not a war on, and if we're not in it somehow, Paladin." He held up a white knight to the camera, then tossed it to me.

I clicked off the werp and muttered, "That was pretty goofy. It'll just confuse me after transit." The chess piece went into a pocket, or my bag, or something. I don't know when or how it got into my space allocation box. I'm pretty fussy about what goes in there.

We joked around a few more minutes. Faint hoot from outside—the robot cab out of Tulsa Dome. We grabbed the bags that were always packed, and our keeper boxes, and went out the door, leaving it unlocked with all the home security software wiped. Better if the place got burgled; it would destroy and scatter more evidence.

The diskster that hovered a few inches off the grass was a first-class job—no point in being cheap—comfortable, spacious, and all ours. We figured we'd catch it all the way south to Mexico City before we got on the maglev to ride down to Quito—a splurge, but this was *supposed* to be a spending rampage.

We took more You-4s and gressors and ordered a big onboard meal. With the extra time to swing by the pickup point for the diskster to grab our meals it would be five hours till the Mexico City station. We left the windows sealed and told the robot to give us lim speed. That meant every so often it lurched wildly when it dodged a bison, didn't see a cactus till the last minute, or had to jump a fallen overpass, but it also meant we would get to Mexico City way ahead of normal schedule, and kind of splashed up with liquor and disheveled. A few cameras were bound to look at us. If they checked the tapes we'd *look* like two guys on a spree.

From Mexico City we took the express maglev to Guatemala City and then the high-speed undersea tunnel to Quito. Since it would take two days for the train up the cable to orbit, no matter what, being in such a hurry to get to Q-town looked pretty goofy too—just as we wanted it to. We partied some more in our compartment with a couple of disposable girls who had just wanted a ride from Guatemala City, Japanese I think, if the recording in the werp of two naked Asian girls was made when it says it was.

We knew we'd done a pretty good job of establishing ourselves as scum on a spree when we got held at the cablehead for a couple of hours and NihonAmerica made us put down a return-ticket deposit.

The train ride out to orbit was just like it always is. You pass the Condor station, outside the atmosphere, in twenty minutes, at the speed you're making, but then it's still forty-five hours till the train pulls in at Supra New York. As you climb the grav falls steadily, which is kind of fun, and there's a couple of hours there in the middle where you can look back at the Earth and see that it's far away, SNY isn't more than a bright star just yet, and the kilometer-wide cable seems to stretch to infinity in both directions. Okay view.

But mostly you just take drugs, hire a girl, or go down and play in the casino car, once you're beyond the atmosphere and it's all legal. Most people on board are tourists; the corporados and plutocks flaunt their money by taking fast private-track cars, or the even more expensive rocket service that leaves from the same station as the Condors.

I spent my time in the cabin by myself, sorting through the mementos, getting drunk and reviewing old records on the werp. I got to feeling extremely sorry for myself, and for the whole world. Maybe I just had some weak You-4 and was coming down off it harder and faster than I expected.

Because I got all sloppy and regretful the whole way up, I read through the werp and found out who Alice was. Thank god not that German girl. Naturally then I checked, hacked a netwide search on her global i.d., and in about an hour found her working—at least pulling wages—in a dance bar up in Supra New York.

When I mentioned that to Sadi, he grinned and said, "Now there's something you can play with."

"Play with?" I took a long sip from a big bourbon and ice.

"Well, you know for all practical purposes you're her dad, bud, am I right?"

"I don't remember her."

"But she remembers you. Except she'd figure you ought to be about eighty years old, right?"

"Something like . . . yeah, that's what she'd figure."

"And she's gotta be what, fifty-two? Good shape, too, if she's still shaking her titties for the crowd, especially in a high-price joint like they have up in the Supra. Well, you're in good shape too, and you don't quite look fifty. Wanna see if she's got an Electra complex?"

"What's that?"

"Like a female Oedipus complex. See if she gets hot for guys who look like dear old Dad?"

I shrugged. Reviewing the records had brought back some stray memories, mostly things when she was a little girl. Nothing that would get me all hot for her or anything. "Sure, I guess. You got something in mind?"

"Just an experiment. Let's see how she takes it when you walk into that club . . . you can't know till you try. It won't be boring I bet."

Nobody ever figured out why the supras were so much like the originals. Supra Tokyo was crowded, rude, and bewildering, but clean and safe. Supra Berlin was badly lighted, cold, and decadent. Supra New York was where everything and everybody was completely for sale, like some old analog sound recording I had when I was a kid said "where they roll you for a nickel and they stick you for the extra dime." I used to love the freedom there.

The dance bar was called Titswingers. The women flipped around in zero g and shook their breasts. Usual lez show. Usual dildo show. Usual bid board so you could buy what you wanted. I got restocked on You-4 and then sat back to see what came out, brushing off a couple of bims that were trying to B-drink off me. Not that I couldn't afford it or that it wouldn't have been good for my cover. Just that I wanted the table free if Alice was working tonight.

Sadi had said he wouldn't come along the first time but he admitted one reason he had pushed me on the idea was that after looking at some of the shots of Alice in my old werp he was a little hot for her. I said she wasn't eighteen anymore and I wasn't so sure that picture was even her but he said he liked her attitude, not her body.

Anyway, so I was in there alone, riding on You-4, though a longterm user like I was doesn't get that great glow a lot of people do—it didn't seem like the place was wonderful, just that I was happy. They said if you kept using it you'd have to take it, like a vitamin, just to avoid depression when you got old. I figured I wasn't going to get old for fifty years. Meanwhile it made me happy.

After a while a bored-looking woman, a fat blonde wearing a pair of fake fox ears on her head and a fox tail on a short stick stuck into her ass, swam by and asked what I wanted to drink. I said lots, didn't care much what. She suggested their champagne, which was going to be outrageous in price, so that's what I took. She asked me if I wanted any company at the table, probably hoping it would be her.

I said I'd know what I wanted when I saw it.

At first I didn't recognize Alice. All I remembered was the pictures, and she'd had herself genaltered, the popular new form of cosmetic surgery, and then surfacted, so that the flesh had grown back according to the new genes. That had given her two big firm tits, a flat belly, and vivid strawberry-blonde hair, but she'd kept her basic face with just a lift. Maybe she liked it, maybe she'd just been afraid of what might go wrong with having that surfacted—every so often you saw a bad regen, a woman who looked like the troll dolls they had when I was a kid. Some women, especially an old bim like Alice, would be scared pissless of that.

She looked as good as thirty-five-year-olds that took care of themselves used to look. I watched her loop around in the central space. She mostly just shook those big tits, no art to it at all, so I figured if I flagged down the fat blonde in the fox rig and sent word that that was my choice, it would be no trouble.

Figure again. "Anastasia never B-drinks," she said. "Is there anyone else you like?"

"Can I just send her a drink and have you point me out to her?" I asked. I had assumed it would be easy, but when had anything connected with that girl been easy?

"We can try that. She *might* take a look at you before she just takes the drink and stays in the dressing room. Then again she might *not*. She tends to treat customers like shit, you know? Like the bitch is too good for anybody. I don't mind telling you the owner's pissed because Anastasia turns away business, and she won't peddle ass on the bid board, either. Treats the place like a fuckin' *job* if you know what I mean. No kind of ho-*stess*."

About five minutes later Alice came out, in a dressing gown, and sat down next to me. She didn't say anything right away, but she took another drink when I offered one. I flagged the blonde in the fox rig, who seemed to be pissed at Alice. Younger women always seem to think they have the right to be the most attractive person present, and they get mad if a guy wants somebody older.

After a minute or two I said, "You remind me of someone I saw in a picture a lot, a real long time ago."

She sipped at the little ladylike drink—something that looked like lemonade—and said, "Funny, you remind me a lot of somebody I knew a long time back, myself. I don't know if he ever had any kids or anything. You any relation to Josh Quare?"

"Uh, you could say that. He was my dad but I never knew him all that well. Wasn't home much."

"What happened to him?" She leaned forward.

"He died working outside on one of the transfer ships, trailed off into the exhaust. I don't even remember which transfer ship. It was a long time ago." That ought to be vague enough, if she checked, but for good measure I added, "I think he was working under some other name."

She sighed. "My first husband's retired now, on Mars, but he was an officer of the Vacuum Workers Union a few years back. He'd have a record of a guy who died outside. Maybe I could track him through that. Or do you know any more about him?"

"Not a thing, and I'm not even sure that's right. My mom's dead too and the thing about Dad dying was one of the last things I heard from her, so I never got any other information. Like I said, I didn't know him well anyway."

"Well, you're the image of him," she said. "When were you born?"

I was in the fog of booze and You-4, just coming down off of it, but I had to answer that one fast, and I couldn't think of a thing to say. I also knew I'd picked up Alice in the Eurowar and she'd left before she was twenty, so I said, "2012, it's just the gray hair throwing you. I'm just a kid really. And of course I've been outside a lot, on the ships and the supras. Would you be, uh, Alice?"

"I used to be. Yeah, I guess so. Alice was the name I grew up under. Your father was my stepdad." She peered at me closely. "You look a lot like him but you sure didn't inherit his genes for aging. It took me a long time to figure it but just from stuff he let slip I figured out he was ten years older than he looked. But you're ten years younger than *you* look. You don't mind my saying that, do you? I mean, you look okay, distinguished and everything, but if you're only about thirty-five . . . well, you've had a hard life I guess, or something."

"Or something. No offense taken." I took a long, slow sip of that cheap champagne—to really appreciate it you had to have your hand on some bim's leg, I guess—and considered. "Yeah, Dad had a lot of pictures of you that he'd taken at one time or another. Four or five, I mean." That was how many were in my werp. "When I was growing up there were five pictures of you on the wall."

"Well," she said. "I guess we can both see how we've turned out. I work in these places, and you come into them."

"Probably his influence," I agreed. Long, awkward silence. I tried thinking about things I could do next.

Start with the craziest possible idea: tell her.

No.

See if I could take her to bed—or even get her alone and make her do something, just to see what it was like? No again. "You ever have any kids?" I asked.

"Three," she said. "Two of them by a rich guy that wanted

me for his toy, but didn't want his kids raised by a bim. He handed them over to the nanny, first thing. One kid that used to write now and then, that I had back when I thought I was going to get on the *Flying Dutchman* and travel with my first husband. I think that kid gave up on me."

To fill the silence I asked, "So what became of them?"

"The older boy's exec officer for the *Dutchman* now; you remember those officers that stopped the mutiny last year? Well, he was one of them. That's how he got promoted up from the engine room really fast. I guess that if he was one of the loyalists, that means he probably helped push some of those mutineers out the airlock like they showed on flashchannel. I scan the ship news for his name; I never wrote back to him so he stopped writing, I think after his dad stopped making him write. Last picture I have of the kid, right before he stopped writing, is from his first date, some kind of a prom or something. I sure hope he didn't marry her because she looked like the puddle you'd get in the road after a four-day ugly-storm. But still he turned out better than the other two. The boy I had by the rich guy is working on drinking himself to death, last I knew, and messing around with a lot of You-4 and all that, middle-aged and fat at thirty and looks like hell and never had to do a useful thing in his life. He'll probably dry out after his old man dies and he inherits. The youngest is on about her fifth divorce. 'Fraid I'm just a pile of fucked-up genes. Murderers, drunks, losers . . . must be my genes because I didn't raise any of them."

"You don't seem like a bad sort to me," I said.

"You haven't seen much of me. Just those pictures and whatever Josh told you."

"He always spoke very kindly of you," I said. It sounded like a line in an old movie. Like something I ought to say.

She nodded, sniffed. I saw her eyes were wet. "He would have."

In zero g, if you want to get out of a chair, you have to unfasten the belt, and though my hand groped tentatively for the fastening, I didn't unlatch it. The moment passed too fast for me to reach and touch or hold her. Don't know why I wanted to. Must've been a memory or something. Probably when she was little I'd had to do that a lot. Maybe because I liked her or maybe just to keep her quiet. Kids are that way.

It made me feel disoriented. Already I was thinking, right now I'm about her age physically and next year I will be ten years younger. It's like everyone's falling down into the well where you start as a baby at the top and you end as a corpse at the bottom, only I get to climb back up every now and then, so I see people whizzing by, people who start out behind me and plunge on down into the darkness ahead of me where I can't see where they go. And here she goes, into the dark ahead.

I have a memory of introducing that kid to her first bathtub in years. It was weeks before I could get her to spend less than an hour in it every night. Alice used to scrub in that hot water till she looked like she'd been boiled. I have another memory of that harsh-smelling Reconstruction soap in her thin black hair, and the feel of her bony arms wrapped around my neck. I think she had a nightmare and I needed to get her back to sleep.

We had a couple more drinks. She proposed a toast "to Josh." It made some kind of sense. The guy she was drinking to *had* been a better guy than me.

It got later, I got tireder, and after a while we had nothing to say except we both missed Joshua. That was all poetic and stupid like a movie. Still, I was drunk enough to appreciate it.

I paid to walk her home early—which meant the owner thought I'd bought her for the night. Probably it got Alice slightly out of trouble and anyway it got her out of there early. The way she thanked me, over and over, on the way, was pathetic.

I let Alice go home by herself when we got to the tram station. We were already out of things to talk about. At the tram station, she hugged me once and said I was a prince. We knew we'd never hear from each other again.

The whole thing had cost me a pile of money, but spending a pile of money was what I needed to do just then. Call it a good night's work. When I got back to the room Sadi and I were sharing, I told him that Alice had been on vacation so I'd just stayed in the club and gotten some action off a dancer. I didn't think Sadi—or anyone else—would get a chance to hose Alice while he was here; "sorry about that," I added.

"Oh, well," he said, and got that faraway look in his eyes like he always did when he was going to make a joke that I wouldn't get, usually jokes about philosophy and that, " 'The best-planned lays of mice and men,' you know."

IV

To Be Born?

i

Sadi's gone from the records. Must have been erased during the War of the Memes. Likely a traceraser—whenever he died or went undercover, a self-replicating program woke up and hunted through the net to destroy any reference to him.

Usually you can still find the person afterwards: gaps in serial numbers, money flowing in and out of banks without specific accounts, parents who wrote down one child more than the system can find, all that. The Copy Transference Recovery Database has nine hundred million numbered trails in the records without names—tracks left by tracerasers. Some of those must have started as fake i.d.'s, some as real people. It doesn't matter to the system. The name has vanished, but the chain of holes in the records still says "someone was here, once."

I run a big search across all nine hundred million. Even with a superMPP built into everyone's werp these days, it takes three full minutes to get back to me.

Not one of those numbered personae could have been

Sadi. Not one probable hit in the search. Must have been a damned good traceraser.

Most can only wipe a name, but this one, after it nailed all the names, went back and built false continuers—hundreds of fake i.d.'s linked to points all over the chain of recorded events that was Sadi. It not only erased the name and made a hole in the records, it went back and filled in the hole.

So Sadi was important enough for the Organization to send a very sophisticated traceraser after him. Maybe he's still alive, maybe even still with the Organization. "I haven't seen weather like this since I was a kid in Ohio." Sadi himself? Some cop who cracked an Organization file? Most likely, the Organization has found me again.

One problem with having a screwed-up memory, and only the kind of record that I can manage to keep in the werp with my lousy writing skills, is that I don't know who I did what to and when. Sadi, or the Organization, or a cop, or for all I know that German chick's kids, might be out to kill me, hire me, anything.

I *have* to reply to that ad, but the idea scares the hell out of me. What if it's Sadi? What if it's not?

I hope his password's as burned into his memory and as scattered through his records as "I haven't seen weather like this since I was a kid in Ohio" is for me.

My little white cubicle has no window. I need to get out. If there's a rebate for not using all my time, it'll track my account down sooner or later.

Walking around Red Sands City, letting my mind drift. Weird stuff I'd rather not think about. Put an audio tour guide on the werp.

Red Sands City is a third-generation Martian city, settled mostly by native-born Martians. It looks down onto the crater floor below, so that one edge of the enclosure's much higher than the other. The whole town's on five excavated ledges plus the rim—the transparent enclosure is in the shape of a gigantic slug just crawling up over the cliff, so water will gather in the top part of the enclosure, filling the little artificial lake on the clifftop.

Within the giant slug: tidy square straight streets, staircases, escalators, all the buildings squarish, pink concrete, Disney cliff dwellers. Outside the enclosure: disorderly mess of q-huts, little pressure domes, pressurized c-block buildings, trash heaps, Sears Marshacks like the one I woke up in. The jumbled heap's plastered all over with solar collectors and baby MAMs, interwoven with thumpered dirt trails, rutted and pitted because nowadays it rains every couple of months.

I watch for a while. Not much difference in the activity inside or out. People in pressure suits outside don't look any more busy, or any less, than people inside on the walkways. Probably there's more illegal stuff out there, and probably the illegal stuff in here is worth more money. That's usually the pattern.

I could go full legit this time, retire, drift through the next fifteen years without doing a thing. Today I'm feeling that lazy. I sit on a park bench up by the top-level lake, stretch my legs out, and look over the city.

After a while I tell the werp "Place an ad. 'Connections and Memories' section. 'Seeking tall male comma thin comma brownish hair comma uh probably gray comma uh vet colon Murphy's Comsat Avengers comma we had a house once in Kansas comma Louie Miller disappeared dear comma quote marks When I see places like this I always wish I was back in New Orleans close quote marks.' Finished. Take out the uhs. Post that and alert me if anything comes in on it."

I sit back on the bench and bask some more. In a while I'll take the elevator down; I can afford any of the three hotels in town. I wonder how I got such a large pile of cash together as an ecoprospector. Reviewing the werp I see again that the life before this, as James Norren, I woke up from transit with my accounts intact but no sign of the Organization. I got into ecoprospecting for no reason I can find evidence of, made a lot of big strikes, spent almost nothing.

There are fewer records of my most recent life than there are of my first two lives, before I had a werp. I think about that. I can prove it was quiet. I can't prove it was unhappy.

I've gone legit before. And life wasn't half bad, if the werp is to be believed. But I know the werp can't be believed. I hope not, there's three places in there where I confess to killing Sadi, one where I say I killed Alice, one where I say Sadi did.

But that doesn't mean any particular thing in that werp isn't true.

But it can't be trusted.

But.

I laugh at it all and stretch. A mother walking with her kid stares at me for a second, as if I might be dangerous. Well, that's the way, I guess.

Somewhere down in Red Sands City I could probably get some gambling, some You-4, gressors, a whore. It would be something to do, but it would take energy. I'd rather sit here on this bench and soak up energy.

People move fast on Mars. A lot of them in here are half running. Out beyond the enclosure the dust plumes of the trucks streak along. Funny, it's not like life's short. With extension technology everybody makes it to 100 or so, and before the transfer ships left the solar system talk was *they* had found a way to live to be 250 or 300.

Probably all the scurrying around, the way people run out to meet the trucks and race up staircases, is a combination of low gravity and just the way Martians are: everything needs to get done right now. Figure they're making a whole living world out of a barren one, there's a lot to get done.

Then suddenly I remember a very dark night on Mars, years ago when they were all very dark, when there was so much less air that it wasn't much different from the moon . . . darker still because I was sitting, with hundreds of thousands of others, on Olympus Mons. And as the thought comes back, I remember the rest of it.

With the collapse and disappearance of the Organization, our suppression of closed timelike curve research must have stopped. And apparently it was an area pretty ripe for study, because the people on the transfer ships got it figured out in just the short years it took them to get out of the inner part of the solar system.

The big barrier to time travel was always causality, the same reason nothing could go faster than light. You can't have the effect modifying the cause, just as people traveling back in time and shooting their grandfathers before they had any children was unworkable. But there was a kind of loophole—you *could* travel into the future faster than regular time. Traveling close to light-speed would do that. And it didn't matter, really, which time you traveled along as long as you traveled along some time or other.

That part confuses me, so I ask the werp. It explains time splits and curves back: where there's a singularity, a place where matter becomes so dense that it isn't exactly in the universe we know anymore, but the *place* it occupied still is. I don't get that part very well.

Anyway, out of a singularity come a whole bunch of lines of time, very much like the line of time that we and the whole universe are in, except that for the "subtimes" both their beginning and their end is at the moment the singularity was created. Those little subtimes start out into the future just like regular time, but they gradually curve backwards until finally they are going all the way backward (relative to our time) and end up at the place where they began. It's sort of like we're on the only highway that goes anywhere, and there are all these big looping exit ramps that come off the interstate of time, but then just swing around and feed back onto the highway right where they left it.

What that means in practical terms is that while you can't reach your own past, you can make it possible for your future to reach you. When it does, there's no grandfather paradox—because what happens is, you get two futures. So you make a singularity, and later have children, and they have children. One grandchild decides to get rid of the rest of the family, gets into that loop, rides it forward as it curves around until it rejoins his own past, and then shoots you. Then, as an adult, he lives on into the future that you never see, which doesn't contain his parents. But because on the whole trip nobody ever moved backwards in the time line they were in, he has parents and grandparents in his personal past, and he continues to exist.

That's why it's called a closed timelike curve. It's "closed" because it only runs through one part of time, eventually bending back to its origin (where our universe is open—it keeps moving forward in time). That bending back is the "curve." And since you can follow it and exist in it just as you can in regular time, it's "timelike." If I got that right.

Anyway, the transfer ships had set off the bomb to make a giant singularity out at 100 AU, way out where the comets come from, and then scattered out to settle five solar systems. A thousand years or more in the future, they would send ships back from those colonies, a whole huge fleet and army, either to retake Earth from Resuna, or at least to seal up Resuna on Earth forever.

We'd had one message from that fleet already—they had informed us they'd be arriving in just about 300 years, and would need permanent accommodations for one hundred million people. *That* was why everything seemed so urgent here; the whole population of Mars was currently that of a city the size LA had been when I was a kid, and somehow in just 300 years they had to get ready to move in the whole population of Japan. They could do it, no doubt—but it was going to be a push.

And that probably percolated down from planners to politicians to managers to bosses to foremen . . . so that everyone got in the habit of running around like they were part of a kicked-over anthill. Hence all these people rocketing by me, or scrambling around out there outside the enclosure, and the occasional dirty look I was getting from people who were walking fast and looking worried.

When I lived at Gwenny's, she used to have a cartoon on the wall, one of those things that migrated from fax machine to fax machine, of a bum on a bench saying "Work is fascinating, I can watch it for hours." Well, it's true.

I sit through the long afternoon, watch the sun go down, and catch the elevator down to the Radisson Red Sands, which is about like every other pricey hotel in the last 150 years, right down to the same room service menu. I order a pizza, watch the news, and go to bed early without setting the clock.

The next morning there's no reason to check out so I don't. I grab a shower, change clothes, toss the dirty ones into the bag to be freshed, send the pressure suit in for routine maintenance, and I'm out the door, just me and my werp, to take a long stroll around the city. I can walk down every street in this town today, if I want to. There are worse ways to kill time.

I eat a long breakfast at a place doing its best to look like a European streetcorner café. As I'm having the third cup of coffee, the werp beeps. An answer to my ad.

It could be something I don't want just anybody to hear,

so I take it on the screen rather than putting it up on voice. The message comes up. I HAVEN'T SEEN WEATHER LIKE THIS SINCE I WAS A KID IN OHIO.

My heart jumps up. Has to be—

IF YOU'D STAYED PUT I'D HAVE COME OUT FOR YOU.

I grin. Glad I managed to make it a little tough. I'd hate to have him think I'm getting soft.

LOOK BEHIND YOU.

Oh god. Oldest werp trick there is, sneaking up on someone and then contacting him via his werp. Kids do that all the time. I turn, ready to say "Sadi."

It's not.

She's wearing a plain black dress, a little out of place on Mars where coveralls are more usual. Her hair, amazingly enough, is still blonde. I can't see her eyes behind the dark glasses—

It can't possibly be Katrina. She was at least ten years older than I was, couldn't look more than five years younger than me now, at best. *This* woman doesn't look thirty.

"It's been a long time, Josh," she says.

It's definitely, really her. I close up my werp case, stand, extend my hand; she gets up, takes it, shakes firmly once, then pushes her dark glasses back off her face. She's smooth, unlined—maybe twenty-five in appearance. "We need to talk," she says. "Your hotel room."

She must know where I'm staying. She heads straight for it though I say nothing.

When we get to my door, she presses her thumb to the doorplate and it opens. For some reason the hotel thinks she's staying with me, I guess. Maybe she is.

I follow her into the room. The maid's already been there. My bag and the returned, tuned-up pressure suit sit neatly in the corner, but the rest is anonymous like any hotel room.

She turns and smiles. "You must be hopelessly confused."

"It's been pretty baffling," I admit. "Are you really Katrina?"

"I have been. Look closer. Study my face . . ."

Like I have no will of my own, I walk toward her, mind blank. My eyes follow the curve of a high cheekbone, the thin lips that seem to be about to make faces at everything, the big, wide eyes. You'd think if she's really 160 or so, and especially if she's been with the Organization all that time, it would show somewhere, around her eyes, in her expression, somehow. But even around the eyes she looks like a twenty-five-year-old.

"You've known me under another name," she says.

I look more closely. Did I read or do I remember that something like this has happened before? Yes. More than once. Not recorded in my werp, but it did.

Shit, I think, looking at her, never wondered what a rejuve job would do on top of that anti-aging stuff. Genaltering and surfacting has gotten so far along that if you're willing to spend six months dreaming in a tank, doped up on painkillers and drifting in a deep virtual reality hallucination, you can come out looking like anyone they can recode you to, but I thought your age caught up with you within a year or two. God, she looks good.

Something in her voice, too. She knows me. Her voice touches me like a hand gloved in soft leather, and holds my heart like—

Then I feel my right hand begin to turn, ever so slightly, the fingers begin to work, and I know that if I held my white knight in my hand, it would be appearing and vanishing between my fingers, neatly, quickly, never where you would expect it.

"Sadi," I say. "Jesus."

"Right on the first guess," she says, and steps into my

arms. My cock gets so hard it hurts. Her tits are soft, heavy, warm against my chest. The muscles of her back are hard and strong. She's undoing my belt even before I sit back, pulling her onto the bed beside me, our mouths still locked.

ii

Scuttlebutt in Murphy's outfit was that the ice dam across the St. Lawrence wasn't going to breach this year at all. We had been wandering uselessly around Syracuse Ruin since May, supposedly waiting to make an attack on a major node across Oneida Bay as soon as the lake drained back and the land was exposed again. But now it looked like what everyone had been saying—that the St. Lawrence was due to stop flowing for good sooner or later, because every summer the time it flowed got shorter—had been true.

This year we were fighting for One True, because it had offered us more money than any other meme had. We were contracted to destroy the Carthage Ruin node—an Unreconstructed Catholic memo running on it was re-infecting millions of AI's and thousands of people. Supposedly if you got infected you'd start hearing PJP's voice telling you that Ecucatholicism was all a mistake and you had to kill everyone who wasn't a strict Catholic, plus you'd suddenly have all these false memories of growing up in a very uptight old-fashioned Catholic school and of being the star student there.

Anyway, if the ice dam wasn't going to break, we'd have to walk around the bay instead of across it. So in little groups of twos and threes, passing word to each other when we met, we had begun to drift south out of Syracuse, up into the hills, then north toward Carthage Ruin. Moving slowly and carefully, doing our best to look like scattered and isolated travelers, Murphy's Comsat Avengers might be able to assemble near the node by late September. Months late and some of us wouldn't get there.

That night in our tent, Sadi was talking. As usual. I was working some passes from the *Boy's Big Book of Magic*. Found it in the storage vaults for a public library, and that white knight I always carried in my pocket was exactly the right size for doing all the little palm-and-finger tricks, which I was getting good at.

After all those years and lives together, Sadi and I didn't really converse. Sadi talked and I listened. I liked it that way. The knight gave me something to do with my hands while I listened to him.

"Trouble is," he said, "we're still losing people. No question about it."

I made the knight slip into my sleeve on the thumb side, out on the little finger, brought him through the middle, popped him into my palm. Years before I might have said, "How do you figure?" or "I don't see how you can know that," but nowadays Sadi could just assume I wanted him to go on.

"Figure our last twelve rendezvous, right?" He totted them up on his fingers. "Four times we met with a party and fought. Twice they snapped out of it—must've been a weak meme. Once we killed them. And once we all had a meme and we attacked each other. Good thing we had a pistol shot that time to jar us out of it. And a real good thing it wasn't you or me getting shot. You saw how tough it was for the guy's partner."

I knew that as well as he did. He liked to tell stories. I liked to hear them. Mama would have called it division of labor. I kept the knight moving.

"So figure one in three times we make contact a meme activates, right? And what, maybe one in four is a strong meme then? So in twelve contacts, about six months, out of a total of, let me think, I guess thirty-one guys counting you and me, three died. That's ten percent per six months. Toss in no new recruits anymore. Not figuring what happens at headquarters, ten per cent dead per six months, figure it's twenty percent or so per year. Used to be if an army had ten percent killed it stopped functioning."

"They're not like old armies," I pointed out, letting the knight slip around and into my other hand, covering the drop by bending my fingers. "The memes just contract us to do a job, and they hire the size unit they need for the size of job. Besides, we're not organized in fire teams or anything; really we all fight on our own. An outfit could die till nothing was left but the headquarters company, and *that* could keep fighting."

"Yeah, but unless they know how many men they have left—"

"They know," I said. "That's why Murphy's sitting behind a wall of bodyguards that are never allowed net access and a bunch of AIs that run on continuously re-encrypted operating systems. So he can use his werp all the time. Sure, *we* stay offnet for safety's sake, but when we check in or when we make our contacts, the count gets relayed to him. He knows."

Sadi sighed. "Right as always, partner. Want me to read you anything?"

I shrugged. "Go ahead and read if you like, but you don't have to read aloud. I'll just sack out."

"Yeah." The way he said it made me think he would go on, but then he didn't. Any time Sadi stopped being talkative something was wrong. I looked up at him.

In the light of the little flickeret, he glowed sort of flame-color. His brown hair was streaked and spotted with gray, now, as if he'd been painting a ceiling not too carefully, and his thin face and high cheekbones made him look like one of those elf-warrior guys on the covers of the books I used to read when I was squatting on my ass in the desert during the First Oil War.

He looked good. Three years till his next transit, five years since my last, we both looked like we were in our mid-forties, though I was almost a hundred and he might have been a bit over.

Sadi stared off into space, started to speak, thought again, stared. Usually when he did that I'd catch him watching me from the corner of his eye, seeing if it was working, if I was about to start saying "What? *What?*" Though a lot of times he just talked, Sadi liked to have my complete attention for something important. So he'd stare off into space to make me ask him.

But this time he really was staring off into space, which I hadn't seen him do much. Finally he spoke again. "Do you suppose that we're going to know when to bail? I mean, get real. The War of the Memes is winding down, bud, has to be. Nobody new joining the armies, memes merging and consuming each other, someday there will be one meme and no soldiers."

"Uh, it's a small world after all," I said.

For years after that I tried to remember whether he had blinked, winced, flickered, had a twitch in his face, anything. I still don't think so. He just smiled as he usually would and said, "Better luck next time."

"It's a small world after all" was our trigger phrase. We'd used some of Murphy's memeware and built a binary chaser for each of us. When one of us said "It's a small world after all," normally it activated an old Disney meme that both of us were carrying, followed by a simple chaser to turn it back off. The whole process of calling it up and getting rid of it took a tenth of a second at most. But if there were a new meme in either of our heads—if somehow we'd been penetrated by something we saw, read, or heard—

the meme-and-chaser cycle would trigger something that looked like an epileptic seizure. That would give the uninfected person time to get us tied up and treated. The most common memes out there nowadays were ones to make you attack the person you were with. If you didn't catch it in time, your best friend could kill you.

Sadi had passed the test, and I sat back. "Okay, I admit, when I thought you'd been memed, I wasn't paying any attention to what you were saying, so what were you saying?"

He shrugged. "Oh, a leading question, I guess—whether we'll have any idea when to get out of the war and go do something else, because pretty soon either One True, or maybe one of its competitors or a mutation, will take over the whole show. The armies aren't getting anybody new and they've attritted like crazy. And think about the way a meme works—basically it's a set of ideas with a compulsion attached, right, that ties into the deep structures, all those places where the brain and mind overlap?"

"Thank you, Doctor Science."

"I'm saying this out loud because I'm trying to think it through. Really, honest to god, Josh, I know I lecture too much but I'm just trying to get this to make sense to me so we can think straight about it. Now, look, the way they work is they attach to existing beliefs. And it's easier to attach to an existing meme, but by now everyone has at least some small memes. Right? And as the number of different kinds of memes goes down—because they combine with each other and take each other over—it gets easier and easier for one meme to sweep the whole system. Right?"

"Makes sense," I admitted, because it did and because I was tired of him lecturing me. I worked a tough faked pass to cover a simple real one. The knight slid around in my fingers like a trusted old friend, always everywhere you want him.

"So the armies are shrinking and there's just a few kinds of memes left. In a pretty short time, there will be just one and it won't need armies—it'll need cops. And the cops will have one job—make sure everyone has the master meme. Right? You know I'm right. It's coming, Josh, I told you this war was going to start, back in Kansas, and now I'm telling you it's about to end and once it does there will be no place for us to hide, whether we're on the winning or the losing side."

"So what's your point?"

"We've got to get out past radio delay," he said.

I didn't know what the hell he meant. But non sequiturs were like the biggest red flag of all. "It's a small world after all," I said, and triggered the backup as well, "To sit in solemn silence in a dull dark dock."

He shook his head as if he'd had a neck crick. Was that the sign? If I had been a little more clever . . .

The trouble was, people were only as clever as they had been during the Paleolithic. Perfectly good brain for mating and whacking animals and running away from tigers. All gravy beyond that.

But memes were getting more and more clever. In the middle of war they evolved as fast as weapons or generals. Of course in a way they were both.

The war had been raging ever since some bright guy had figured out how to write a program that could analyze any operating system it talked to, figure out how to penetrate, and get in and take over AIs. Whoever it was, he'd probably never realized that to a program like that, a mind's just one more operating system on a slow-running massively parallel processor—probably he only meant, as a loyal cybertaoist in the chaos of religious violence sweeping Earth, to make all the banks, autopilots, navigation software, and medical robots go cybertao.

Whether he intended it or not—and for that matter I had

no idea whether or not it was a "he"—he'd about conquered the world for cybertao before Ecucatholic memes had turned up to fight back, quickly joined by Sunni and Shi'ite memes and the mad-dog guerrilla memes called Freecybers. Now the whole First Generation—cybertao, Ecucatholicism, RPs, Newcommies, Freecybers, Slammers, every meme that had begun the battle—was long extinct, except copies in museums.

It had to go that way; the most effective thing for a meme to do was to take over, copy, or digest another meme. Competition was fierce and fast; nothing lasted long.

Mercenaries like Sadi and me, and everyone in Murphy's Comsat Avengers, worked for memes but didn't talk to them. We did what they told us to do and they paid us.

Probably three quarters of the world's human population was now running One True or one of the other memes. They weren't exactly *not* themselves but they weren't exactly themselves either. Like after a religious conversion, kind of.

I stared at how Sadi rolled his neck after I triggered our chaser and our backup chaser. Strange move for him, but it really looked like just a crick. No use *asking* him. Memes could lie better than people. "Well," I said, "what is it you'd like to do?"

"I want to power up a werp and check the situation. If the numbers don't look good we bail. And from now on we watch for when we should get out, before it's too late."

"Too late for what?"

He shuddered—or maybe it was a spasm. "I don't think the memes—or the meme, let's face it, One True or something descended from it's going to win—will let any uninfected minds exist after the war's over. I think once the profit's been made from the wars, we want to get out to where the radio delay's significant."

"*Space?*" I asked. The memes had not been able to take

hold in the terraforming projects, the asteroid cities, or the transfer ships because radio lag provided a natural barrier. A meme needed to interact with what it was infecting, quickly enough so that the person or AI under attack would accept the responses for an instant or two without question. An AI or person who was more than a few light-seconds away had too much time to think between responses for the meme to get a grip. It helped too that when the War of Papal Succession had turned into the War of the Memes, the space people had seen what was coming and started all kinds of quarantine measures so that nobody could send them a whole copy of a meme.

"*Space,*" Sadi agreed. "And the question is, when is it time to jump? Figure Earth is going to be effectively cut off from space at the end of the war. This Resuna idea that One True has won't work if ideas are dribbling in from space and stirring the pot, because the idea of Resuna is everybody gets the same personality, and if some of them are talking outside the system they won't stay the same. So no question in my mind, once Earth is all Resuna there's going to be an embargo, blockade, call it what you want but money in our Earth bank accounts won't be worth crap. The question is *when* we want to take our muster out, catch the next transfer ship, and end up rich out in the solar system somewhere. And if we wait too long, we'll end up here as happy little processors running One True, thinking One True thoughts and doing whatever it likes."

"Well, then maybe we should jump now," I suggested.

"I've thought about that too." He glanced down. The flickeret shone off his face, making it look warm, though nowadays in upstate New York it rarely got above freezing on a summer night. "But let's be honest about this one, bud, hunh? If we wanted to play it safe we'd have gotten out a while ago. We're as rich as we could ever need to be, you know. We ought to just bag it."

"Let's."

"You're kidding, right?"

"Naw." I hadn't thought about it for anything like as long as he had, of course, but then thinking about things for a long time was something he did for fun. I didn't want to be one more copy of One True, and as soon as Sadi pointed it out it was obvious—stay on Earth and I would be, sure as all hell. Yeah, when I left there'd be no coming back. But that doesn't matter when you really *have* to leave. I've had houses I loved but if they were on fire I left.

He sighed. "Just like that. Should've figured you would. Can we still run the werp real quick? I just figured out what numbers would tell us when to jump, I think. We could just pop onto a flashchannel for a second, depth it to get statistics—and you know stats are safe, they have no power to compel attention at all—and be back out before anyone knows we've been in."

I shrugged. "Suit yourself, but why bother with the numbers? No point in waiting around when running out now will work just as well. And it seems to me that any number you get off a flashchannel has probably been buggered a dozen ways by memes, for their own purposes."

Sadi said, "You're right in principle."

Sadi always said "You're right in principle" just before he did something dumb or pointless. "You want to check?" I asked. "Keep it short."

"Sure, sure." He uncased his werp, set it up so we could both see it, turned it on, passworded it, waited a second. A picture sprang up on the screen, I don't know what of. I sat back for a long breath. The edge of my little frame cot pressed my leg, my pants were rubbing my thighs, I could feel the very slight tingle of some grain of pollen that I was just a tiny bit allergic to in my left sinus, the one that runs between your nose and your mouth—

I *knew!*

Sadi was not my friend he had never been he had never intended to be what he was was a useless parasite who talked too much and always talked down to me like I was a goddamn *moron* or something and he'd shat all over my memory of what I had done to that German girl that poor kid I'd raped her mouth in front of her babies and then shot her dead with my sperm still dripping from her lips and that had made me feel like shit like total evil I had been burned by guilt and he'd just laughed at that laughed at my guilt at her babies just encouraged that just wanted to hear about it because it got him so fucking hot and horny to hear about that girl she was so young and so pretty and she was probably devoted to that poor stupid fuck who rescued her I blew his head off and then I found she was just getting fucked when he got up to see who had kicked down his door so I was hot to see her like that and I kidnapped her and killed her kids except I kept the girl and raised her and named her Alice and that was all Sadi's fault he wanted me to tell him those things and that Alice left home when I raped her like I had her mom and Sadi made me take him to the club at SNY and afterwards he fucked Alice and told me how it was she was a snotty bitch he said so he had to hit her and hit her and then it felt so good when she sobbed he got done he cut her up bad and then slapped her around and humiliated her he married her that summer and they didn't invite me he made all the guests do her on the floor he spread himself out and had them all do him he had eaten my shit and deserved to that was what he wanted I had had such a good time been such a good boy done good things done things good grew up killing and raping he made me feel bad about it I wasn't innocent when he was done I was always in fear of him that was why I did it he made me ashamed of what I had done he made me like it he did it all because he knew it was bad for me he did it all to make me evil to make me not guilty to leave me without the love of

God and now I saw Little Lord Jesus look down from the sky Jesus and Lenin and my mother Sadi raped Mama Sadi raped Mister Harris Sadi raped Grandpa Couandeau Sadi made me say I wasn't sorry Sadi kept me from going home Sadi was evil Sadi was all evil Sadi evil Sadi evil Sadi evil Sadi evil Sadi evil

flashed into my brain in less time than it takes a breath to catch. Just as I was vowing to Jesus that I would not let Sadi lead me astray anymore, just as I was understanding that I had a personal commission from Comrade Lenin to deal with Sadi's betrayal, just as I was calling Mama and telling her I'd be home for a visit—

That son of a bitch grabbed my throat and tried to choke me.

I struck back, hard, with everything I had. We got our grips and sank them in. Our little shelter went crashing and rolling. He tried to dig out my eye with his thumb; I got a hand free and slammed him in the side of the neck. He beat the back of my head against the hard edge of my cot frame; I kicked him in the belly, turned him over, got a full nelson, and pressed with the whole strength of my body . . .

The human neck is strong, and Sadi was a big, strong man in good condition. It takes a lot to break a neck, but I did it.

His neck crunched like a joint of frozen beef breaking in half, and I wrenched and twisted his head, bucking it back and forth to make sure the spinal cord severed.

I felt his body go limp. For good measure I slipped into a carotid grip and held it for a two-minute count, as hard as I could. When I finally dropped his battered, twisted body onto the floor of our shelter, among the strewn mass of our possessions, his face was contused by the internal blood pressure I had cranked up on his neck.

I put my head back and laughed, laughed, laughed, for the pieces that made me up had at last found each other again, after migrating into these two bodies and then calling up the third piece, and it was a good trick on Sadi and me, and it was *funny* to see him dead like that—

And then, too late, the chasers won out. Sadi was dead. My hands were still warm from where they had clutched his body to squeeze the life out of it. The last laugh strangled as I fell to the floor of the tent, weeping, screaming, clawing my face with my nails.

iii

It's past lunch time before we're really done with each other's bodies. We call up room service but otherwise we just lounge around in the afterglow.

No question. Katrina and Sadi are the same person, and physically she's in her mid-twenties or so.

"All right," I say, "you owe me some explanations."

"Oh, I agree," she says, her voice purring and warm. She snuggles against me and adds, "After a nap, you know."

Drifting off to sleep I think I will wake up and discover that this whole thing's a hallucination. But when I wake Sadi's in my arms. Her eyes are open. We rise without speaking.

It's three in the afternoon. "Let's get dressed and take a long walk," she says. "I'll tell you everything, but we have tons and tons of time. There's no reason to rush *anything* anymore."

We end up on the bench, up by the lake, where I sat yesterday. I suppose if anyone looks at us they must think I'm her grandfather, or maybe her customer. She checks something on her werp and says, "Okay, there's no listening device within a hundred meters, and we have the net bugged—if anyone starts recording us the werp will sing out. Say something distinctive."

"Uh, clap your hands if you don't believe in fairies?"

"That's if you *do*. Every time some child somewhere says 'I don't believe in fairies,' a fairy falls down dead."

"Well, you would know children's literature better than I would. It looks like you just got out of childhood. It's been awhile for me."

She giggles. "Yeah, I suppose so. All right. I have three great big bombs to drop on you, things that will change everything, and I'm just trying to think what order I should go in. I guess I'll start with the smallest bomb first, the obvious one. If it had been entirely up to me I'd have always worn this female body, but I got the surgery in the early years of the Long Boom, because when I got assigned to go out among the vags, back in 2021, it just seemed like being an attractive woman would be dangerous. So I figured, well, here's one whole lifetime as a male and then at the next transit the sex change will undo—that happens, you know, as part of the regeneration—and that will be fine. But instead I ended up partnered with you, and—well, it's hard to explain. You got to be important to me."

"That's not hard to explain," I say. "You got to be important to me, too."

"Yeah, I know. Well, anyway, the thing was, it was a male-to-male friendship and I wanted to make sure it kept going. So I managed to get some stuff through a back channel to keep the sex change from undoing, and I went through transit, and there you were, taking care of me."

"You looked like hell," I said, remembering, "but it felt good to care for you. And it was such a relief when you finally were lucid and could talk again."

She nodded. "That's what it's like for us, isn't it? We need the care and the help and we need it from someone we can count on. Anyway, then once I'd done it the first time, decided to be a man, I found there were other advantages. The male body is clumsy and awkward but it's a good body for violence, and that was mainly what we were going to do. And obviously it's the only body for serbing. I never much cared for sex like this but you know all those old feminist bitches were right, it *is* about power. I love the way they look after you're done with them, you know, girls or boys, you've stolen their soul, left your mark on them forever. Do you remember some of the things we did?"

"Just what comes up when I look in the werp." I look out over the terraces of Red Sands City, full of quiet people doing their quiet business, and say, "I know I enjoyed a lot of it but all that stuff's behind us now. Earth is two billion Resunas without crime or violence, and the space cities and the ships were never very violent or dangerous. I don't see what there could be another war about. I think it's probably about time to put all that shit behind us, don't you? And to tell you the truth what I remember, and read off the werp, of my past two lives is that I slept a lot better and it didn't feel awful to be me."

She sighs and snuggles against me. "Yeah," she says, "it was always a little trouble to get you back into having fun whenever you transitted. You'll see when we take you through revival."

"Revival? Is that what the process is called that makes you, uh—"

"The apparent age I am? You bet. Congratulations, you just set off bomb number two, the middle-sized bomb. Here's the short on the deal: you get to live a lot longer than you thought you would, and do it with a young, healthy body. Not available commercially and with luck never to be discovered elsewhere—we've got people working on making sure that it's not discovered independently, you remember, the same kind of work you and I used to do on CTCs." She giggles. "Remember Doctor What's-his-dick and his little wifey and their daughter? That kind of thing. Every so often just for kicks I go along on one. It's almost as much fun to watch, I think; like I said I was never into that male body but I love that feeling of male power.

"Anyway, yes, we have the revival technique now. Works on any longtimer. I don't understand a lot of it, but apparently if your body already knows how to transit, then they can push you into a transit, and then make the transit go all the way to completion so that you end up with a completely new body, instead of about a ten-year regeneration. While they do that there's some stuff they do with the brain so that not only do you keep all your memories, you get all your old ones back."

"You mean like now, you have a perfect memory till the next time you transit?"

She beams at me. "You don't suppose the Organization stopped doing research after the longtimers took over? They found a way to bring back *all* your memories—except for the transits themselves—completely accurately. Including your memories of what you thought happened while you were still reconstructing them after every transit, if you see what I mean. You'll be able to remember both what you believed and what was actually true, and keep them sorted out, just the way you know the difference between what was a dream, what was real, and what you remember from someone else's stories. Not perfectly—most people get a few false memories out of it—but good enough so that you can figure out what actually happened to you. Your past life's going to make some sense to you, finally."

My eyes get wet, yet I don't feel much inside. She holds and cuddles me for a little while and though I still don't feel much, I sob a few times. "Completely normal," she says. "You never forgot those things, you see; it was more like every time you transitted, the pointers got reset so that you couldn't find most of them. It's all still in there, wanting to come out, and you want it back, so even though you don't 'know' what's in there, you're emotionally overwhelmed by the possibility of getting it back. It comes out physiologically but you can't touch the feelings yet. It will all be a lot clearer and easier to deal with once you go through revival."

"Does it hurt?" I asked.

"You go into the tank for six months and have a lot of nice dreams. The time passes like nothing. Then you come out and you'll remember everything. And you'll be physically somewhere between nineteen and twenty-five. For maybe a month after that you'll need to sleep a lot to sort it all out. And even though your memories are very clear at that point, you'll spend a few years finding which ones you want to access—there will be just too many to go through all at once. But that's all the trouble it is. And after that you're just like anybody, except of course that you're living for hundreds of years, physically in your mid-twenties. You're going to love it, Josh—I've talked to you in the future, and you're going to have so much fun."

"You've talked with me?" I take a very deep breath, lean way back onto the park bench, and let it out.

She smiles at me again; she has hardly stopped smiling. "I said I was going to drop *three* bombs on you. Number one was my being a woman. Number two was revival. But number three is bigger than both. Have you gotten around in your reading and remembering to recalling where the transfer ships went?"

I think about it and I do remember—and once again, I'm overwhelmed. The fleet of five transfer ships, out at 100 AU from the sun, set off a matter-compression explosion that created a singularity, the base point of a "closed timelike curve"—a thousand-year loop into the future. Now any spacecraft could simply take a turn over into the adjoining, backward-running temporary universe which had extended out into the future from that singularity. And once in that backward-running universe, anything could move back in time as far as the original singularity, re-cross to our universe, and thus enter its own past.

Of course you needed a really big nuclear bomb for the initial energy to establish the singularity. Bad idea to make a big singularity—one large enough spatially for the five-kilometer by one-kilometer cylinder that was a transfer ship, and extending a thousand years or more into the future—anywhere within the solar system, so they'd waited to construct their singularity for a couple of years until they got out to 100 AU.

With the singularity in solar orbit, the transfer ships would be able to return to that point in solar orbit at any time within the thousand years before it merged back into ordinary time. It was the doorway back.

That doorway built, the five ships—each with its crew of ten thousand—had scattered to the nearest stars where the light-speed probes, launched fifty years before for Deepstar, indicated solar systems which had both habitable worlds and minable asteroids. Drives running flat out, the transfer ships would reach the star systems they were heading for in a couple of centuries. That would give them some more centuries to get civilization under way around the new stars before dispatching fast ships back to the Earth system, traveling toward Earth backwards in time around the closed timelike curve. The hope was that a huge, technologically advanced force from the future could at least help the colonies to confine One True to Earth, and perhaps by the time the ships came back, they might even be able to think about invading and freeing the Earth itself.

If they didn't do it, sooner or later One True would find a way to break out of Earth, swallowing up the solar system colony by colony, bringing them all into Resuna. In a few thousand years One True might even spread to the stars.

According to the fast probe that had popped out of the singularity a decade ago, the ships from the future were still three hundred years away, but when they got here they'd need accommodations for a hundred million people. That was the last that had been heard from that source. Meanwhile, observations of Resuna from covert flybys seemed ominous; at a minimum they were putting up fifteen more supras, and why build a space port if you're not planning to go somewhere?

I realize I've been sitting here slackjawed while all of recent history runs through my head. I had read it a bit and a piece at a time, to explain parts of newscasts or to understand fragments of memory, but this is the first time I've thought of the whole story.

Sadi's still looking at me, smiling patiently. At last I say, "Yeah, I do remember. The first time I remembered was the other day. I was just wondering why Martians always seem to be in such a hurry, and then all of a sudden I remembered why—everybody's just trying to get it together for when the ships come back, three hundred years from now or so, and they aren't sure they can get their terraforming done in that time. So it's all focused into the future and hardly anybody pays any attention to what it's like now."

"That's it." She stretches, yawns, and pulls my arm around her. "All right then. You're about ready for bomb number three, the big one. You'll probably guess it as soon as I say, making a singularity was something almost anyone could have figured out how to do ever since the first atomic bombs and the first rockets that could get outside the atmosphere, right? Because all you have to know is how to position the reflectors to form an infinitely regressing perfect virtual image. When the image gets dense enough for phase reversal, the whole thing instantaneously converts to exotic matter; it's not really any more complicated than an ordinary hydrogen bomb, phase reversal MAM, or single-massive-photon laser, as long as you know what you're trying to do.

"Right." I suddenly realize what the truth must be and blurt it out. "So the *Soviets* made a singularity and used it?"

She nods. "Back in March 1987, when the Soviet Union was decaying fast but they still had an effective space program—and while the Americans were pouring all their effort into dealing with that space shuttle that exploded and had no time for anything else—there was a semi-covert robot mission, carried out by teams from the space program, weapons research, and KGB. The weapons research people had only figured out that they might be able to make a singularity, that it was dangerous, and that therefore they might be on to a new weapon; the KGB was in it because they were into everything."

"You said 'semi-covert.' "

"Unhhunh. You can't hide three missile launches in a period of days, especially not ones big enough to leave Earth orbit. The Japanese, Europeans, Chinese, and Americans watched it leave and monitored the transmission but they still didn't know what was going on.

"The Soviets put three satellites into solar orbit. The first one was just a relay station, something to relay signals back to Earth, concealed as an unannounced, failed Venus mission. They leaked information that the second one was supposed to be a secret solar observatory for the Soviet Navy to provide early warnings of solar flares that could cripple their communications. That one was really a scientific station that went all the way 'round the sun, to a point just short of 180 degrees from Earth in its orbit, so that it was hidden by the sun. And right at that 180-degree point—"

"The third one must have been the singularity constructor," I said. "So they fired that off on the other side of the sun. Of course. It took them what, more than a year to get there? But it was too dangerous to try on Earth and you couldn't hide it in near-earth space, so it had to be somewhere where the traces would be lost in the glare. So that's how they found out how to make one?"

"That's how they made one. The singularity implosion didn't look very useful as a weapon, so they gave up on it and left the data in the files, not knowing what they had. But they had produced a closed timelike curve, just like the ones the transfer ships made for themselves, though much smaller—only 144 years in diameter and only big enough for a small ship. They didn't know how to use it at the time, of course—because the theory of a singularity producing a CTC wasn't yet developed. And they thought their data was hopelessly scrambled because it looked like a lot more matter came out of the singularity than had gone into making it—but there was nothing wrong with their instruments. What they were seeing was a steady dribble of spacecraft sailing out of the singularity. All very small craft. And a lot of those were *us*, Josh. You and me. We just keep going around the loop, making the twenty-first century more and more the way we want it."

I thought about that for a second. . . . "How long do we actually live?"

"Oh, well, when the Organization figured out how to use a CTC, back in the early 2000s, we went back and looked at the Soviet observation satellite's records of the singularity, and we put up an observation satellite ourselves. And the answer seems to be that about fourteen thousand ships went through. Figuring most of them are you, me, or both of us, say we each make ten thousand trips through a loop of a bit over a hundred years, that's a million years." She shrugged. "Once you get used to the idea you stop caring. But you're always you, and from your own local perspective time is always running forward, so what else matters? Maybe somewhere in that sequence we find a perfect version of the twenty-first century, and decide to fire off another singularity constructor so we can do a billion times through the twenty-second. The point is, thanks to relativity, we can skip over the bad parts, and thanks to revival, we never get old. We get to be together at our favorite times in history, *all* the time."

She's looking at me very intensely, like it's important that I be happy with this. I don't know why I'm feeling funny about it. Finally I say the first thing that pops into my head. "That seems like a lot to do for a couple of employees. The Organization must really have changed while I wasn't watching."

"Oh, you were watching," she says. "You just didn't *know,* the first few times through. While the struggle was still going on I had to conceal my operations from both you and my earlier self, mostly for your own protection since there would have been people looking for you if they knew you were important to me. But nowadays, Josh, since around 2070, all there is to the Organization is me, plus the hired hands. I own it, it's all mine, now."

iv

Every time before, Supra Tokyo had been grim, orderly, quiet. You knew you didn't fuck around, they knew you'd behave.

Today the air stank of fear. My ears ached with the cacophany of thousands of people trying to argue a reason why they should live.

My best reason had just failed—I'd pulled out enough platinum to make anybody a billionaire and Captain Space Prick had just sneered and gone on the next. I'd been smart enough not to try drugs, the people on the transfer ships never used them much—a few decades before when the Organization tried to get an in that way, our organizers got massacred.

So though I didn't understand it, I knew they didn't like drugs there. I had never realized they didn't like money, either.

Fuck 'em then if they didn't want to make any sense.

I passed back through the crowd to the waiting area. Lots of people were trying more than once but since the only people at the admissions table were the same two spacers—a snotty rat-faced bitch named Rodenski and a pompous fat bag of shit named Harrison—and they seemed to have good memories, it looked pretty stupid to try to get in by iteration.

The year before, the transfer ship *Albatross* had been almost grabbed by the Unreconstructed Catholic meme on its last Earthpass; they'd had to kill twenty of the crew in the process of keeping it out of the control of that meme. That freaked the *Albatross* crew—there's practically no violence aboard the transfer ships, usually nothing worse than a punch in the nose, and what with all they had all been teenagers or younger when the adults left the ships in 2024, and with life extension, whole decades went by without anybody dying on one of the ships. Twenty in a day, shot, left them in hysterics, though any realistic person would've known that was nothing.

The hysteria was really unnecessary anyway, because the Unreconstructed Catholic meme was extinct by the time the next transfer ship arrived. One True had won the war and taken control of the Earth—which it was rapidly turning into Resuna—but the transfer ships had vowed they'd never trust a meme again, no matter how many assurances One True gave them. They were all modulating orbit so that they would not pass nearly as close to the Earth as they had before, which meant a longer radio delay and hence made infection much more difficult. But it also meant it was going to be much more expensive to get to Mars, Venus, Ceres, or the Jupiter or Saturn systems.

But they had been willing to strike one very limited deal with One True. They would take all the people they could carry in one trip to the colonies—any refugees who did not want to join Resuna. All you had to do was be at one of the supras during the last pass of a ship, and get far enough up the list.

All you had to do.

All the people they could carry was hardly any, compared to how many wanted to go. The bottleneck: short time to load—the transfer ships didn't even come within the moon's orbit. The shuttles to and from them could only run for about six weeks (four weeks before and two after the Earthpass) at most, and it took a shuttle around a week, round-trip. Fifty shuttles times five passes times six round trips per pass times 1800 passengers per shuttle worked out to 2.7 million. About half a million on each of the five transfer ships.

Total. One-way trip. Coming back for nothing.

There were at least twenty million people packed into each supra during each pass. And out of the sixty million who were lucky enough to get to a supra, 2.7 million—fewer than one in twenty—would actually escape. The rest would go back down the cable into the One True society where everyone would be Resuna.

The trick was figuring out how to get to be one of the 2.7 million, especially since I was older, male, single, with a criminal record two meters long if they happened to check my thumbprint against their database. Which they were bound to do. They *needed* reasons to reject refugees.

All that was why Supra Tokyo echoed with keening, wailing, shrieking. People pleading. Showing pictures. Rejected families selling their children to those yet to apply. I had been in this vast steel cave before—it had been advertised as "the largest dance floor in the solar system," on the flashchannel. (They cheated, in zero grav you could count all the surfaces.) I had never seen it so crowded or so loud.

The queue was messy. You can't keep kids still anyplace. In zero gravity it isn't even worth trying. The line wound around the inside of that giant box like a spring coiled in a can, people hanging on handholds, and with the person on one side of you a thousand people ahead in line, the temptation to muscle in got pretty strong. There were fights and squabbling all over all the time.

The Supra Tokyo cops were already One True, and that helped, because One True was fairly gentle, for a meme, and took better care of bodies than some of them did. Still, the cops had their hands full and if you looked around at the coated walls along which the long spiral of humanity ran, you could always find a fight someplace.

As I drifted through the center—the exit route—I thought, my platinum coins might as well be chewing gum wrappers for all the good they were apt to do. Not sure why I was doing it yet, I pulled out a couple handfuls of platinum coins and flung them all around me, letting myself tumble as I went and not worrying. I hit the catch net at the end and scrambled out. The noise behind me had just started.

I guess I'm sort of sorry. There were fifteen dead or so from me doing that, most of them kids. Once people saw that much money—one platinum coin was worth more than most people made in a year—they went for the coins. But their place in line was just as precious, and a lot of people grabbed places rather than coins, triggering fights. I hadn't pulled myself more than a hundred yards along the corridor outside before the screaming din behind me got even louder.

Then the screaming was drowned in thunder.

A long life of healthy habits had me moving fast before I thought what the hell that might be.

I had heard something like it before, but not as loud. I remembered. People zero-g dancing, when a place was really crowded. They made that sound by springing off the sides. But this was a thousand times louder.

Feet and bodies, slamming into the walls. Those with some zero-g skills were leaping back and forth, grabbing coins and places. Those without were getting beat up and thrown around. Most of the thuds were made by feet and hands as people bounded against walls, springing off to change direction. But a lot of them were people ramming into the walls at high speed, smashing on protruding handholds or thudding heads onto the unyielding metal. The inside of that room rang like a giant drum.

I moved faster. No idea how many people had seen that I was the one responsible, but for sure once they figured out platinum coins had started the riot, Rodensky and Harrison would tip Supra Tokyo cops off and they'd be looking for me.

Then I realized why I had done it. Instinct, on my side again. Nineteen shuttles docked at Supra Tokyo. Major riot underway. Not enough cops to guard shuttles, for the next few minutes anyway.

I had no idea how anyone could stow away. But I would.

Either I was going to find a way to get on board one of those things in the next couple hours, or they would catch me. Supra Tokyo was a few kilometers across nowadays—maybe a tenth the width of a full moon from Earth's viewpoint, not the mere bright star it had been when it was first built—but it was still a space station, with so many internal checkpoints, airtight doors, cameras, and microphones around, that anything I did I'd better do quick.

Or I could always go back down to Earth and become part of One True, be Resuna. Like shit.

I wished Sadi were here. According to my werp he'd always been quick with an idea when you needed one. And I had expected him when I last woke up from transit, eight years ago, but the Organization (before the memes had destroyed it) had only said that he was busy and it would be a while before we could be assigned together, on the werp it said I'd killed him, but also it said he'd killed me—he said he needed my werp to help me and had to kill me to get it.

Well, he'd never showed up, and my Organization pay had stopped coming. One True had killed four Organization agents that I knew about. And we'd never been able to hit back. Why it hadn't killed me, I had no idea. So I was all alone in the world, just me and my wits, like back when I was starting out.

It worked out simpler than I had thought it might, once I decided to trust my gut and improvise. I found a big secure area, with many waiting rooms for people cleared to board the shuttles. Then I heard alarms going off and realized there must be twenty other people trying to slip through and setting off guard beams. I slid under a guard beam that no cop was backing up and I was in the secure area.

The people in the waiting rooms kept their boarding passes where they could watch them. Small wonder, they were worth killing for.

I slipped into a men's room by the waiting room nearest the next shuttle to depart, and waited in one stall, floating in a curled ball so that it might look like it was just locked for maintenance, carefully maintaining a position where through the crack of the door I could just see the entrance.

Guys came and went. Lots of them. Mostly just from boredom, I suspect—taking a piss is about the only thing you can always do. A lot were in groups; forget them. Guys way older than me. Little kids. All that. A very tall blond guy, my age but nothing like me. Ditto two dark black men, one after the other, and an Asian. I sat, floated, waited. Relaxing all my muscles, getting ready to move when I had to, I watched through the tiny crack as men came and went.

Finally a good one: by himself, about my height and weight, near enough my hair color. I sealed the toilet and flushed it as if I were just finishing. He had just pulled out a length of disposable hose from the dispenser, slipped it over his penis, and plugged it into the vacuum urinal. He was pissing, not looking at me.

As I went by him, I grabbed the urinal hose and yanked as hard as I could. It probably didn't hurt much—the things were lubricated to fit comfortably—but it startled him and the spray of urine droplets caught him in the face. He cried out, half a breath, half a scream, a little sound lost in the slurping roar of the urinal drain sucking air.

I pulled the hose off its connection and whipped it around his neck. Legs around his waist so that I was riding his back, I arched my back to stretch him out as I hauled the hose as tight as I could, snugging it up under his jaw.

He was in lousy shape and had no idea what to do in a fight anyway, so his arms just waved around ineffectually, and he didn't manage to push me against a wall hard enough to do anything, as we rode around the room. His face got all screwed up and funny looking, and I couldn't help noticing that what they used to say when I was a teenager was true—getting strangled really does give a guy a massive woody.

He passed out in a few seconds. Carotid cutoff is a fast way to go. I took his limp body and slammed the back of his head on the wall a couple times till I felt something give. Then I stomped his larynx, kicked his kidneys, and knotted the urinal hose tightly around his neck, to make sure he wouldn't be waking up later. Didn't matter which he died from as long as he died.

I shut off the roaring vacuum urinal so it wouldn't draw an attendant, and searched my pigeon's corpse. Sure enough, he had a boarding pass and an i.d. that I could use.

Better still, nobody traveling with him. I floated the corpse into the stall I'd been in and locked him in.

That would sure be a surprise for whoever cleaned this place later. Well, Supra Tokyo had always been kind of dull. This would liven it up some.

Only took a few minutes. Nervous about it anyway. If anyone had walked in I'd've been in deep shit.

Instead of a thin mist of piss, I thought to myself, and giggled. This was going so well.

His i.d. showed this was Dr. David Stroup, M.D. Most people just went to medical AIs but there were still a few M.D.'s who did research, and to do research they had to treat patients. I suppose the idea was that his skills shouldn't be lost to the human race. Well, they were. On the other hand the human race would be keeping *my* skills. Win some, lose some.

Stroup's i.d. showed he was traveling alone. Nobody would come looking for him, which meant I could use this pass and wouldn't have to wait and try for another one.

I checked his boarding-pass time. Thirty-eight minutes away.

Forty-one minutes later, precisely, having established by watching that three minutes was really close, I raced up to the gate, looking like I was panicking, jammed the i.d. and boarding pass under their noses, said I'd been caught short in the bathroom. I figured if they smelled piss on me so much the better. It would seem more like a guy who'd been in a panicked hurry in a zero-g bathroom.

They waved me aboard.

I wasn't going to go to Stroup's berth—for sure they'd find and i.d. that body within hours. So I looked around for one that had a "still vacant" light on, and found one for George Pillbrenner. I put Pillbrenner's name plate on Stroup's berth—no passenger would ever check the number against the name—and wedged Stroup's name plate, and the urinal hose I had used to strangle him, down between the bunk and the wall. Maybe I'd get lucky, and when they found Stroup's body, they'd check the berth number he was supposed to be in, search this berth, find this stuff, and waste a couple days interrogating George Pillbrenner.

Next step: find somewhere to be during acceleration, and ideally for two days afterwards. I could steal water and food, or since it was just two days manage without them. Save the problem of getting off the shuttle and onto the *Flying Dutchman* for later. Right now, get somewhere to not get caught.

Every acceleration couch in every berth would be full, one way or another. The shuttles didn't boost hard—nothing like taking off from Earth's surface—but they still pulled a good two gee for the first twenty minutes, and you could crack an ankle or get a hernia in that. I wanted somewhere soft to lie down.

I ended up sacked out on top of a pile of wrapped meal packets in a storage bin—they were all being held to the wall by a piece of cargo net. I wasn't sure but figured that probably they'd put them on the engine-side wall, which would be "down" whenever the engine was on. I tucked my feet under strands of the netting, grabbed two more, and held on.

I waited a long time. It got to be an hour past departure time. Nervous, breathing slow to calm myself, more nervous. Always possible they'd found Stroup, put together the timing of the riot and Stroup's death and maybe some evidence I hadn't been careful enough about, were searching for me, were just about to open the door . . . right now. . . .

The catapult shoved us and I lurched into the pile of meals. Then the engines cut in. It felt a little weird as I sank into the slippery pile of wrapped meals, but it beat being dead or back on Earth.

When I slipped out of the storage bin, I had half a dozen meals tucked into my werpsack, along with my werp and my space allocation box. That, the clothes I was wearing—and maybe thirty million in platinum coins—was all I owned. It would do, if I could get anywhere with it.

It was easy enough to fix those meals. You just had to get some water from a bathroom, put it in the vent on the meal, and microwave the meal a few seconds. This shuttle had been a luxury liner—there were a lot of little lounges with microwaves. No problem that way, if I could avoid getting caught.

Mostly I just circulated around, looking like I had somewhere to be, talked to no one. Lots of people still in shock. Easy to avoid conversation.

Late that first day I overheard some of the passengers talking about a stowaway. Some poor bozo had killed George Pillbrenner for his boarding pass and then tried to take his cabin. He'd disposed of the evidence of Pillbrenner's murder, and he had Pillbrenner's i.d., but for some mysterious reason he hadn't gotten rid of the urinal hose he used to kill Dr. Stroup, as well.

The shuttle captain gave him a two-minute trial and then tossed him out the airlock. The shuttle was moving at above Earth escape velocity, so the stowaway's freeze-dried body was on its way into solar orbit. He'd be out there a good long while.

Anyway, with him gone, they stopped looking. The second day they weren't checking i.d.'s in the mess, so I got regular meals. I still tried to stay out of sight a lot.

Poor stupid bastard. Going to sleep in the berth of the i.d. he'd stolen. Obvious amateur. They'd have had him for murdering Pillbrenner, anyway, eventually. No skin off mine if they threw him out the lock for Stroup, instead.

V

Revival is kind of fun. If you've led an active life imagine literally having six months to catch up on sleep. After that, with my new twenty-year-old body to play with, Sadi and I settle down to a "honeymoon" in a big private house she has way out in the Martian desert.

I'm still troubled by all the memories. Now that I know what happened, I feel it, it doesn't seem so bad to me, but it doesn't seem so good either. I don't want to take antidepressants to get rid of the feeling. Sadi's very patient. For some reason this bug or blues or whatever it is makes me horny all the time, and she's willing to have sex with me as often as I want.

Many nights I put the heated suit on, go out, lie in the rust red sand, look up at the stars, and finger the emergency venting valve. Hit that one twice, speak the right codes each time, and I'd be fresh out of air instantly. The transponder would summon Sadi but I'd be dead before she could suit up and come out to me.

The thought's not exciting or comforting or anything. Just a thought.

I've searched the records more completely in the last couple of months. Alice died of old age a while back. Her transfer ship officer son, the one she had with Joe Schwartz, paid for her to come as his permanent guest on the *Flying Dutchman*. The odd thing is, I came to Mars on that ship, though they kept us in the cargo hold and wouldn't let us talk to the crew for fear of memes. I was maybe three hundred feet from Alice and neither of us ever knew.

The report that she was dead came from the *Dutchman*, en route to Epsilon Indi, a few years ago. They were fourteen years out from Earth, then—around 63,600 AU, almost a light-year away. That's a long way from anywhere.

She was a hundred two years old, not bad for an old bim that never took care of herself, when she died.

With my memories back I realize Alice and Sadi were the only people that ever counted worth shit to me.

Alice has been dead, now, for twelve years. Thirteen, I keep forgetting about radio lag. That is, dead in this time line I am living in. There were many other times when I believed she was dead, when I have vivid memories of having seen her dead. Sadi says those are false memories, like the way I remember her killing me and me killing her, or that I remember so many different Boy Scout knives or two different times decades apart when I learned magic. Sometimes I just lie out there in the desert night, staring up at the stars through that thin atmosphere, and try to sort out all those memories.

There's a small river named for Alice, most of the way around the world from here, where I found a good artesian vein while prospecting, during my years as Kindness O'Hart, just before I transitted, time before last. Mars Development Inc. paid me to open it up and let it flow.

The Alice River winds south from the equator, across the highlands, before plunging down a two-kilometer fall into the Mariner Sea. There are Marsform frogs and otters and trout in it. She always liked animals, so I guess she'd have liked that. And since I did that about twenty years ago, if she ever looked at maps of Mars, she might have seen it. She wouldn't know that she was the Alice, of course. I'm really sorry she didn't.

I named it during the time I was Kindness O'Hart; right after I did that, I started to work really hard to make the James Norren i.d. full legit. When I woke up as Norren I spent fifteen years wandering around in the desert by myself, just thinking things through. Didn't like what I thought. Never saw any way to think different. After a while I was just kind of "present," not really thinking at all. So I didn't write much down.

I liked that a lot. I wish Alice could have seen as many Martian dawns and sunsets, as many great plains thinly dotted with green and brand new seas and rivers rolling, as I've seen.

I wish, instead of Quito, we could have shared my years as an ecoprospector in the Martian back country. They were good years. They were miserable years of loneliness. Both.

I wriggle to get a bit more comfortable. The iron sands crunch under my butt and shoulder blades. The stars are as bright as ever—a clear night on Mars is like the Arizona mountains, squared and cubed. I sigh, think about it all. More trips through will mean a chance to meet more people, but am I going to care about any more of them?

I never had any friends.

There have been times I've been so tired of Sadi I've wanted to kill him. Her. I guess it'll be her from now on. We've got a million years together. I can see what she likes about me: I listen. I do what she says. I'm all a god needs, an audience.

And she's a god. Every trip through she gets to fix more things and try more experiments. The world's getting to look like what she likes it to. Lucky me that I'm part of it. I mean part of what she likes. Because the parts she doesn't like are going away, and she's really enjoying getting rid of them.

The valve's right there under my finger. I'm very tired. I lie there and finger the button. I feel the words rehearse on my tongue, I know what it would be like to press twice. Then I wouldn't be able to breathe and I'd be panicky and thrashing, and then the lights would go out.

"Josh?" Her voice in my headphones.

"Yeah."

"Just wanted to see how you were doing. Want to come in?"

"I guess. Anything up?"

"Not really. I just kind of missed you. It's been a lot of years without you and now I want to see you all the time. But if you need time to yourself, say so."

"Guess I'll come in."

We get into a fight over something stupid, and we end up sleeping separately that night. It's always the same question—why I don't want to jump back to 1988 together and start it all over again. I point out that if she knew me before, she must know when we will. She won't say a thing about that.

She gets into her Doctor Science mode of lecturing me about the jump for the hundredth time. Never did know when to shut up. Like the problem's that I don't understand the deal. I mean, I understand it just fine. What I haven't decided is whether I want to take it.

"You're just impossible," she screams. She's dressed the way she likes to dress around the house—like something out of a porno movie. Looks uncomfortable to me and I don't see how you can get horny from what you're wearing—I mean, if you're inside, how can you tell?—but she says it makes her feel good to do that in front of me. Don't get me wrong, I like to look, but I wish I knew why she does that.

So I'm looking at this bim screaming at me in a little leather swimsuit and a pair of thigh-high boots, and I'm thinking that maybe I should've just opened that valve.

"One more time," she says. "There's nothing irreversible about this. You can just do it once and then decide not to. You can just be a timeline that only went around once. But just try it. Get on the ship with me, and with relativity it will only be about a year subjective, and then we arrive more than a hundred years back. And then we can do whatever we want for a hundred years, or come back forward if we get bored. I swear to god, Josh, I don't know why you won't try it at least once."

I won't try it for the same reason I won't suck cocks—I'm afraid I might like it, I think. *I don't want to be locked in a tin can with Einstein the Psycho-Slut,* I think. Neither of those is the real reason. I don't know the real reason. But it has something to do with remembering too much.

She's shown me holos and everything else about this. I understand it completely, I understand everything except *why* I would want to do this. You get on the little very fast ship with some dingus on it. As soon as you're far enough from large masses, the dingus goes "bing" and then you're moving backwards in time—or you'd be seen as such to anyone outside your ship. Since there's nothing close to you out in space, from your standpoint it just seems like a hundred-year spaceship ride—at relativistic velocity so it only seems to be a year—while the planets go backwards and broadcasts from Earth are time-reversed.

When you re-enter the inner solar system and pass through the singularity, there you are, back in whatever year you aimed for.

She repeats it all twice, screaming. Her makeup runs all over her face from tears. It's like being reamed out with a physics lecture by a hysterical streetwalker. When she's all done, I just say I haven't made up my mind and maybe she's in the wrong timeline.

vi

The big night, half of the population of Mars gathered on the slopes of Olympus Mons, in our pressure suits, to watch. Of course there were better views on the vid, but so what? We wanted to see the actual flash.

It took a big bomb for a singularity that size, and a lot of matter got sent through some very strange changes. Even out beyond Pluto's orbit, the bomb that could make a big enough singularity—forty gigatons—would be more than visible from Mars. So we all sat and watched, knowing that near that flash would be the five transfer ships, now starships, bound outward.

They would have to get to where they were going on their own, at their miserable crawling acceleration of about one percent of a gee. That meant it would be centuries to reach the star systems, and even with life extension it would be the current generation's grandchildren that would get there.

But if this technique worked, they'd have a way back. A singularity opened up a big loop in time, a "closed timelike curve" so that there would be a backward path in time available from the moment of the singularity until the loop's farthest reach, a thousand years in the future. They could go out, settle the new systems, build a civilization, and then send a ship backwards in time, back to our solar system, to enter the past. The resources and knowledge of the future would be available to civilization back here—and with those, perhaps Earth could be taken back from Resuna, or at least the colonies could be better defended against One True.

Some people were watching because it was going to be an important event in human history. Most of us were watching because it was the last naked-eye-visible sign of the transfer ships, where so many of us had friends and relatives. Alice was on one of those ships. Lots of people had such reasons. I read later that there were four hundred thousand of us on the side of Olympus Mons that night.

True, the flash would not be *exactly* where our friends and relations were. They were firing off the singularity ten million miles from the ships—but ten million miles was nothing at all compared to nine billion miles from us to the ships. That flash would be as much of a wave goodbye as we would get.

Strange to think, too, that the die was already cast—when the light at last reached us, it would be fourteen hours since it had already happened.

Even after this flash, I could theoretically write to Alice, of course—the ships and the home system would still be in communication for decades to come. But I had had to scramble a lot to establish an i.d. The only thing that had saved me was that so many of the refugees had decided to give themselves new names for Mars, it was like a fad, and that made a lot of noise and confusion in the records, giving me somewhere to hide. It had been tough enough getting onto and off of the *Dutchman,* and creating the i.d. of Kindness O'Hart (the kind of silly name that went with my previous forged i.d. being from Frisco). Because I'd had to improvise I hadn't done it at all well. My i.d. as "Kindness O'Hart" was already shaky enough, all too apt to connect me to Stroup's murder and god knew what else, without giving any possible listener a clue to who I really was.

But god, I wanted to write to Alice.

The flash startled me because it was over so quickly; the bright light burned for an instant, like a star that had been turned on and off with a switch, a dot underlining Casseiopeia's W. That was all.

Everyone had been told it would be like that. I was glad that we had only digital com. I didn't have to listen to people who had missed it by looking away at the wrong time, or kids griping, or anything.

I had two years to go before I would transit again, and the i.d. I was building for that transit would be a good, tight, solid, clean one. Not good enough to allow me to write to Alice, never good enough for that, sorry Alice, sorry. I'd have had to explain being alive at my age, especially since she thought she knew when and how I had died.

Well, the choice would be out of my hands soon enough. She was old, she'd die. They figured it was hopeless for the ships to communicate with the Solar System after about a light-year or so anyway—though that distance kept getting rolled back as the technology improved. The old Deepstar probes had had to come all the way back, but the new series were good out to a light-year.

I got up and walked down the mountain to where the excursion planes were parked, showed my ticket, got aboard. The plane was weird looking, built with seats on top in a passenger compartment open to the air. Usually it transported hikers and climbers. The open rows of seats on top, where we sat, took up about as much room as the passenger area of an old Earth airliner, but this ship had eight times the wingspan. The wings themselves formed one big delta wing, extending almost as far behind us as out to the sides, and looked all the stranger because that giant wing was not a solid structure but a hydrogen-inflated balloon. With so little oxygen in the air, there was no fire hazard, and hydrogen lifted more and leaked less than helium.

The electrostatic pushers cut in, vectored downward, and we rose from the side of Olympus Mons, then glided silently away at a gentle angle, headed for a railhead a thousand kilometers off. We weren't taking off from from the top, but we were three times higher than the peak of Everest, and Olympus Mons is steeper; it was like sliding into a night sky full of stars. The dark bulk of Mars hung below us, and the sky—now empty of anything but stars—was all around.

In a way this voyage into deep night was the best part of the excursion. I was glad I'd decided to do it. Probably just that I'd been thinking of Alice, especially the way she'd been when she was a kid, but I thought about how exciting she'd have thought it was when she was nine or ten.

She'd have made a good partner for an ecoprospector. She was always really into all the enviro-stuff, and wandering around finding places to help life take hold would have appealed to her. Ecoprospecting would have been a better job for both of us, really, than the ones we actually ended up with. We wouldn't have talked much or anything. Just had company for the sunsets, and sunrises, and all the wild Martian landscape.

I had an expedition coming up, ecoprospecting for a place where I could plant a bomb and start a river. And maybe Alice looked at a map of Mars now and then. I thought maybe she'd get a kick out of it if she happened to see her name on a map, though of course she'd never know that it was me, or that I meant her.

I sat back and enjoyed the long, slow, silent crawl across the Martian sky, said hello to Phobos when it rose, drifted off to sleep a while before we touched down. One of the best naps I ever took, I think.

vii

Sadi and I stopped yelling at each other, gradually, a while ago. I guess Sadi, as a woman, doesn't like to yell. I don't like to yell at women. Reminds me too much of my old man.

So we circle each other in that house, getting close to each other, avoiding, getting close, avoiding. We sulk, so the other one can see we're sulking.

We don't fuck much anymore.

I keep wondering about the memories of killing him, of him killing me, her killing me. I think about the memory problem a lot because now that it all links together, I notice that if I try to recite any long block of it to myself, I get—loops.

Loops, like continuous timelike curves, I find myself thinking.

A million years of time. And she's been around the loop many times, had to have been to have changed the world so often.

And I finally ask myself the question that I should have asked before: am I that sure that this is *my* first trip? I try out the perfect memory: I think about my fortieth birthday, in 2008. I remember Alice and I went to a movie, I remember Alice had a bad cold so we didn't go to the movie, I remember a little blonde girl, not Alice at all, I remember— It falls into place, right there and then, as I'm sitting with my arms folded trying to think of a way to carry the argument on. We're having a big joint sulk-off. "Sadi," I ask, "how many times have I been around the loop?"

She starts to cry, and won't let me hold her or touch her. Finally she says, "I thought you were ready, I thought it was all going to work out. I thought this time we could be really together, that I wouldn't have to hide the memories from you anymore, that I could let you have the revival treatment so you wouldn't get old. That's what I thought. I thought, you change the world, you change the person in it, and I thought I had changed the world enough."

"So you *have* taken me around the loop before?"

"I wouldn't have gone without you, Josh. I mean maybe I'm kind of crazy and I know you sometimes get bothered about things that I like, but you know, you've got to know, I have always loved you. I never felt any other way. You can't say I didn't love you."

"I believe you."

"Well, I tried, Josh, I really tried. And this time I thought yes, yes, he's ready, let him have revival, it's time to be really together, to stop picking you up and trying over every trip through. I really thought that."

"But it didn't work out," I say. I am thinking about what

is in my memory. Sometimes we killed each other. Sadi has killed Alice more times than I know. Sadi did get me to kill Alice, and I was remembering that on the night I killed Sadi. It's the opposite of it all falling into place; suddenly it all falls apart, and I realize that "apart" is the only way it fits.

"It didn't work out," she agrees. "But you can come around the loop anyway, Josh, just take the ride on the CTC with me, and then we can work it out together through the rest of the century. We have lots of time. It can be good, we just have to use the time to work it out."

"Let me think," I say.

Then she won't talk about it anymore, but that night she comes down to the small side bedroom I sleep in now. She's naked. She hands me some short lengths of rope.

I'm not sure what she wants, and I stand there with those in my hands, till she says, "You're angry with me."

"Yeah."

"Tie me up and hurt me. Do what you want. I worked so hard to get you here, like this, you, young, with all your memories. I love you so much. I'll let you do whatever you want with me. You can hate me, you can kill me. Just don't ignore me."

I throw the rope aside, hold her, cry into her beautiful soft hair, let her cry on my shoulder. We cuddle for a long time, and then it turns into giggles and flirting, and finally into wild, screaming sex. It's very late when we fall asleep.

When I wake up the gravity's all wrong.

I get disoriented and dizzy when I stand up, the way it used to be confusing to walk in the Mushroom, the high-gravity area of the *Flying Dutchman* where they made us work out to keep us healthy during the voyage.

I don't remember much. The prick of a needle? The shot

of an airgun? Where is Sadi? (Where's Alice? I think, and then I know how stupid that is).

My werp's there, and my space allocation box. When I open it, the napkin, the holo, and the old dogtag are gone. One thing has been added: a holo of Sadi, as a young woman, naked, positioned for doggie style so that her tits look huge from the front side and in the back you can see right up her vagina. A note clipped to it says *Remember this is waiting for you.*

The kind of funny sideways feel to the gravity can only mean one thing, I realize. I'm in a spaceship that's using centrifugal gravity.

She'll have left a message. If there is anything she *can't* do, it's *not* explain. I turn to the werp and say, "Play the message."

Sadi's face comes onto the screen. She hurried about her makeup, didn't get the lips right.

"I really do love you," she says. "By now you've figured it out, haven't you? I would think you would. While you were still asleep from the drugs, the time shift was initiated. You're on your way back to the singularity, Josh. You were never going to make up your mind, and you know it. But you have to do this. It's taken me centuries—all the twenty-first" (she giggles at her own joke) "to get it to this point, where I could offer you a chance to really share the century together, where I could let you have a permanent revival and all your memories and know you would come back to me. You can't just give up on it now.

"This is costing a third of the budget of the Organization, and it's worth it.

"So you're off at near light speed, going out almost sixty light-years and coming back, 120 years that will pass like fourteen months. The ship you're in is not under your control. Don't try to hack the control systems—you could screw up life support. Besides you're not an astrogater.

"When you pass through the singularity, after your return to the solar system, I'm sure you'll be happy to find yourself in 1988. The ship will drop you off on a low hill in the New Mexico desert. Head *west* on the two-lane road at the base of the hill. Take everything you need from the ship, because as soon as you're out of sight, it's going to take off and go hide in a long orbit.

"You will be three miles from a small town with a Greyhound station. You will arrive there, at a normal walking speed, about an hour before dawn and three hours before any business opens. In the ship's safe—which is keyed to your thumbprint—there are six ATM cards, each with a million dollar balance to draw upon. You've also got an apartment in San Francisco—keys and details also in the safe. Use them and enjoy them, bud.

"I finally realized how unfair I'd been. I've been around the loop thirty times with my memories, several before I ever found you. Of *course* my mind's made up, and of *course* you'll need time to think. So I'm giving it to you. The ship will give you five years back there—right up to when the mutAIDS plague hits—to play around and think. After that there will be a message for you, mailed to that San Francisco address, so if you move be sure and leave a forwarding address. That message will be a letter from your ship's AI, setting you up for pickup and return.

"If you're ready then, fine. Come on back and we can talk about what it would be fun to do together. Or if you want to stay longer—why anyone would want to do mutAIDS or the Eurowar again is beyond me—go ahead. The ship can park in a long orbit, way away from anything that might detect it, for as long as you want to stay. After the first time it returns for you, in 1993, the ship will place itself under your command. You can even repeat all or part of a loop.

"Enjoy your trip, Josh. Take all the time you want, because you have it. I won't be lonely. Whenever you get back, in your time frame, it'll be just minutes for me. Sorry to pull a trick on you, bud, but you know, you'd never have done it otherwise, and we had to do it. For me it's always been you."

She blows me a kiss and waves. My werp clicks off. Alone, in this metal box, fourteen months to go.

I'm sure she has provided plenty of ways of amusing myself; I can probably dream most of the time away in virtual reality, and there's probably a big library and a lot of movies and music and so on. Any kind of food I want. Some kind of gym. All that. I don't bother to look just yet.

1988. I can go see Mama, Gwenny, Grandpa Couandeau. Ambush Daddy someplace and kill him if I want—I have all kinds of skills now. Be a serial killer, billionaire (I remember the brand names on about ten things that ought to make me rich if I want to pick up a quarter million in stock), politician, anything. Go to college and spend a hundred years reading to see if there's any worthwhile shit in books—not that I need that long to find out there's not.

Wonder if the information in my werp and my memory is adequate to find Alice's mother? Get her out of Europe early enough, might make big differences.

Other thoughts hit, and I start to really smile. That little German housewife. All the places where there's going to be no law at all. Or set up a pickup with the ship so I know when and where I'm getting out of Dodge, go do ten things for the hell of it, go catch the ship, presto, twenty years into the future or past. Never take me alive, coppers. Never even take me *existing*. I have total, complete, freedom to be me, to be as many kinds of me as I want. All kinds of chances.

Sadi was a fool. (Love does that.) She figured if she gave me this century to play with, I'd get bored and run back to her. Or maybe she thought I'd be so in love I wouldn't give a damn for all the stuff that's here.

I laugh and slap the steel wall of the ship. "Yes sir?" the AI asks, in Sadi's voice.

"Steady as she goes and hold your course," I say.

"I am not authorized to alter this flight plan on your commands, sir," the AI says. "Would you like something to eat, or some entertainment?"

"Not just yet." I lean back and consider falling back asleep. Lots of time. Worlds of time.

I can do good things for Mama, Gwenny, Alice, everyone, if I want. I can party for a hundred years. I can kill someone every month just for fun. And if it ever starts to look too hot for me, I can always get on this ship again.

Knowledge is power and I've got that. Power is being able to touch and not be touched, and I've got that.

Hell of a century coming up, I realize. Best one so far. I have to wait fourteen months to get started, but even that's okay. More time to plan, think, dream. Then off the ship and all my dreams come true.

Yeah. It will be the best century so far. This time it will all be different. The next century is fucking *mine.*